A VALLEY TOO FAR

JULIE DOHERTY

SOUL MATE PUBLISHING

New York

A VALLEY TOO FAR

Copyright©2019

JULIE DOHERTY

Cover Design by Fiona Jayde

Published in the United States of America by
Soul Mate Publishing
P.O. Box 24
Macedon, New York, 14502

ISBN: 978-1-64716-027-2

ebook ISBN: 978-1-68291-945-3

www.SoulMatePublishing.com

For my mother,

whose steadfast love for her children

would carry her across any wilderness.

Acknowledgments

Special thanks to my editor, Mary Harris. I may bake the cake, but she patches the holes in my fondant. To Connie Flauaus, Jessie Walsh, and Betsy Davis, thank you for reading scenes and offering honest opinions. I am obliged to Leigh Ann Oullette for answering many questions about 18th century garments. As always, I am deeply grateful to my Facebook followers. You reassure me when I'm filled with doubt, offer advice when I need it, and share my latest news without being asked. I could not do this without your generous support. Finally, a deep curtsy to my biggest supporter, Aunt Rosie, who now whispers encouragement from heaven.

Chapter 1

Catrina Davis ran her hand along the mare's underbelly, blazing a trail of worry through sweat. When a tiny hoof finally knocked against her palm, she closed her eyes and exhaled, straightening her back and uttering thanks to God in German, the language of her youth. She wiped her hands on her skirts, then patted the mare's neck, thick with muscle. "Good girl, Willow. Good girl."

Willow.

Trees made absurd names for horses, but no one could tell Jacob that. No, her son-in-law knew everything about their fine plow horses, including when to breed them.

Willow was far too young.

"Jacob should name your baby something more fitting, like Mercury or Hercules, *ja*?"

It was a silly wish, of course. *If* Willow carried the foal to term, and *if* it survived, Jacob would call it Ash, Poplar, Elm, or some other ridiculous name, leaving Catrina to bite her tongue.

Again.

Ah, well, silence seemed a reasonable price to pay for keeping a roof over her head. She owed Jacob amenability at the very least. He could have taken Marie and little Hans to the frontier without her. He hadn't. For that kindness, she would tolerate many wrongs, including the nonsensical naming of superior horses.

Willow whinnied through the open stall window.

Heinrich, a stallion named long before Jacob's arrival, answered from the pasture.

Willow danced in place, raising the acrid scent of urine and obliging Catrina to dodge trencher-sized hooves.

"I know, girl, I know." She longed to turn Willow out of the humid stall and even suggested it at the morning meal, but Jacob—using the vast wisdom gained in his six and twenty years—refused to relent. The pregnant mare must be confined until she foaled.

Catrina pushed Willow to the back of the stall, then seized the manure fork, its shaft smooth from heavy use. *It's the Sabbath*, she thought as she flipped manure and urine-soaked straw into a barrow. *I should be at worship.*

She would be, her brown hair smooth and smelling of rosewater, if Jacob hadn't uprooted them to follow Sam Bigham into the infinite forest, where God existed but churches did not. Piety and respite had not followed them across the mountains. Here, in the Godless Tuscarora Valley, they toiled all day, every day, even on the seventh.

She slipped out of the stall, latched the door, then gathered up her skirts and pushed the barrow toward a dung heap steaming in the morning chill. How many women her age were spending today—the Sabbath, *Gott* forgive her—mucking out stalls? Not many, she reckoned. *Ah, well. Keeps me young.* Besides, Marie was at the dough board. Nothing made chores less wearisome than knowing warm bread awaited at the end of them.

Inside a split rail fence, the heavy stallion showed off by thundering in a wide circle with its meaty neck arched and tail held aloft.

"*Ja*, Heinrich, *wir sehen dich.* The mares are captivated. The birds are captivated. We are *all* captivated."

Heinrich bucked, expelling a blast of wind.

She laughed. "You are as suited to grace as I am to marriage."

The unembarrassed horse tossed its tow-colored mane

and galloped away to join the six mares grazing unseen in the stubborn fog.

The mist cloaking the valley banished Catrina's good cheer. She despised murky mornings and moonless nights. Death prowled in both. Not a peaceful death surrounded by loved ones, but a measured execution carried out by barbarians.

She shuddered, remembering the shock of last October, when the devils shot the horse out from under Jenny McClain as she fled toward Fort Patterson, just fourteen miles away. No one had seen Jenny since, nor did they find the women and children abducted from the Penn's Creek settlement the same month.

She tipped the barrow, determined to think no more on their perilous situation. What was the point? She lost the argument for returning to Chester County months ago. A woman's opinion held little value. A widow's held none.

Staccato hoofbeats carried all seven horses out of the fog, their ears pricked and nostrils flared. They fanned out with military precision to inspect the valley below, where the Tuscarora path stretched unseen across the backcountry. Once a narrow track, the path had broadened three years ago as land-hungry settlers migrated west. It grew wider still last autumn, when Indian raids sent those same men racing off the frontier carrying what little they could.

Only the desperate or foolish remained in the valley now. Jacob fell among the latter, believing God would reward him for persevering. The women under his roof wept bitterly while rational men bolted off the frontier. They cried again when the stream of deserters dried up. They were abandoned, left in the care of a reckless man blind to the blood-tinged blades slicing ever closer to their throats. As summer's weeds choked the path, erasing their lifeline to civilization and safety, Jacob's obstinacy strangled their hope. In time, both disappeared, leaving the women of the Meyer household with nothing but rancorous acceptance.

Catrina strained her eyes to determine who or what used the abandoned path now. She felt a presence as surely as the horses smelled it. It could be a traveling preacher, or maybe a trader, though those were few and far between now that the governor banned all trade with Europe.

Heinrich snorted and stamped a feathered hoof.

Her father's advice, given long ago, returned to her. *Watch the horses, Cat. The horses always know.*

Danger.

"Jacob!" She balled up her skirts and ran for the open door of their log cabin, nearly stumbling over an exposed tree root.

Jacob's face appeared over a musket aimed from the doorframe. "What is it?"

She raced past him to pluck a second firearm from the wall above the hearth.

"What is it, Mama?" Marie stood behind a mound of half-worked dough on the board, golden ringlets escaping her linen cap. She pressed Hans's cheek to her hip, leaving streaks of flour on his skin.

"I know not." Panting, Catrina crept behind Jacob, who still aimed the long barrel through the doorway. "The horses—"

"Something's got them worked up." Jacob pulled the hammer of his musket to half-cock.

Catrina did the same with hers. She would hand the heavy gun to Jacob the moment he fired the one he held. If he fell first, she would defend the cabin to her last breath. God's grace, she would *not* outlive her child.

Jacob squinted. "It could be a bear."

"Or deer." Marie traded fear for excitement. "Or the pigs!"

Many fleeing settlers had been unable to take their livestock with them. One feral pig already hung in Jacob's smokehouse. He'd been trying for weeks to shoot another.

"Ja," Catrina muttered, furious at their predicament. "It could be a bear or a deer, or it could be the thing no one wants to mention; the thing that cleaves skulls and takes scalps. It could be *that* thing."

Marie's blue eyes widened. She covered Hans's ear with her hand. "Mama, please . . ."

"Both of you, shush," Jacob said, his angular cheek still resting against his gunstock.

A whinny floated up from the valley, sending Heinrich into a rampage.

Catrina's heart banged in her chest. A horse meant a man. She tightened her grip on her weapon.

Jacob pulled his musket's hammer to full cock, steadied his aim, and waited for the mist to present him with a target.

Chattering teeth exposed Marie's terror. "God-d, help-p us."

Catrina turned to reassure her daughter, but Marie had already sunk to her knees to embrace five-year-old Hans, whose suppressed sobs racked his frame.

Heinrich's ropey haunches bulged as he hammered the ground along the fence. He stamped, neighed, and tossed his mane.

The incoming horse answered him, much closer now.

Blood roared through Catrina's ears. Her knees turned to soup. She trembled and stared at the fog until dryness forced her to blink.

Behind her, Marie lost the fight to keep Hans silent.

He wailed into her bosom.

"Quiet, Hans," Jacob hissed.

Marie tried her best to calm their son. "H-Hush-a-b-bye, H-Hans."

Pins and needles pricked Catrina's arms. The hair stood up on her neck. She blew out a breath, hoping to conquer her escalating fright, then sank to one knee to avoid the flash that would come when Jacob fired his musket.

Outside, a shadow in the fog deepened and took the shape of a man on horseback.

"Meyer, ye up?"

Jacob lowered his musket. "Praise God."

"Meyer," the voice called again.

Catrina rose to her feet, her fear giving way to relief, then annoyance as she recognized their visitor's voice. She glared at Marie. "It's Stewart Buchanan, that no-good Indian peddler."

~ ~ ~

Marie knelt under the oak tree, a scowl carving lines above the bridge of her nose. She wrapped a cabbage leaf around a dough ball, then nestled it among the other loaves baking on the coals of a dying fire. "Mama, I beg you, do not call him an Indian peddler again."

Catrina stirred a pot of broth hanging from a tripod. "Pray, why not? Is that not what he is? He probably supplied them with the very guns they use against us, you know."

"You have no way of knowing for sure. Regardless, it is not a nice thing to call him." Marie looked over her shoulder toward the cabin door, left open so the men inside could take advantage of the daylight. She lowered her voice. "I fear you will offend him."

"You need not worry he'll hear us, Marie, what with Jacob's mouth running like a swollen river. Besides, men do not care what women talk about. They think us altogether incapable of meaningful conversation."

Her work finished, Marie sat back on her heels, her scowl giving way to a wry smile. "I think him handsome."

"Have you lost your wits?"

"He looks . . . distinguished somehow. It is perhaps the gray at his temples."

Catrina guffawed. "A distinguished Irishman. Indeed, I pray you jest, daughter."

"Surely, you must admit he's robust for a man of his years."

She would admit no such thing.

"His eyes twinkle when he smiles. Have you ever seen eyes so blue?"

Catrina stirred her broth, though it was no longer necessary over the low heat. "*You* have blue eyes. So did your grandsire." Sorrow provoked the bear hibernating deep inside her. "Need I remind you it was an Irishman who took him from me?"

"Surely, even you would not blame an entire race for Grandpapa's death. The neighbors left to us in this valley are nearly all Irish. I find them altogether decent."

Catrina pointed the dripping spoon at her. "Mark me, they have passions like powder kegs. They are easily riled and not far removed from wild beasts. Hannah Dieffenbacher once suggested I marry that awful James McHenry, remember? The ghastly man who bought your father's coopering tools?"

"He seemed nice."

"Nice, indeed! He was a no-good scoundrel, which is exactly what I told Hannah Dieffenbacher at the time. I maintain, Marie, any deutsche Frau who falls for the wicked charms of an Irishman—"

"Walks a valley too far." Marie rolled her eyes. "So you have said. Many times."

"It is true. We are better off among our own kind."

Marie cocked a brow only slightly darker than her golden hair. "Were *you* better off among your own kind?"

"I do not know what you mean."

"I think you do. You blamed the bruises on the horses, but everyone knew better. I certainly did."

Catrina's voice abandoned her.

Marie suffered no similar want of words. "I hated Father for what he did to you." She stabbed a wooden wedge under a loaf of bread to lift it for inspection, sending up a deliciously fragrant puff of steam. "I still hate him for it."

In a bizarre contradiction, the men inside the cabin laughed.

It was Catrina's turn to lower her voice. "This is no way to talk about your father, Gott rest him."

"Why should God give him rest? Did Papa allow *you* any rest during your twelve years of marriage?"

"He was good to you, Marie."

"He was not *bad* to me. There is a great difference."

Catrina laid the spoon across the top of the pot and looked toward the cabin. She whispered, "Now is not the time to—"

"Like you said, they cannot hear us. Mama, do you know what I did the day Zeus kicked Papa? I thanked God. I thanked Him for saving you when I could not. Whilst everyone cried and whispered prayers in the drawing room with Reverend Klossner, I skipped to the barn and fed Zeus an apple."

Catrina pressed a hand to her belly, thankful for the stiffness of her stays. "Let us turn away from unsavory matters. We are not to speak ill of the dead."

"Why?" Marie scoffed. "Does being dead make them better?" She flinched at an exploding spark. "I thought *we* might die today. It bothered me that I might never talk to you about this. I was just a girl when Father treated you so poorly. I *wanted* to save you, but I did not know how. Zeus did. It is like you say, the horses always know."

Catrina obeyed her weak legs and knelt beside her daughter. "Had I known you bore witness to . . . I would have . . ." *What? Run away? To where?*

She took Marie's hands in hers. They were hot from the fire. "Women have so few choices. What about you, Marie? Pray, be truthful. Does Jacob . . . what I mean is, is he . . . is he at all . . . like your father?"

Marie jerked her hands away to stifle a giggle. "Mercy, no."

"Praise Gott. If a man ever laid a heavy hand on you, I would cut off his slaw bag and serve it to him between two johnnycakes."

"Mama!"

They giggled behind their hands.

"I believed Jacob kind, but one cannot know what truly happens behind closed doors. Even the best marriage can be rather"—she searched Marie's face for comprehension—"relentless."

Marie screwed up her face. "Indeed. I submit as I must. Hans is my reward." She cast another glance toward the cabin, then leaned in to whisper, "Rebekah Todd once told me some wives find their duty tolerable. *Pleasurable*, even. Can you imagine, Mama?"

"Elizabeth Todd would die of shame if she knew Rebekah discussed such matters."

"It does make you wonder though. Mayhap, some men know how to make it less . . . troublesome."

There was definitely a trick to it, Catrina believed, although she'd never say so aloud. A skilled eavesdropper could sometimes pick up fragments of bawdy conversation during social events, when matrons chattered in secretive corners. At weddings, they often frightened young brides with unsolicited insights. "*You're about to find out something you never knew!*"

How right they were. Catrina would never forget Matthew's crushing weight as he grunted on top of her, or the rasping of her unaroused sex, or his fury when she bore Marie two miscarriages later.

I need a son, not a worthless girl!

She wondered whom she would have married had the choice been hers. Maybe Yellow Bear, the Conestoga boy she played with in her youth, if he'd survived the pox.

The silence stretched until Marie broke it with a new subject. "I love to hear him talk."

"Jacob?"

"No, silly. Buchanan."

Though men like Buchanan considered themselves Irish, thanks to a few generations in Ulster, their burr-festooned speech and confident swaggers marked them for what they were: stiff-necked Lowland Scots barely out of the heather and whin.

"He wears a fine coat for a ruined man," Marie said.

That was a rumor delivered by Thomas Martin, the last trader to pass through the valley. Nearly every one of them lost at least one warehouse after Braddock's defeat at the Monongahela last year. Many were now bankrupt. If Buchanan wasn't already insolvent, he was perilously close.

Catrina could not forget the look on Martin's face as he stood next to his string of empty packhorses.

"I'm ruined, thanks to the governor's embargo," he'd said to Jacob. *"It's back to Philadelphia for me, and from there, who knows?"*

By banning European trade, the governor meant to stop unscrupulous men from supplying the Indians with rum and weapons, but the embargo did not discriminate. Honest traders spiraled toward insolvency along with the rest.

"I would wager Buchanan's better off than folk think," Marie said.

The lean horses tied to the chicken coop suggested otherwise. Catrina would waste no sympathy on Stewart Buchanan, but it was a shame for his horses, which looked underfed and hard used.

"He would not leave the safety of Carlisle unless he had to," she said. "Only desperate men cross the mountains nowadays."

Marie touched a finger to one of the loaves. "We shall soon find out. The bread is done. Bring the broth." Halfway to the cabin, she turned, looking apprehensive. "Try to be polite, I beg you."

Catrina rolled her eyes and carried the pot into the cabin.

Marie set her loaves on the table, where Buchanan sat with Jacob. "Will you stay the night?" she asked the trader.

Dear Gott, say nein.

"My thanks, Mistress Meyer, but I must press on." He doffed his hat, revealing the gray streaks Marie found appealing. Stubble on his face painted shadows of a mustache and beard.

Catrina set the pot on the table and unintentionally met his gaze.

A slight grin lifted the corners of his mouth, deepening his crow's feet and igniting an impish flicker in his uncommonly blue eyes. There it was, the Irish charm.

She pressed a hand to her stays and whirled away, mouth agape, her face and chest flushing. At the cupboard where Marie kept the bowls, she paused to compose herself.

Surely, the light in his eyes had been nothing more than a reflection of the open door and not . . . *desire*. She was long past her prime, a widow, and a Deutsche one at that. Didn't he know their cultures simply did not mix?

If only she hadn't spun away. She should have met his gaze with indifference or even hostility. Had he noticed her undignified reaction?

". . . should try to make it to Patterson's before nightfall," Jacob was saying. "If you cross the Juniata too late, you risk a welcome made of lead."

Buchanan laughed. It was a nice laugh, the hearty kind reserved for the self-assured. "Right enough, the Pattersons are trigger-happy, and deadly accurate, thanks to plentiful targets and two fine, rifled muskets."

His chair squeaked as he turned in it.

"Your father made those guns, aye?"

Though she still had her back to him, she knew he addressed her. "Indeed." She pretended to search for something inside the cupboard.

"Few Schneider guns come to me for repair. It is a testament to your father's skill, mistress."

The mention of her father brought the crush of grief, as always. She spent her life's happiest moments in his shop carving gunstocks. No one knew that, of course. Girls didn't carve gunstocks. At least, not after their fathers took new wives. When their fathers took new wives, girls didn't ride horses bareback or play with Native children, either, even if they *were* Christian converts. No, when their fathers took new wives, girls donned silk gowns and learned to sew and cook. And, when their fathers died, they were married off to the first man to consider fifty pounds and three draft horses an acceptable dowry.

An eternity seemed to pass before Catrina mustered up the strength to lift the bowls off the shelf. She set them on the table, careful to avoid Buchanan's gaze.

Marie ladled broth, then gave thanks.

"Amen. Och, I nearly forgot." Buchanan pulled a bilbo catcher from a leather bag. He handed the toy to Hans.

"For me?" the boy squealed, his face brightening.

"Aye." Buchanan rumpled Hans's flaxen mop. "Go on and gi' it a wee try whilst the broth cools."

Catrina eased onto her chair, smiling in spite of herself.

"How generous of you." Marie frowned at Hans. "What do you say to this good man?"

"Thank you, sir! Thank you!" Hans hopped off his chair to swing the ball on its cord. He caught it with the tiny cup on the end of the stick, then looked around to make sure everyone witnessed his grand feat. "I got it on the first try!"

"Why, ye're a lad of unparalleled talent," Buchanan declared.

Hans swung again and missed.

"Suffer no shame, sir. Many's the lad who tried the cup in front of Old Buchanan, and ye're the only one to get it on the first clip."

The praise pleased Hans, who grinned and seemed to grow two inches taller.

Jacob's dark eyes turned stern. "One more try, Hans, and then you must sit up to the table."

When Hans had used up his last attempt, Buchanan patted the boy's back. "Well done. Now, then, let us see how well ye can fill up that wee belly."

Catrina marveled at his skill in guiding Hans back to the table. She knew him to be a widower, but recalled no mention of children. His easy manner with Hans suggested he had some. Where were they now? In Carlisle? Or, had he gone deep into the woods to drop blue-eyed babes among the brown?

"What brings you over the Tuscarora, Mister Buchanan?" Marie asked.

"Deerskins. Meeting a man by the name of Thomas Downey at Patterson's."

"Another Irish peddler," Catrina mumbled.

Marie glowered and gave her a mighty kick.

Buchanan shot Catrina a triumphant look. "He's an Oneida half-breed by a French father. George Croghan gave him the nickname because he looks like an Irish shipping merchant Croghan once knew."

Catrina sipped her broth, its steam worsening the heat spreading across her cheeks.

If Buchanan noticed her chagrin, he ignored it. "Downey wrote to say he would be at Patterson's by the end of May.

I figured a week extra could nae hurt, what wi' the trouble brewing in these parts."

The hard angles of Jacob's jaw pulsed as he chewed a bite of bread.

"Do ye come by much news?" Buchanan asked him.

Jacob swallowed. "Very little."

"Ye *do* know aboot Jenny McClain and the attack at Penn's Creek, I hope?"

"We do. God preserve them."

"And that a month later, warriors attacked McDowell's Mill using weapons taken from Braddock at the Battle of the Monongahela?"

The color drained from Jacob's face. His lips pressed into a taut line. "They stripped the bodies?"

"Always do." Buchanan delivered more bad news. "And in March, a band of Delawares used those same weapons to fire upon Fort Patterson. They carried off Hugh Mitcheltree."

Catrina clamped a hand across her mouth. That was just three months ago and only fourteen miles away. Maybe now, Jacob would move them off the frontier. She exchanged a hopeful glance with Marie, whose eyes were beginning to well.

Buchanan slid to the edge of his seat. "I hope ye plan to move your family to safety."

Sense. From an Irishman. What was the world coming to?

Jacob flopped back in his chair, hugging himself. "We have never had problems with the Indians. Besides, we have forts, three of them now, all within a day's easy ride."

"All three are short on men and munitions. The Assembly refuses to fund our defense. Why should they, when they are nae the ones sleeping wi' one eye open? Three months ago, the Ohio tribes took up the hatchet. They use Kittanning as their base now, a village along the Allegheny River. Each week, they range oot a wee bit farther to kill and capture folk."

Jacob's fist hit the table, bouncing everything sitting upon it. "Governor Mifflin must do something!'

"He did. He declared war on the Delawares. There are rewards for Indian scalps now and promises of fair pay and land bounties for any man willing to enlist. I, masel', drill in Carlisle. To be plain, we're naught but a ragged force of backwoodsmen who caught the scent of wages. It's only a whiff we've had thus far, I might add. If the Assembly does nae soon send the paymaster, the men will abandon the forts and go back to their farms. I tell ye this, sir, so ye know the full measure of risk ye take by staying here. At any moment, ye could be entirely isolated and at the mercy of Providence alone."

Jacob closed his eyes and shook his head. "I take no issue with men defending their homes, but war is never the way."

Buchanan leaned on his elbows. "I would expect a Quaker's son to say so. Mercy, man, it is one thing to hate war, but it is another thing entirely to farm the damned battlefields."

He blushed and bowed his head at Marie. "Pardon the oath, mistress. I forget masel' at times." He sat back in his chair. A long silence passed before he addressed Jacob again.

"Ye must have kin who could take ye in until this madness passes."

Catrina and Marie looked at each other, then at Jacob, who pursed his lips as though he might yet be swayed.

Oh, please, Jacob. Listen to sense.

Jacob stood, then walked to the doorway. "Come."

Buchanan swallowed a bite of bread as he joined him.

"What do you see?" Jacob asked.

Buchanan, shaking his head, returned to his seat. "Save your words. I know what ye're gonny—"

Jacob's voice turned resolute. "A mare in foal and the most promising crops I have ever—"

"What aboot him?" Buchanan gestured toward Hans, who had seized the opportunity to abandon his broth and play unnoticed with his new toy. He pointed at Catrina. "And her?" Then Marie. "And her? Send *them* to Carlisle, or to Bigham's fort, if naught else? By all accounts, sir, the Delaware chiefs, Shingas and Captain Jacobs, mean to invade every valley between Kittanning and Carlisle. They can call upon—"

"I can spare no hands."

Buchanan sighed, clearly exasperated.

Jacob returned to the table. "I am glad of your concern, but we will fare well."

Catrina could stand no more. In all the years she knew him, Jacob never once listened to reason. He was a stubborn, foolish man who would get all of them captured . . . or worse.

She found Buchanan's news disturbing, though not unexpected. Everyone knew the Delaware tribes longed to reclaim the lands sold by the Iroquois to the Penns. What nobody wanted to discuss—at least, not in front of their poor, mindless women—was that Britain had another enemy in America: France. *Both* wanted the contested, fur-rich lands of Ohio and Pennsylvania. How long before the French united with the tribes against the settlers?

She longed to add her opinions, to beg Jacob to see the wisdom in Buchanan's advice, but she was a woman. Worse, she was a widow, resident in her son-in-law's house by his mercy alone. Frustration overcame her.

"I beg your leave, gentlemen." She stood. "I must see to the horses. Hans, do you want to go see Angela?"

"Can I take my toy?"

"Of course." She was glad he wanted to join her. It was not good for him to hear such frightening things.

She took his tiny hand and led him to the barn. "Shall we give her a treat?"

"Aye."

"You mean *ja*."

She hated how quickly her family absorbed the language and mannerisms of their Irish neighbors.

Hans was not as tall as the grain barrel, so she set a crate beside it for him to use as a step. With the barrel rim cutting into his midriff, he retrieved a scoop of oats.

They took it to the fence, where Hans stood on the bottom rail while Catrina whistled.

Angela abandoned the grazing herd to trot over to them. She was knock-kneed, ungainly, and downright pointy in places.

Catrina recalled with sadness the fluid movement of the mare's youth. Angela had been her father's best brood mare, one of three given to Matthew Davis as a dowry.

When the old mare stuffed her grass-scented muzzle into the scoop, her probing tongue sent Hans into a giggling fit. His laughter faded as an idea struck him. "Here," he said. "You hold it."

She took the scoop from him—it was nearly empty anyway—and watched him pull his bilbo catcher out of his pocket.

"Look, Angela." He skipped a few feet away, then tossed the ball.

Catrina rubbed the warm spot under the mare's mane. "How is my old girl, eh?" In spite of plentiful food, Angela's backbone grew more pronounced each week. Copious gray hairs flecked her chestnut coat. Five summers ago, her muzzle, belly, and hoof feathers turned white.

According to Jacob, Angela wouldn't see the coming winter. She was too old for breeding and, like a widowed mother-in-law, now a burden. He made it clear last week that his stores of clemency were depleted. No amount of weeping would force him to feed the worthless mare past the first frost.

Tears pricked Catrina's eyes as she thought about losing the last of her father's original stock. She couldn't bear to think of Angela hanging in the smokehouse, covered in salt.

"I hope what I said in there did nae frighten ye."

She reeled, dropping the scoop at Stewart Buchanan's feet.

He picked it up.

She sniffled and turned her back to him, not wanting him to witness her tears.

His voice turned panicked. "Och, Mistress Davis, I did nae mean to . . . I see I've upset ye."

Well, there it was. He knew she was crying. So what? She would not allow him to take credit for it.

She wiped her cheeks and faced him. "The tears are not your fault, Mister Buchanan. They are hers." She gestured toward the horse.

"Aye, she's seen better days." He rubbed Angela's blaze. "Haven't we all?"

The mare stretched out her neck to sniff him. Her velvety lips made a smacking noise as she nibbled his cheek.

He chuckled. "She likes me."

The horses know.

"Grandmama." Hans tugged on her skirt and jabbed a chubby finger at the rooster, a hostile bird he loathed.

"Ja, Hans, I see him. Take your toy and go back inside."

He raced away, his fine curls bouncing.

Buchanan scratched the mare's neck. "Your daughter married an obstinate man."

"Do you know any other type of man?"

He ignored the question. "Leave wi'oot him."

"What?"

"Leave wi'oot him. Toss the lad on top o' this old horse and go wi' Marie to Carlisle or Shippensburg."

If he had any idea how much she longed to do just that . . .

She said, "We have seen Indians before, even fed a few—"

"I know you probably believe your past benevolence will preserve ye. That is a very Christian hope, Mistress Davis. Shingas and Captain Jacobs have nae mercy in 'em."

"You cannot be certain. Perhaps—"

"When ye left the hoose, I told Jacob aboot a man named Sheridan."

"The Quaker in Sherman's Valley?"

"Aye."

"I know him," she replied. "We watered at his spring on our way here. He and his sons came over to help us raise the barn."

"Aye, well, I'm sorry to say they're all dead but one."

"What?"

"Scalped and left for the buzzards to pick clean."

"But . . ." She swallowed rising panic. "The Quakers have been friends with the Indians since William Penn first set foot upon this land."

"Aye, precisely why Sheridan felt safe enough to invite the bastards in for a meal." He looked at his shoes. "Apologies, mistress. I forget masel' so easily these days."

"Pay no mind, Mister Buchanan. My late husband swore often." *Whilst he beat me.*

"Regardless, I do regret my poor manners. My anger overwhelms me at times."

Passions like powder kegs . . . too easily riled.

Without warning, he gripped her shoulders.

"Unhand me, sir!"

He ignored her. "What if I stop on my way back from Patterson's to help ye o'er the mountains? If it's the horses ye're worried aboot, we can take them to the corral in Carlisle, and then, on to Chester County. Surely, ye still have kin there? Someone who could take ye in until things settle doon."

She shrugged his hands off her shoulders. "And Jacob?"

"It might convince him to follow."

"Ha! Convince Jacob? Like all men, Jacob finds no worth in anything a woman does."

He smirked, reigniting the tiny fires in his eyes.

For a moment, she entertained the notion that he was indeed quite handsome.

He made a small bow. "He could use a lesson or two from a good Irishman. We appreciate a woman wi' her own opinions."

She spat a thoughtless reply. "Many battered Irish wives would disagree with you, Mister Buchanan, women who raise children on nothing whilst their husbands drink up the wages."

Though she intended to discourage his flirtation, her words did more than wipe the smile from his face.

His lips parted, but he said nothing.

"I . . . I . . ." She pressed her palms to her cheeks and sought a way to express her remorse, but found none.

He shook his head, turned on his heels, and muttered, "Well, then," leaving her alone with her shame.

Why had she been so cruel? He was only trying to help. Oh, if Marie ever found out . . .

Disgrace chased her into the barn, where she hid for an hour or more, too embarrassed to face him. By the time she'd contrived a fitting apology—and practiced it several times on the grain barrels—he was gone.

~ ~ ~

By the light of a grease lamp, Catrina looped a thread across a coin and tugged.

Cat, her father once said, *if trouble ever comes, sew your money into your shift.*

Hans snored beside her on the straw-filled mattress, his curls glued by sweat to his temples. How unfair that his earliest years would be marked by constant upheaval and fright. If he lived to adulthood, he would despise the stubborn father who plunged him into the terrifying world that formed him.

Her gaze fell to the bilbo catcher, still loosely clutched, even in sleep. It was a kind gift to a disadvantaged boy—his first, she believed. Disgrace scorched her cheeks. She owed its giver an apology. God willing, she would survive long enough to offer one. With luck, Buchanan would pass by on his way back to Carlisle. If not, someone in the valley would eventually go for salt or gunpowder. She could send a letter to Buchanan with them.

On the other side of the bedchamber wall, Marie beseeched Jacob, "What about our boy, Jacob? You heard what Buchanan said about Sheridan."

"We do not know the whole truth of that story," Jacob replied.

Marie sniffled.

Catrina fought the urge to comfort her only child.

"Jacob, I beg you," Marie sobbed. "If not to Chester County, then to Carlisle. We can take the horses to Philadelphia and sell them on market day."

"Marie, I have had enough of this."

"At least, let us go to Bigham's fort."

"We will, at the first sign of trouble."

"Do you mean it, Jacob?"

"I mean it if it shuts your yap, woman. Now, can we please go to sleep? I want to get an early start on the upper field."

"Do you promise?"

"Promise what?"

"That we will go to Bigham's at the first sign of trouble?"

"For the love of man, Marie, I promise. Now, say your prayers, and go to sleep."

It was an absurd promise. If Indians attacked, Marie would never make it past the apple tree, let alone a mile away to the fort. They should go now, *before* an attack.

The lamp sputtered. Catrina knotted her thread, then bit it off. Five shillings sewn fast to her shift were better than none. The rest would have to wait until sunrise. She dared not refill the lamp. In Penn's wilderness, grease was too precious to squander.

She slid out of bed. In the dying light, she lifted a floor plank to return the clay pot to its hiding place, pausing a moment to savor the coolness rising up from the ground beneath the cabin. Except for the five shillings weighing down her shift, the pot held all of her savings. No one else knew about the cache, not that it was substantial by any stretch. Her father's farm had gone to Anna, who still lived in Philadelphia, as far as she knew. Matthew's debts gobbled up everything else but a few horses. Those now belonged to Jacob.

She replaced the plank, then blew out the lamp, sending the windowless room into smoke-tinged darkness. Just past the deerskin curtain separating her tiny bedchamber from the main room, the low fire they kept for light crackled softly, adding to the suffocating heat. Outside, a chorus of crickets and frogs trilled a resounding opus stretching to infinity, underscoring the vastness around their little cabin.

She crawled back into bed, where the memory of Stewart Buchanan's astonishment stole her prayers. He winced at her words. She rolled onto her side and tried to recite The Lord's Prayer. "Our Father . . ." Buchanan winced again.

It would be a sweltering, turbulent night.

Though nothing would cure the heat, an apology would expunge her guilt. She calculated the number of days until she might offer one. Two, she guessed. He should be nearing the river now. Would he cross at night? There had been a lot of rain lately. The creek was swollen, and if the creek was swollen, then the riv—

A horse screamed.

She sat up, the roar of her own blood instantly obliterating every other sound. Painful sparks shot to her fingertips. Her heart lashed against her breastbone. Sweat trickled down her back.

There. There, it was again. A horse. Screaming.

She leapt out of bed and into her shoes, then ripped the curtain aside. Dashing into the main room, she nearly collided with Jacob.

He tipped the backlog to raise the light, looped his shot bag and powderhorn around his neck, and then plucked the musket off the wall for the second time that day.

"Jacob?" Marie trembled in her shift at their bedchamber door, the shadows of her face elongated by worry and dim lighting.

More horses screamed.

Marie's hands flew to her mouth. Firelight glittered in her eyes.

Bile rose to the back of Catrina's throat. "What should we do?"

"Get dressed," Jacob said.

Marie's voice turned shrill. "Why?"

"Just do it!"

Catrina could not bear to tell Marie that surviving the exposure of captivity might depend upon a decent set of clothes. She dressed quickly, though she was sure the dimness and her shaking hands caused the crooked pinning of her stays.

On the other side of the bedchamber wall, Marie squealed for more light.

"No," Jacob barked when Catrina went to the mantelpiece for the lantern. "The light of the backlog is enough. Any more will make it hard for my eyes to adjust to the darkness when I open the door."

Marie reappeared, her eyes frightfully wide. "Open the door? What do you mean when you open the door?" She rushed to him, her partially fastened stays drooping like a daisy petal. "Why would you open the door? Why would you open the door, Jacob?"

She turned her back to him and wept into her hands. "My baby. What will they do to my baby?"

Hans toddled out of Catrina's bedchamber, the wooden ball of his bilbo catcher knocking across the floor as he dragged it behind him. "Mama? Papa?"

Shrill war cries sent him flailing against the blue and white stripes of his mother's petticoat. Satan's own death halloos pierced the night. The shrieks surrounded the cabin. They lassoed the Meyer home and pulled the noose tight.

Marie pressed Hans's keening face into her skirts. She stared openmouthed at her husband, who stood with rounded shoulders regarding the family he murdered by sheer pigheadedness.

Catrina ran to lift the spare musket from the wall. Wheezing with panic, she aimed it at everything—and nothing.

Outside, the horses still screamed.

Gott, der Allmächtige, how long does it take a horse to die?

She dropped to her knees and sat on her heels with the musket balanced across her thighs, then slapped her hands over her ears. *Please, merciful Gott. Silence our poor beasts.*

Jacob paced, bumping into furniture, knocking baskets off of tables, and tipping chairs. His expression was dismal. "I have to do something." He cocked the musket and headed for the door.

"No, Jacob. No!" Marie leapt for him, dragging Hans—who clung to her skirts—along with her.

"I have to. The horses!"

"No, Jacob." Marie pulled on his arm. "You need to stay here and protect us. Our son! You cannot let them take our son!"

The milk cow went next. It bawled pitifully, accompanied by cackling chickens.

An orange glow shimmered below the door.

"They've fired the barn," Jacob said.

Marie stared at the light, her expression of terror replaced by something far worse: acceptance. "The house will be next. We will die. We will all die. Our Father, which art in heaven—"

"They will take the animals and leave us be," Jacob said.

"Hallowed be thy name—"

"Marie." Catrina rose from the floor. She reached for her daughter with an arm made of lead. "Listen."

There was nothing now but a deadly calm broken only by chirping crickets and her own thrashing heartbeat.

Marie's cheeks glistened. She clutched her belly. "Merciful God, have they gone?"

A thump on the roof provided a reply.

Marie lost all sense. She screamed until her eyes bulged. A shadow blossomed on the hem of her skirts as homespun linen wicked up her urine. Smothering Hans in her arms, she paced from one log wall to another, squealing like a branded sow.

Smoke coiled into the room.

"Damn them, they plugged the chimney!" Jacob fired the musket at men thudding across the birch shingles above him, adding more smoke and the sulfuric stench of spent gunpowder to the room.

Catrina looked up through the haze, her ears ringing from the shot.

Flames.

They coughed and rubbed their eyes as blazing shingles fell around them.

Marie dropped to her knees, rocked her inconsolable child, then began singing a German lullaby.

"I . . . can barely see . . . to reload," Jacob sputtered.

Catrina buried her face in the crook of her elbow and held the heavy musket out to him. A falling shingle narrowly missed her shoulder.

He took the musket, looking rueful. Fire brushed its crimson sheen across his forehead. "I have to open the door." He coughed. "It is our only chance."

"Jacob, no!" Marie crawled toward him, dragging a yelping Hans through mounds of burning shingles.

Jacob flung open the door, waving the barrel of his musket left and right as he sought a target.

Welcome air poured into the cabin . . . and nourished the inferno.

A shot rang out.

The back of Jacob's skull exploded, sending a spray of brains and blood sizzling onto burning shingles.

He fired his musket by reflex alone, hitting nothing, then fell across the threshold, making it impossible to close the door.

With both muskets fired, they had no hope. Catrina screamed and ran to Marie, who gawped at her dead husband.

"Marie!" Catrina shook her. "Marie!" Her hand stung as she slapped Marie, returning her to sense.

They locked their arms around Hans and, choking on smoke, huddled against the back wall.

More shingles bashed against the floor, showering the room with sparks. Marie's skirts caught on fire.

Catrina coughed and stamped out the flames. Her lungs burned with want of air. The skin on her face would soon blister and split.

Through the open doorway, she saw the barn, now fully engulfed. Lithe silhouettes frolicked in front of the flames. Two of them hauled on a rope and tried to bring down a rearing horse.

Heinrich.

The screaming stallion thrashed its head and wheeled its front legs.

"Mama." Marie coughed and gestured to Hans, now limp between them.

They would die here.

A warrior's shadow darkened the doorway. He yanked Jacob's corpse outside to the woodpile, then bent with another man to retrieve Jacob's spent musket, powderhorn, and shot pouch.

Their ghoulish work finished, they tramped into the cabin, waving away smoke.

Marie fainted on top of Hans.

In spite of the heat, Catrina's limbs turned to ice. She crawled in front of Marie and Hans to shield them.

The two men rushed at her, their eyes only visible in their faces by the reflection of firelight. One of them twisted her arm and heaved her to the hearthstone where she struck her wrist. She rolled onto her back, coughing and burning her hand.

The room began to close in.

One warrior scooped up Hans. The other tossed Marie over his shoulder as though she weighed no more than a sack of grain.

Nein!

Catrina wobbled up to her hands and knees, then lunged for the warriors' ankles as they headed for the door. She missed, pitching forward, and then slammed against the planks.

They dropped Marie and Hans onto the grass next to Jacob.

Ignoring the smell of singeing hair and the agony of burned palms, Catrina patted up the wall. She found the handle of Jacob's broad axe, which hung to the left of the hearth. Mustering all the strength left to her, she hoisted it off its pegs, then dragged it, staggering, to the doorway. In the shadow behind the door, she knelt to cough into the crook of her elbow and gulp fresh air.

A rod away, one brute straddled Jacob and sliced off his scalp in a single, violent cut. Two others fiddled with a length of cord near Marie and Hans. The taller of them carried a curved club with pewter studs that brushed against his thigh and reflected the horrors of the night. He hauled Marie to her feet by her hair.

Fueled by rage, Catrina ground her teeth together and charged at him, swinging the axe.

His eyes flashed white. With the speed and grace of a panther, he parried her blow.

Momentum sent her tumbling to the cool grass, where the heel of Jacob's axe head sank harmlessly into the ground.

Half-naked men gathered around her, bringing with them the reek of bear grease and vermillion-stained faces decorated with black stripes and circles. All of them laughed except the tall warrior, Catrina's intended victim. He spoke, and the rest fell silent.

Their leader.

A stripe crossed his face just below his nose. From there up, ebony dots decorated skin so red it looked like he'd fallen headfirst into a cauldron of melted tallow. The only hair left to him was gathered at the top of his scalp and adorned with a crimson deer's tail fluttering in a breeze made by fire. The rims of his ears were cut free and stretched into grotesque rings. In them, he wore copper baubles matching the band encircling his sinewy arm and the triangle dangling from his nose. All of his trinkets seemed to vibrate—all but one, a beaded sheath hanging from a cord at his breast.

His scalping knife.

She stared at the weapon until he yanked her to her feet. She squeaked and cupped a blistered hand over her shoulder.

He towered above her glaring with the heat of a blacksmith's forge.

Insanity spread across her like butter on fresh bread. "*Du tierisches*," she shouted. "*Du schmutziges Schwein*! Think you the first to strike me? Ha!" She rose up on her tiptoes to get as close to his face as she could. "Do you want my fear? My pleas for mercy? How about you take *this* instead?"

She gave him what Matthew always deserved but never received—a mouthful of her spit.

Disgust contorted the warrior's features, then seething hatred as he wiped her saliva off his face.

She stabbed a finger at him. "Mark me, if you lay one greasy finger on—"

He shoved her against a fellow warrior, and that one shoved her against another, a terrifying man with one eye. His deformity created no handicap, for he pushed her more brutally than any other.

"I will kill you with my bare hands!" she wheezed. Ignoring dizziness, she cursed in German, her arms clawing at their faces like windmills.

They took turns heaving her for sport, the disfigured man laughing as one of her wild swings barely missed his good eye.

The tall warrior put a stop to the spectacle with a single word in a language she did not know. Then, he cocked his war club.

Darkness swallowed her.

Chapter 2

"Mama!"

A man's arms bound Marie like a barrel hoop, robbing her of air. A second tyrant tied cord around her wrists.

"Unhand me!" She kicked at her captors and thrashed her head, whipping golden ringlets across her face. "I said unhand, me, you wicked devils! Mama!"

Mama's form lay crumpled on the ground beside Jacob's broad axe.

"You depraved fiends! You sinful wretches!"

A well-built man with a studded club—now dripping with blood—charged at Marie, his fist cocked and his eyes full of loathing. He struck her.

She awoke amid a cloud of fireflies to find her knees denting the ground. She stared at the tiny insects, charmed by their curious display, and swayed to indistinct thuds keeping time with her pulsing temples. There was another noise, too, faint at first, a low whistle that grew too shrill too quickly, lifting her out of fantasy and dropping her before the fiery gates of hell. Panic slammed her hard as she recalled the horrors of the night. Smoke stung her eyes. The fireflies became sparks. They landed on her arms, singeing her. She gasped, sucking in air made sharp and hot by the fire consuming her entire world.

Moccasins zoomed past. Everywhere, beaded moccasins.

Something tickled her chin. She tried to swipe at it, then remembered her wrists were bound by cord. She used the back of her hand instead, depositing a red smear across her knuckles. *Blood.* She tasted it now, wincing as her tongue explored a cut inside her mouth.

Hans. Where is Hans?

He sat a musket length away, his shoulders rounded by the weight of years not yet lived. No scream or cry parted his lips. Arms once capable of delivering slaps during fits of temper now hung flaccid at his sides. He stared blankly at his father's shattered skull, detached by trauma, a boy incapable of feeling anything at all.

Marie crawled to him on her elbows, dragging her skirts through muck and past moccasins. She looped her arms around his neck, then drew him to her breast.

He sagged against her, broken by distress.

The club-wielding man pulled a glinting knife out of a sheath. He kicked Mama onto her belly, then bent to grab her hair. As he snapped Mama's neck to an unnatural angle, Marie's constricted throat turned her breaths to wheezes. She closed her eyes and crushed Hans's face against her heaving chest, determined to spare him *this* memory, at least.

Household goods clattered as men carried them off, cherished items they'd labored to haul across the mountains. Candlesticks, brought from Germany, once owned by a grandmother she never knew, would be among them. Grandpapa's carved bracket clock, too.

Plunder. It was all plunder now. And Jacob and Mama were dead.

Behind her, where fire consumed the barn, Heinrich's screams turned guttural.

"*Couvrez la tête de ce cheval!*" a Frenchman shouted.

She understood French well enough to know he said something about Heinrich's head. Were they about to shoot the valuable stallion?

A moccasin booted her ribs, narrowly missing Hans. She opened her eyes, careful not to look at Mama.

"You, up." A short warrior yanked on the cord trailing from her wrists. Pain stabbed her shoulder as he hauled her cruelly to her feet.

Hans burrowed into her skirts.

"You're all right, Hans." She tried to sound calm. "It's going to be all right." His chances of survival, she knew, depended upon his acquiescence. She didn't care what happened to her anymore, but Hans . . . her boy . . . He must live.

"You, come," Shorty said. He looked ridiculous in an open scarlet coat with yellow cuffs and long skirts, a garment doubtlessly stripped from an ill-fated grenadier at the Battle of the Monongahela.

"You no come, I make like her."

He pointed at Mama, but Marie did not follow his gesture. No barbarian would dictate what her last memory of her mother would be. Mama would remain an ironclad woman, a sturdy oak in a forest of pines, not a disheveled heap left for the buzzards to pick clean. Mama deserved dignity. She would desire it above all else, and Marie would see it given.

"I say you come!"

Despite his small build, the man jerking the cord seemed more fearsome than the others. Deeply set eyes conveyed infinite fury. He wore red porcupine quills in his top knot to match his coat, his painted face, *and* his prickly temperament. Sinewy muscles covered limbs like carved hickory. He was hard, inside and out, except for three sagging tiers of earlobes that jiggled as he flicked his chin toward Hans. "You him carry. He cry, you scream, I make long sleep."

She nodded, knowing what he meant in spite of his broken English. She slipped her arms around Hans, then lifted him so he sat on her wrists.

He fired warm whimpers against her neck.

"Shh, Hans. Be a good boy. It will be all right." Would he find love among the Shawnee? A wife and children among the Delawares? Sorrow gripped her throat, cutting off her air, as she imagined the grandchildren she would never know.

A Frenchman approached.

"What do you want with us?" She twisted to protect her precious cargo.

The Frenchman drew a knife, then reached for her petticoat, his eyes gleaming.

"What are you doing?" she demanded, her voice turning shrill.

He sliced away her petticoat, laughing, leaving her ankles exposed below the hem of her shift.

She stumbled backwards in shame, hitting the end of the cord.

No woman abducted from the frontier by Indians ever returned with claims of rape. The same could not be said of those captured by the French. Marie's stomach tightened. "Pray, sir," she cried, "not in front of my son."

The Frenchman smirked. "*Je n'ai aucun goût pour les femmes allemandes.*" He hailed a warrior struggling to roll a brass cauldron past the woodpile. Jacob once wrestled with it, too, at the Susquehanna River, and later, at Sherman's Creek, where they nearly left it.

You and this blasted pot!

Mama must have it, Jacob.

It was the first and last time he capitulated to their wishes. Now that same cauldron gleamed in firelight beside the cordwood meant to heat it.

The warrior claiming the prize jogged over. When his eyes met Marie's, his expression softened. He lifted a strand of her hair, rolling it between his fingers as though he'd never seen anything so fine.

She squeezed Hans so tightly she feared she might

suffocate him. They would strip him from her now. She was to be scalped. Raped, and then scalped.

*My poor, dear Han*s . . . He would be alone in this merciless world.

Shorty shoved her from behind, causing her to trip and fall into Cauldron Man's arms, smashing Hans between them. "I'll do whatever you want." She trembled against his chest, slick with grease. "Just don't harm my boy."

Cauldron Man pushed her away gently to deliver an assurance contradicting his formidable appearance. "Stop cry. No one hurt." Full lips the color of wine lifted into a smile, sparking kindness in his eyes. He gave her a reassuring nod, waving the ruddy deer's tail fluttering at his crown.

The Frenchman balled up the ruined petticoat and stuffed it into Cauldron Man's arms. "*Prends ça. Jetez-le sur la tête du cheval.*"

Cauldron Man backed away, keeping his gaze locked on Marie's until he reached the panicked stallion. There, a second Frenchman stripped the petticoat from his arms, then threw it over Heinrich's head.

An argument erupted next to the horse. Mama's murderer fumed at a French officer. The baubles in his ears and nose danced as he heaped more weight on Heinrich's back.

The officer pointed at the stallion's hooves. "*Ils nous trahiront, imbécile.*" He made sweeping motions with his arms as he spoke, gesturing between the upper ridge and the valley below.

Marie guessed the quarrel had something to do with the load on Heinrich's back, but Shorty kept her from finding out. He slung a bulky sack across her free shoulder, then shoved her toward the upper pasture. "We go. You drop, I make sleep."

She wobbled ahead, faltering under the combined weight of Hans and the heavy bag, silently beseeching Cauldron Man to see her plight and save her.

"Go!" Shorty lashed her back with a switch.

She squealed and swayed uphill. In the field Jacob planned to plow at dawn, she turned her ankle.

The switch stung her backside.

She limped onward, sweat stinging her eyes. The intense heat and ruddy light of the barnyard faded, and with them, all hope. She was enslaved now, bound to a man whose cruelty compensated for his pocket-sized build. Her former life was a memory, burned up in a godless wilderness. The new one would expire soon. She had only a few days remaining, maybe less, with nothing left to treasure but the boy in her numbing arms. Even he would be taken from her soon. Of that, she was certain.

When they reached the tree line, Shorty lashed her back with his switch. "You stop."

Marie set Hans down. She leaned against the shaggy bark of a hickory tree to catch her breath.

The valley below glowed red. Five shadows carried plunder up the hill. Three more followed with sticks, swishing them back and forth to lift the trampled grass. They plucked and rearranged everything, erasing all evidence of their departure.

Oh, blessed Jesus, let them miss something.

The absurdity of her prayer punched her in the gut. What difference did it make if they left clues when there was no one alive to follow them?

Chapter 3

James Patterson had not seen Thomas Downey since winter, but a German in his company had—mere days ago, at Fort Granville, sixteen miles upriver.

Stewart left Fort Patterson immediately, which meant no sleep and a moonlit trek across a perilous stretch of unbroken woodland. It also brought a few shillings to his coin bag, as luck would have it, since Patterson sent a letter along with him for Captain Ward.

It was just like Downey to march to his own fife. If he had only sent word that the skins were at Fort Granville instead of Fort Patterson, Stewart could have bypassed Tuscarora Valley—and the sharp tongue in it.

The widow's insult still smarted.

Had he misjudged the glimmer in her eyes at Meyer's table? Their connection had been brief, sure, but potent enough to risk dipping a toe into German waters. And what had it gained him? A thorough scalding up to his Irish balls.

He smirked, oddly charmed.

Rumor had it Catrina Davis refused three previous offers of courtship, two from decent and prosperous men. She seemed altogether uninterested in a second marriage, especially to an Irishman, whom everyone knew she despised. What a crying shame. She was just the sort of wildcat Stewart found irresistible. Her intelligent eyes matched the dark curls she kept properly covered. Her oval face boasted high cheekbones, long lashes, and a pouting mouth any man would pay to kiss. Childbirth had not destroyed her waist. She was, in short, physically perfect in spite of her years.

It was a wicked crime she discounted all Irishman, for in Stewart's opinion, a passionate son from the Old Sod was just what the woman needed.

She would be in her bed now. He imagined her there, covered only by her shift.

He fidgeted in his saddle, admonishing himself for fantasizing at a time and place demanding vigilance. A long journey alone allowed a man too much time to think, particularly one whose most recent taste of a woman was a whore six months ago.

He *should* be thinking about Rachel Campbell. A cherished member of a well-connected family, Rachel was splendidly trained in the arts of ladylike behavior, which included, of course, knowing when to hold her tongue. *She* was the kind of woman for Stewart Buchanan. It certainly didn't hurt that her dowry would more than satisfy his debt.

The thought of money scraped his attention back to Downey. He could forgive the scoundrel's noncompliance if caution lay at the heart of it, but Downey's reluctance to meet him at Fort Patterson likely had more to do with rum than anything else. James Patterson allowed no spirits at his fort. Upriver, at Fort Granville, Captain Edward Ward did; in fact, he stored the fiery stuff for trading with their elusive enemy. Stewart knew this because he and Thomas Martin delivered many casks of spirits just a few short months ago.

Because of rum, Stewart left the reasonable safety of Patterson's stronghold for a fort teetering on the sharp edge of the world. Because of rum, he would push six frothing horses across the same river thrice in one night. Because of rum, he would beat Downey senseless.

A wise man would return to Carlisle, but empty packhorses pointed to looming insolvency, a circumstance that would instantly purge him from Rachel Campbell's list of welcome suitors. There was truth in the rumors of his impending ruin, a reality spelled out in the letter in his bag from his Philadelphian merchant. Isaac Gratz's demand left no room for confusion: Stewart must make a payment by July or risk debtor's gaol.

By the time he reached Granville Run, his backside ached and a rosy strip of diffuse light was erasing the stars. He reined in his horse and cocked an ear, but found it impossible to hear anything over the earsplitting birdsong.

Ace, his winded gelding, pawed at the ground, no doubt as eager as he for a meal and some rest. It had been a long night—too long, thanks to Thomas Downey.

Stewart patted the gelding's neck, then stood in the stirrups to stretch and sniff the air, finding only the scent of horse sweat, now soaking his leggings.

Two steep ridges of the Northern Appalachians pinched the creek here, creating a bottleneck on rising ground—the perfect place for an ambush.

Anxious to lay his head down within the safety of an oak palisade, Stewart clucked his tongue and tapped his stirrups against the horse's sides.

The animal groaned and dragged the pack train onward.

As his gelding picked its way through the murky gap— the last obstacle before Fort Granville—Stewart imagined balling up the letter and shoving it down Downey's rummy throat. His violent thoughts kept anxiety at bay and made the hours pass quickly. In no time, the path leveled out, left the mountain, and then crossed a plain. A mile later, it veered away from Granville Run and stretched north to a loop in the Juniata River, where George Croghan had built Fort Granville on the western riverbank last year.

The smell of mud and a deafening chorus of frogs marked his nearness to the river. Stewart dismounted. He pulled his horses into a grove of brush to await daybreak. The famished animals ripped at leaves while he sat on a log and took the edge off his own hunger with a few bites of dried venison.

As the sun rose, so did his nervousness. In the rising light, he noticed smooth dents speckling the mud around him. *Moccasins.* He eased off the log, then slipped his musket from his packs. He carried it downriver, slinking from tree to tree, wondering what to do if he found the fort destroyed.

When he reached a huge sycamore tree, he peered around its knobby trunk. Across the river, on a steep knoll, wisps of smoke rose up from a stockade with windowless blockhouses overhanging its corners. On the stockade's interior platform, a sentry paraded back and forth, his face visible as he passed each loophole cut into the logs.

Stewart exhaled and leaned his forehead against the tree, noticing many feet had pounded the mud into a slab here. He took a moment to settle and listen for danger before returning for his horses.

He trotted his pack train to the river crossing and then fired a shot from the saddle to announce his arrival. He winced at the waste of powder and a perfectly good ball. Had it not been for footprints, he would have taken the time to assemble his ball puller and save the lead. It could not be helped now.

The stockade bristled as men aimed muskets through loopholes. A few seconds later, a white flag waved above the sharpened tips of the logs.

"Git up, Ace."

The horses splashed across the water.

An ungodly stench greeted him as he rode through the open gate, turning his relief to dread. He lifted his neck cloth as the great door slammed behind him.

Displaced settlers huddled with their meagre belongings at the mouths of drooping tents. Every square inch of earth inside the stockade had been turned to mud. At twenty or more low fires, women in grimy aprons stirred pots and eyed him curiously. None could stretch out her arms without touching another.

"Mercy, man." He handed his reins to the lean soldier patting Ace's neck. "It stinks like the devil's breeks in here."

"Ye get used to it. Private Alasdair Matheson."

Stewart dropped his neck cloth, then shook the hand offered to him. "Stewart Buchanan."

"The gunsmith?"

"Aye, and trader."

"Injun came lookin' for ye last week."

Thank Providence. "He still here?"

Private Matheson shook his head. "Got into a scrap wi' the mornin' watch. Left two pigs dead and a man wounded. Captain Ward thrashed his drunken arse and sent him packin'."

Stewart's face burned. "I deeply regret the trouble. He was supposed to go to—"

"Make no apology on my account." The private grinned, revealing a gap between his front teeth. "We ett pork for three days straight."

Stewart hoped Downey stayed sober long enough to store the skins someplace dry.

The private pointed to a rickety shed. "Ye can put your horses in there. There's a barrel full of water. Some grain and sweet grass in the loft."

Stewart slid out of the saddle. When his feet hit the ground, he winced and reached for his hip.

"Ye come a long way?" the private asked.

"From Carlisle, by way of Patterson's."

"Through Tuscarora Valley?"

"Aye."

". . . whilst their husbands drink up the wages."

He rubbed his forehead as if trying to push the widow's insult from his memory. Sleep would cure him. A refreshed mind was an unsullied mind. First, business.

"I have a letter for Captain Ward from Fort Patterson."

He unbuckled a leather pouch to withdraw the wax-sealed missive.

"He's in the far blockhouse. I'll take it to him. Get your horses settled, and then go on up. He'll want a report of what ye seen on your way in."

Stewart relinquished the letter. He would be glad to talk with Ward again. The young captain had yet to see his thirtieth year, but an insatiable lust for distinguishment meant he already boasted a long list of accomplishments. When the French demanded surrender at the forks on the Ohio, Ward negotiated the terms. Later, he served with George Washington at the Battle of Fort Necessity. If anyone could preserve Fort Granville, it was he.

Stewart slogged through the village of tents to the shed barely capable of accommodating his pack train. If the day turned hot, the beasts would be miserable. He saw no other choice for them. The stalls at the western stockade wall held too many milk cows. Next to them, pigs wallowed in what used to be a decent corral.

He untacked and tended his animals. They would need food and a full day's rest before carrying the heavy skins back to Carlisle, then a good week before hauling the load to Gratz's warehouse in Philadelphia.

He climbed a wobbly ladder to the loft, where two grain barrels guarded a mound of sweet grass. He brought his own grain, but his horses could do with some grass. It would cost him a few pence, but his pack train had earned its grub.

With his animals devouring grass, he left the shed to rummage through his goods for the crate packed with sawdust. Inside, he found the bottles of wine intended for Downey as a bonus. They would go to Ward now, along with a heartfelt apology for the trouble the scoundrel caused.

"Buchanan!"

Stewart nearly dropped the costly bottles.

A young man with devilish good looks flashed perfect teeth. "Don't shite your breeks, old man." He wore the evergreen coat and crimson waistcoat of Pennsylvania's Second Battalion. At his breastbone, a brass gorget reflected the sunlight.

"Armstrong." Stewart pinched a bottle between his arm and side so he could shake the lieutenant's hand. He genuinely liked Edward Armstrong, who was nothing like his standoffish older brother John, or his cousin Joseph, Carlisle's most prominent citizens.

John commanded the entire Second Battalion. Joseph was a respected member of the Pennsylvania Assembly. Young Edward could have entered a similar career, a lucrative one befitting his station. Instead, he took up a musket and followed the fifes and drums across the frontier.

"I have nae seen ye since Croghan's," Stewart said.

Edward adjusted his tricorn hat, crushing the double row of flaxen curls above his ears. "They're calling it Fort Shirley now."

"Aye, I'm having a hard time getting used to it. Croghan still up in New York?"

"Saw him there not long ago. He's with Johnson, interpreting for the crown. Hugh Mercer commands Fort Shirley now."

"I heard. If anyone can gi' the heathens a good scutching, it's that bawdy Scot." Stewart chuckled and gestured to the tents. "Where did these folk come from?"

"The valleys, mostly. Sherman's and Tuscarora."

"How do ye feed them?"

"We have barrels of salt pork left. About once a week, we send out a hunting party."

Stewart thought about mentioning the moccasin tracks, but decided Ward should know first.

Armstrong leaned in, his hazel eyes penetrating. "Folk grow restless. Worried about their livestock and crops, you see, and who can blame them? Captain Ward's been talking about taking half the company out to guard whilst men do their reaping."

"But the fort is already short on men."

"Small in number"—Armstrong patted his gorget with both hands—"but big where it counts."

"Buchanan!" someone shouted.

In the shady northeast corner of the stockade, Captain Ward stepped up and out of his blockhouse in a serious state of undress. He wore only a linen shirt over tan breeches with stockings and buckle shoes, but no waistcoat or leggings.

Stewart would be glad to doff his own leggings, which were soaked, stinking of horse sweat, and growing hotter by the minute.

"There's our captain now. He's some pup, isn't he?" Armstrong asked. He flicked his chin toward the buildings in the middle of the stockade. "I'm in the nearest barracks. Stop by when Ward's finished with you . . . unless you require a nap first."

"Do I look tired?" Stewart asked.

Armstrong made a small bow. "I merely assumed a man of your advanced years needs a bit of sleep after a long journey."

Stewart feigned offense. "A man of my advanced years is about to break a bottle o'er your noggin for calling him a man of advanced years."

Armstrong grinned. "Well, that would be a wild waste of good wine, wouldn't it?" He slapped Stewart's shoulder. "I jest, but not about the visit. It will be good to have the truth from home. I fear my brother does not tell the whole of it."

~ ~ ~

Captain Ward shared the log and chinking blockhouse with seven of his men. The only hint of his superior rank was a table where quills and an inkwell stood ready. In all other aspects, his quarters were like any other—cramped and stinking of stale smoke. Tiers of narrow bunks flanked a central hearth. The dirt floor was damp in spite of scattered rushes and bits of straw accidentally kicked out of the beds.

The captain had an aristocratic face with a patrician's nose and a high forehead. His dark eyebrows matched his hair, which boasted three rows of curls so rigid Stewart thought he might use them for an anvil. Only Ward's hands betrayed his low birth. They were as calloused and scarred as a plowman's.

Ward motioned toward a worm-ravaged chest serving as a bench at a table. "Take a seat. It is good to see you again, my friend. Last time was at Carlisle, was it not?"

"Aye." Stewart sat gingerly.

"Your man Downey made quite the ballocks of himself."

Heat pricked Stewart's cheeks. "A matter I deeply regret. Three pigs is a great loss when there are so many hungry mouths to—"

Ward flashed his palms. "No one finds fault with you." He pulled a shard of birch bark out of a cupboard pegged to the logs, then laid it on the table. "He left this for you."

Stewart picked up Downey's primitive note, unreadable in the feeble light of the open door.

Ward lit a candle lantern, then slid it across the table, illuminating Downey's scrawl.

Bookanun,

No skins. French better gifts. I come back spring.

Stewart slammed his fist down on the message, splitting the fragile bark. "Damn him!"

He was ruined. His packhorses would haul nothing but shame to Carlisle. He may as well hang a debtor sign around his neck.

"I read it, of course," Ward said. "I take it you were counting on those skins to pay for goods already delivered to the cunning heathens?"

Stewart rubbed his eyebrows. "Word of a man's ruin travels fast."

Ward's voice took on a sympathetic tone. "I know by experience, not by rumor. Any man who braves the frontier for a load of deerskins in these trying times is either desperate or mad." He looked down his nose. "I know you're not mad."

There was no point in lying to the astute captain, who had crisscrossed the frontier for many years with his half-brother, George Croghan, wilderness diplomat and King of the Traders.

"I lost nearly everything after Braddock's defeat," Stewart admitted.

"As did many, myself included, though General Braddock paid a higher price than anyone, God rest him. It's the bloody French I blame, always meddling. And on that account, I confess I have some concerns about your man Downey. Why would he come here at all, if he had no skins?" He did not wait for Stewart to reply. "I believe he came to gather intelligence for the French. Or, mayhap, they sent him so they would have a man inside the fort during an attack."

Stewart could not picture the dumpy mongrel as a spy. "It is just as likely he came for rum alone."

"Nevertheless, I believe it prudent to alert Captain Mercer at Fort Shirley. Would you be willing to deliver an express to him and another to Colonel Armstrong upon your return to Carlisle?"

"It's the least I can do to make up for the loss of three pigs." More importantly, it meant a circuitous return to Carlisle. He would avoid Tuscarora Valley . . . and Catrina Davis.

Ward clasped his hands behind his back. "There is another matter I wish to discuss, one perhaps beneficial to both of us. The settlers here grow restless. Who can blame them? A single event stands between them and prosperity."

"The reaping."

"Aye, their fields are nearly ready, fields watered with their very blood and sweat."

Having just lost the one thing that would set him to rights, Stewart understood all too well. He would ride to Canada if it meant bringing back a load of deerskins. "What do ye have in mind?" he asked.

Ward put his hands on the table and lowered his voice. "To put it plainly, I need your horses. I would like to take a detachment across the mountains to guard whilst men reap, but until today, I did not know how I would manage it. Your horses would allow us to return swiftly."

"I have no saddles or bridles. Only hauling tack."

"The men can ride bareback. We have a smithy. He'll make the bits in less than a day. You will be paid for the use of your animals, of course."

"How long will ye need them?"

"The harvest will be over by August. I will send them to Carlisle then. I give you my word they will not be hard used."

Hope blossomed as Stewart mentally tallied his potential earnings. He nodded.

Ward stood upright. "You have my thanks. Would it trouble you to look at a few muskets whilst you are here? Two in particular will not fire properly."

Stewart bowed. "It would be my honor."

Ward pulled a sheet of foolscap from his cupboard. "What I wouldn't give for an aide-de-camp." He sat, dipped his quill in the ink, then scratched a few words across the page. He handed the document to Stewart. "This makes our arrangement clear. I think you'll find it fair." He took out a second piece of foolscap and spoke as he wrote more. "I am deeply grateful and not a little sympathetic to your plight." He signed his name with a flourish, blew on the ink, then slid the missive across the table.

Stewart's heart lurched when he saw Lieutenant Francis Campbell's name. Delivering it would mean an opportunity to see Rachel, the lieutenant's ward and orphaned niece.

"I am recommending you to Lieutenant Francis Campbell for all of the Second Battalion's gun repairs," Ward said. "There will be many needed, given the circumstances."

Stewart could not believe his luck.

Ward laid his quill on the table. "I can afford no detachment to accompany you on your journey to Fort Shirley."

"I prefer to travel alone."

"Good, good. Now, let us discuss what you saw on your way in."

~ ~ ~

With Ward sufficiently briefed concerning the abandoned valleys and the moccasin tracks near the river, Stewart tucked the captain's letters into his pouch and made his way to the barracks.

Armstrong was getting ready to go on watch. He sat on a bottom bunk and pointed to another across from it. "That's my bed. Crawl in and get yourself some sleep. I'll be out for a few hours."

"Is a man of your rank not spared the watch?"

"Not in this blighted hell. To be truthful, I rather like it. My cheeks need a bit of color. This day looks prepared to oblige."

Stewart sat to untie his leggings and kick off his shoes. "Mercy, what a relief. My feet are like overripe pumpkins."

"Smell like them, too." Armstrong rolled a tiny cask out from under the bed. He pulled the bung, took a swig, then held the container out to Stewart. "Here's to your safe arrival."

". . . *whilst their husbands drink up the wages.*"

The smell of rum wafted up to him. He rubbed the back of his neck and stared at the cask. How long had it been since his last drink? Nine years? Ten? The memory of his wife's ashen face draped the weight of a blacksmith's apron across his shoulders. He licked his lips, then shook his head. "Not just now. Too tired."

Armstrong swiped the back of his hand across his mouth, then patted the bung back into its hole. "Private Mosebey nearly ran me over when he saw you ride in. He wants to know if Rose still lives with you."

Stewart had seen the young man making sheep's eyes at his Seneca housemaid on more than one occasion. "Tell him aye, but only until next week, when she weds the new Presbyterian minister."

Armstrong nearly dropped the cask. "She's to be married? It'll *kill* him, man."

Stewart laughed. "I jest, but do ye not think young Mosebey should make his intentions known before someone *does* marry her? I find him altogether agreeable, and I am quite certain Rose returns his tender feelings. I do nae fancy losing the woman, as she keeps a good hoose, but I should like to see her content wi' a man."

In fact, he'd been wondering what to *do* with Rose when he married Rachel Campbell.

Armstrong returned his rum to its hiding place. "One does wonder how Fate expects an illiterate man to court his sweetheart from the confines of a remote fort. I say, Buchanan, I am bored to distraction in these endless woods. What say you to helping our fellow man? I shall write a letter on Mosebey's behalf. Indeed, I shall make our love-struck private a Romeo to your Juliet—with his consent, of course. If he agrees, will you do your part and read my letters to her?"

"As long as ye do nae make them so sappy I boke up my guts."

"You truly believe Rose returns our young friend's affections?"

"She never fails to ask aboot him."

"I always wondered . . . That is to say, she seems rather . . . attached to you."

Stewart laughed. "She is most assuredly attached to me, but only because I saved her life. Edward, she manages my hoose and looks after Thomas for me. That is all."

"Ah, young Thomas. How is the naughty grasshopper?"

Stewart stretched out on the buggy mattress. "As addled as e'er. Many question why I keep an indolent servant."

"You must teach him to act as a true apprentice, make repairs and such, at least whilst folk watch."

"I have, and believe it or not, he is quite skilled. The difficulty lies in keeping him on task. Only Rose can manage him. He would much rather play wi' wains half his age than stand at the forge. I confess, Armstrong, I fear my secret will soon be revealed."

"And your late wife's only child dragged off to an asylum."

"Indeed. There is the heart of it."

Armstrong stood, then seized his musket. He slipped the straps of his powderhorn and ball flask around his neck. "When I get back to Carlisle, I will talk to him. He may listen to me."

"I would be glad of it."

"I'll see you in a few hours." Lieutenant Armstrong left the barracks.

Stewart closed his eyes and listened to the low murmur of too many people in proximity. A cow lowed, a rooster crowed, pots banged, and spoons scraped. A hammer pounded on metal. The blacksmith, already making bits.

He imagined the money he would receive in August, when the provincial forces returned his horses. Tomorrow, he guessed, Captain Mercer would send his own letter from

Fort Shirley to Colonel Armstrong in Carlisle. That meant another few shillings. By July, Stewart would have a decent payment gathered up. By early autumn, he would have a sizeable one—enough to toss Gratz off his back.

Best of all, though, was the letter for Lieutenant Campbell recommending his gunsmithing skills. If that didn't impress Rachel's guardian, nothing would. First, he had to pass through the hazardous expanse of lands stretching between Forts Granville and Shirley, then find his way home to Carlisle. With Shingas and Captain Jacobs on the warpath, every gloomy hollow and spine of rock ahead of him held the potential for danger.

For reasons he failed to comprehend, he would rather face them than the razor-sharp tongue in the valley behind him.

Chapter 4

Catrina grimaced at the light. A pounding headache kept time with her heart.

Mein kopf.

A fierce burning seared her crown, and for a moment, she wondered why she wore a cap of molten lead. A voice like hers moaned. She smelled smoke, grass.

My arms. Where . . . are my arms? One of them served as a numb buffer between her cheek and the ground. The other bent at an odd angle across her waist, dropping her hand somewhere behind her back.

Her parched lips tasted sweet, metallic. *Blood.*

She lifted her aching head to call for help, but managed only a squeak before collapsing.

Flies buzzed close to her ringing ear.

Am I dead?

Answering that meant opening her eyes, and opening her eyes drove a dagger through the bridge of her nose. Through the haze of pain, she found the barn, now nothing but a ribcage against a clear sky. One corner of Jacob's pride and joy remained upright. The rest lay in a smoldering heap.

Willow . . . She was still in the barn. *Must save Willow.*

Catrina rolled onto her belly, pressing her breaths into staccato pants. Blood rushed in painful stings to rediscovered limbs. Defying her agony, she drew her wrists and knees under her torso. She pushed, rocked up, then vomited bile. Her head bobbled weakly, pitching a dripping curtain of hair in front of her eyes to block all but a sliver of the scene. Pinpricks of light distorted even that. Her face felt taut. She touched it and found the tackiness of blood.

What happened?

She closed her eyes and tried to remember.

Jacob. Marie. Hans. They should have noticed her trouble by now. Were they injured, too?

She sagged to one hip to search the yard for the cabin, finding only a smoking lump behind their formerly meticulous woodpile. Next to it, a man with a head made of pounded meat sprawled on the ground.

Jacob.

Panic delivered memories in flashes. She fixed her gaze on Jacob's mutilated corpse and screamed the scream of nightmares: Soundless. Strained. Useless.

She collapsed and curled into a ball. "Marie," she moaned. She cupped her skull to quell its racking throb. Her fingertips touched her sticky crown and turned the burning there to blinding agony. She withdrew her trembling fingers. They were covered in blood.

She tore open her mouth in a silent wail.

Marie.

The child who changed everything was gone, along with sweet, innocent Hans.

Catrina glared at Jacob's corpse, anger erupting in labored breaths that sprayed blood-tinged saliva. How unfair of him to deny her the satisfaction of killing him for this. Was it not enough that his wife and son were now captives? Was her own certain death insufficient for him? Must he also send her to God with resentment in her heart?

Bitterness raged until it burned itself out. Fury yielded to profound acceptance that poured over her like warm wax. What good was hatred now? For that matter, what good was salvation?

She turned her face away from Jacob, closed her eyes, and waited for death to claim her.

~ ~ ~

Something blocked the sun.

Lord?

Velvety lips blew grass-scented breath on her cheek.

Catrina patted the ground until she found a hoof. She grabbed a fistful of coarse feathering and, eyes closed against infinite pain, used it to pull herself up to her knees. She slid her hands, sticky with seeping blisters, up the horse's leg to a knobby joint.

Angela.

Had their attackers deemed the mare unworthy of stealing? Unlikely. The horse must have slipped away unnoticed while they fought with Heinrich, a meatier prize and one better suited for fireside tales of valor.

Catrina swayed to her feet. She seized Angela's mane, then pressed her forehead against the horse's shoulder until a bout of dizziness passed. She opened her eyes to a world seen through bubbled glass, her poor vision distorting everything, even the bloodstain left by her brow on Angela's coat.

Resolve pushed despair aside. If she could mount the horse, she could reach Bigham's fort. Men there would help her. They would rescue Marie and Hans. But how would she mount the horse when she could barely stand?

She retched as another wave of nausea gripped her. Her arms and legs trembled. *I need to lie down.*

Nein. Angela might wander away.

Time was running out. She needed help. Soon. She *must* mount Angela now, while she was at her strongest. It was her best chance of survival and her only hope of saving Marie and Hans.

The woodpile. The splitting stump would make a decent mounting block.

She dug her fingers into Angela's mane. If she lost her grip, she would fall. If she fell, she would never rise again.

She pushed.

Always obedient, Angela responded by turning in the right direction.

Catrina clucked her tongue, wooziness threatening to overcome her. She held on with all her might as the mare dragged her toward the cabin ruins.

Catrina could not bear to look at Jacob, who, by the sound of things, was beginning to gather flies. "Whoa." Her vision blurred. Her legs turned feeble. It was now or never. In a single movement, she stepped up onto the axe-scarred stump and threw her leg over Angela's back.

Pain sliced through her head and stabbed her neck. She pitched forward onto Angela's prominent backbone. With the last of her strength, she laced her fingers into the wiry hairs of the horse's mane and clucked her tongue.

~ ~ ~

Trees. Running water. The sleek hairs of a horse's neck.

Something bruised her sex. A backbone. A backbone of a horse heaving under her. *Angela.*

"Git up," she murmured. She tried and failed to kick the mare's sides.

The mare took a step, then faltered. It took another and stumbled, pitching Catrina onto a pile of last year's leaves.

Catrina howled and reached for her head, then remembered why she couldn't touch it.

The mare groaned and dropped to its knees. Only then did Catrina notice a blackened hindquarter and a puckering slice along the animal's underbelly.

Angela's rear crashed to the ground, narrowly missing her. The old mare rolled onto its side, its legs stiff and straight.

"Nein. Angela, *steh auf.*" Catrina crawled to the mare's

head. She stroked its silky cheek. In the reflection of the horse's dimming eye, a bloody mess stared back at her.

Angela's nostrils flared, expelling a final breath and leaving Catrina alone in a forest that never felt more immense.

~ ~ ~

It took time and effort to tear a strip of cloth from her petticoat. She used it to dab her scalp, turning the linen bright red.

She began to piece together the extent of her injuries. Her left palm was burned. Her head ached unmercifully from the devil's club. That fiend was probably responsible for the bleeding at her crown, too, where she was missing part of her scalp. If she didn't find a way to close the wound soon, she would bleed to death.

Those were her *external* injuries. As gruesome and severe as they were, they hurt far less than her heart. Jacob festered alone on the frontier. Marie and Hans were probably alive, but for how long? The farm—their beautiful tract of fertile land—lay in ruin. Her father's line of superior horses . . . Hans Schneider's dream . . . dead when Angela breathed her last.

The mocking treetops soughed a single word: *Gone*.

The sounds of the attack echoed through her mind—the horses' screams, the crackle of fire, Jacob's brain sizzling on shingles, Marie's rattling prayers, the frenzied chickens, even the bawls of Moo, their poor milk cow.

Oh, how she longed to cry, but her skull would bear no weeping. She sat motionless, staring at nothing in particular, the temptation to admit defeat circling like a buzzard. She need only lie down next to Angela . . . *Angela, steadfast Angela, strong to the end*. Could *she* do less than her horse?

Nein.

She *had* to live. Her loved ones needed her.

Like all dying animals, Angela sought water, collapsing beside a spring trickling through nettles.

Though she wasn't hungry, Catrina mashed up nutritious nettle leaves, then swallowed them with a handful of water. When she was certain the meagre meal would stay down, she rolled onto her back. She shimmied toward the cold spring, careful to keep her head off the ground. When her open wound touched the water, she fainted.

She awoke to a numb head and hair limber enough to tie in mimicked sutures across a pad of linen. Her crude self-treatment seemed to stop the bleeding, but the effort wore her out. She crawled to a sunny log, hoping the sunlight would dry her hair. The brightness worsened her headache and made her sick again. She hugged the log and concentrated on keeping the nettles down. When her nausea passed, she tied a strip of petticoat across her eyes for shade.

Exhausted, she leaned back and dropped her arms to her sides. Hours—or was it days?—later, she awoke to a chorus of crickets. She removed her blindfold. Her hair was dry except for seepage from her wound. Twilight was descending, and with it, the promise of a chilly night. Her neck was stiff and aching. Heat would cure it, but a fire would draw the enemy to her. Besides, she had no flint or steel. Starting a campfire without them required pine sticks and strength, two of the many things she lacked.

How she longed for warmth . . . *Angela*. The horse wasn't finished saving her yet.

With the sun dipping below the horizon, Catrina bound her head with strips of petticoat. She crawled to the mare, which had not yet lost all of its body heat.

Tomorrow, she would follow the spring downstream. With luck, it would empty into Tuscarora Creek, a waterway flowing toward Bigham's fort . . . and help.

~ ~ ~

A fly tickled her nose. She swatted at it . . . and instantly remembered her injury. It was much later than she realized. The sun was almost directly overhead.

She sat up stiffly, anticipating the dizziness that followed. A murder of crows cawed in the treetops. They came for the horse, and in all likelihood, her. Why shouldn't they? She smelled dead, thanks to the blood and urine soaking her tattered garments.

Angela looked leaner in death, a pelt stretched over jagged bones.

Catrina pulled a fallen tree branch out of the leaves, relieved to find it straight and solid. Using it for support, she wobbled up to her feet, then leaned against a tree until stars stopped swirling through her vision.

Putting one uncertain foot in front of the other, she followed the spring, stopping only once to eat her fill of blackberries. She tried to calculate the number of days since the attack. *Nearly two?*

Fever would set in soon. Help was only a mile away, less if Angela went the right way.

Two days.

How far could men drag Marie and Hans in two days? They were probably already at the village Buchanan mentioned. What had he called it?

Two days.

Did Buchanan say he would be back in two days? She couldn't remember. What did it matter? He would never find her this far off the path.

She staggered on, her head like an angry boulder on top of her sore neck.

The sun began to set. Again. This time, in the wrong end of the sky.

It's supposed to be over . . . She shielded her eyes with her hand. *Am I going the right way?*

If the spring didn't lead her to the creek, it would certainly lead her to the river, where James Patterson would protect her with one of her father's fine guns. Buchanan might still be there. He would go after Marie and Hans.

The temptation to rest was great, but the need to help her loved ones far greater. Were they alive? Surely, they were. She would feel something if Marie died, wouldn't she? A mother sensed such things.

A chill raked her spine, an ominous symptom not associated with the setting sun, for it remained a warm day. A new enemy stalked her, one pushing her onward at a turtle's pace in spite of her exhaustion.

When darkness fell, she stayed within earshot of the spring and felt her way through the forest until the moon rose and cast yawning shadows on the steep sides of the hollows. A few days ago, the frightening gloom would have sent her cowering behind a rock. Not now. Nothing frightened her now, not after surviving a mother's worst nightmare.

She spied a bank of moss and considered resting there.

Nein, walk on. Crawl, if you must.

Who said that? Had Papa come to take her to heaven? She was certain she heard his voice.

She teetered against the rough bark of a tree and searched for her father among the shadows. Though she shivered, her face and arms burned. A trickle of sweat dribbled between her breasts.

An owl kept time with a whip-poor-will. Crickets and frogs trilled. She added her hoarse plea to their chorus. "Papa, I'm not ready yet." She had to save Marie and Hans first. "Help me, Papa."

Papa gave no reply.

Chapter 5

In Carlisle, Stewart balanced the Schneider gun across his thighs. Lieutenant Campbell sent it for cleaning immediately after reading Captain Ward's letter. Cleaning a rifle was not a repair—Schneider rifles rarely needed those—and it was a task most men undertook themselves. Stewart guessed Campbell sent the gun as a gesture of good faith, validation of Ward's sound recommendation and a promise of ample work to come.

Pretty Rachel Campbell made no appearance at the lieutenant's fine house, a nonoccurrence Stewart expected, since he knocked at dawn.

The journey back to town had been uneventful except for small bands of Indians encountered near Fort Shirley in a ravine called Shadow of Death by the locals. He went several miles out of his way to avoid a group of them gathered around a campfire only to meet five warriors hauling home a freshly killed bear. Luckily, they took no pains to remain silent, and he was able to hide with his horse in the thick laurel along Aughwick Creek until they passed.

His head ached from sleeping too long into the day. Rose should have roused him sooner. He rebuked her for that. She fell into brooding silence afterward, only breaking it to proclaim he could expect no help from Thomas today, who was out by the beaver dams playing with the Monroe twins again. They'd been building a stick fort since Stewart's departure on Sunday.

Stewart attached a square patch of ticking to the rifle's rod and rammed it through the bore to wick up excess moisture. The cloth came back dry on the third pass. He ran his fingers along the graceful stock, where an engraved patch box matched the brass of the butt plate and trigger guard. Intricate carving adorned the curly maple around the cheek piece; it reminded him of the magnificently etched standing stones from his homeland. The rifle tapered in at its wrist, just behind the hammer. The dip, like the curves of a woman's waist, gave the gun a remarkably feminine quality. How intriguing that something so beautiful could be so dangerous.

Stewart smirked. "Not unlike your daughter, Herr Schneider," he whispered to the late gunmaker. "By God, man, ye knew how to make fine, deadly things."

He hoped Jacob Meyer had reconsidered his decision to stay on his farm and wondered what Hans Schneider would say about the matter. Based upon the quality of his work, Schneider had been both intelligent and passionate, the sort of man to box a son-in-law's ears if need be. What a shame the gunmaker died, and worse, by an Irishman's hand.

He turned the final screw on the lock plate, then ran an oiled cloth over the gun's lock and barrel. With the gun gleaming, he hopped off the stool. Pain shot from his backside into his legs. Unplanned treks were better left to the young, he decided.

He replaced the flint in the hammer's jaws. Lieutenant Campbell would be glad to have his weapon returned so quickly. It would obligate him to invite Stewart in for a chat, a pleasing prospect, since Rachel would be long awake.

~ ~ ~

If Stewart was going to convince Campbell he was wealthy, he couldn't go traipsing around Carlisle wearing a homespun hunting shirt. In the warehouse built onto the back of his house and shop, he overturned piles of goods. "Rose!" He tossed a stack of strouds aside.

Rose glided to the doorway, ever the silent Indian. By her countenance, he knew she had yet to forgive him for chastising her. He paused his search to look at her. "I would have your forgiveness, Rose. Ye know I am of foul mood when first awake."

She grunted and looked away.

He pulled a letter out of his pocket and waved it in front of her aquiline nose. "Would a letter from a certain private at Fort Granville loosen your tongue?"

Her fingers flattened across the floral print covering her ample bosom. The gown he brought from Williamsburg was too extravagant for a housemaid, but with trade suspended, what else was he going to do with it? Besides, he enjoyed spoiling Rose. Since the day he pulled her from the icy waters of the Allegheny, she gave much and asked for nothing. He could never manage Thomas on his own.

"Who sent us a letter from Fort Granville?" Her ebony brows rose above the darkest of eyes.

"Not a letter for *us*, Rose. It is a letter for ye alone from one Henry Mosebey. If ye finish sulking, I shall happily read it."

Her smile replied for her.

"Come, then. Help me find the French weskit meant for Shingas. I lost it in this hopeless mess."

"Thomas was in here playing—"

"Wi' the Monroe twins, I reckon."

"Aye. You should speak to their father, Stewart. I have enough to do without those naughty cubs under my feet."

"Of course. I will." He didn't relish the idea. Monroe was a hothead, and usually drunk.

". . . *whilst their husbands drink up the wages.*"

He rubbed his forehead.

"Does your head ache?"

He nodded. "I slept too long."

"You made that clear enough already."

"That is not what I . . . Oh, Rose, let us not fall back into argument. Come, help me find the weskit. I wish to take a bath."

"Not as much as *I* wish for you to take one." Rose strolled to the far end of a table, past a pile of kidney-shaped canteens. "Here." She pulled out the silk waistcoat, probably the finest on the frontier. "I take it you are going to Campbell's?"

"Aye, well, I canny dine wi' the king, can I?"

She folded her arms and scowled.

"Forgive me, Rose. My recent journey has left me as pleasant as a bag of rats. Come." He extended a hand. "Let us go to the fire, where I shall happily read your suitor's letter."

~ ~ ~

Stewart walked along High Street feeling ridiculous in the silk waistcoat and wondering if Rose was still bent over the smelling salts. Young Mosebey—or rather, Edward Armstrong—had a gift for romantic poetry. His words affected Rose deeply, and certainly uncorked her mouth.

"Do you think Henry could be killed? When will he come back to Carlisle? Could you write a letter for me? How will we get it to him? Is there enough food at the fort? I heard Granville lacks powder. Do you think they lack powder? Is Henry a good shot? Did he look healthy? Do they need a cook? I could go there and cook, you know, if you think they need a cook."

Stewart couldn't help smiling. Love flourished in the most wretched times.

Just past a tavern, the Sign of the Sword, a stockade ringed a fort on the west side of the town square. Unlike Granville, the fort boasted swivel guns at each corner. It had a strong inner clapboard platform for gunners to stand on. The single building in the center of the fort could not accommodate a regiment, though the Second Battalion was in the process of constructing another. Most of John Armstrong's company slept in tents while their officers stayed in Carlisle's grandest houses. Volunteers like Stewart slept at home or in the long line of wagons flanking the road south of town. They entered the fort only for drills.

A stonemason at Stephen Duncan's rising house wished him a good day. By the looks of things, the structure would outshine Lieutenant Campbell's when finished, though neither could rival the grandeur of John Armstrong's blue limestone mansion at the corner of Bedford and High.

Stewart turned up a cobbled path leading to Campbell's door. He rapped on the solid oak.

The lanky English servant who opened the door looked disapproving, even hostile. "Come in." He stood aside to allow Stewart to enter a small but dignified hall. "One moment, if you please." The servant disappeared through a door, then returned a short while later. "This way."

Stewart followed him into Campbell's drawing room.

"Buchanan." Campbell stood at a polished table where he'd been writing a letter. He had a high, sloping brow, a straight nose, and piercing eyes. His provincial coat, with its many brass buttons, hung on the back of his chair. He wore the red waistcoat of his uniform, but strangely, not his gorget. His wheaten wig had three curls above each ear.

Stewart handed him the rifle.

"So soon? No wonder Ward recommends you." He caressed the cheek piece, then hoisted the rifle onto the pegs awaiting it above the hearth. "Such a fine weapon. I would give my eye teeth for another five just like it."

A gunmaker would consider the trade fair; Campbell's teeth were flawless.

Rachel's placid eyes peered above her sewing. She offered a nod and a pleasant smile.

Stewart bowed. "Mistress Campbell, a delight, as always."

"Sit, sit," Campbell said. "I was just finishing up some letters. Dawson!"

The peevish servant reappeared.

"Bring us some sweet cakes and something to drink." He asked Stewart, "What is your preference? It is yet early, but perhaps rum? Brandy? Madeira?" A smile brightened his eyes. "Or, do you have a taste for that rot-gut Monroe distills out by the beaver dams? I myself can find no use for it but starting a fire or cleansing a wound."

Stewart raised two fingers and shook his head. "Water will do."

"I would offer tea, but there is none to be had in this desolate wilderness." Campbell nodded at Dawson, who whirled on his heels to retrieve the refreshments.

Rachel pretended to concentrate on her work while the men discussed the state of the province.

Stewart sought her opinion twice, but she merely replied, "I find such matters best left to men," and returned to her stitching. Her ambiguous smile offered no clue as to her judgment of him. Refined ladies like Rachel were well trained in the art of indifference. For all he knew, the mind past the golden curls was imagining him naked and groaning on top of her. It was possible, wasn't it? Some found him desirable, or so he'd been told, though by whores, and quite long ago.

It was just as likely—indeed, fairly probable—that another suitor occupied her thoughts. His competitor would be striking, eloquent, rich . . . younger.

He refused to succumb to envy. It didn't matter what Rachel thought of him, really. He hoped she at least *liked* him, but it was more important to impress her guardian uncle. Judging by the lieutenant's animation and generosity with refreshments, he was suitably swayed.

". . . were three thousand people living in the settlements last year," Campbell was saying. "And how many are left now?"

"Less than one hundred, certainly." Stewart's gaze remained fixed on Rachel. "And of those, most are at the forts."

"I fear Carlisle will eventually fall," Campbell said. "Colonel Armstrong cannot get the townspeople to participate in a picket guard."

"I am his humble servant, day or night." Stewart searched Rachel's face for a reaction to his brave decree, but she remained expressionless.

"I shall convey your pledge to the colonel when I see him."

"When ye talk to him, ye might let him know the situation at Fort Granville is quite dire. I tried to see him this morn' when I delivered letters from Captains Ward and Mercer, but the sun had yet to rise. The brash, wee banty cock he calls an aide-de-camp would nae let me past the front door."

"Colonel Armstrong is a man of many burdens and little time. Let me assure you, the letter you brought from Captain Ward makes Granville's needs abundantly clear. Armstrong will take the captain's requests seriously. Remember, too"— he winked—"he has a young brother there. If it was up to the colonel, we'd have a wagon train of rifled guns heading west. The confounded *Assembly* is our real problem. Wringing a sixpence note out of that dour passel is like trying to get milk from a duck."

"The problem with the Assembly," Stewart said, "is that it is made up almost entirely of pacifists—"

"Mhm. Mhm." Campbell nodded vigorously. "Quakers."

"—living in the safe zones around Philadelphia. Why should the plight of a few hundred settlers concern them?"

"Indeed. They force destitute men to take matters into their own hands. Look at the Robinsons over in Sherman's Valley and Sam Bigham along the Tuscarora."

Stewart winced at the word.

"Why, had it not been for their own toil in constructing their own forts," Campbell continued, "they would be left entirely defenseless. I say, Buchanan, we are not whipped yet. The people in these backwoods shall give their very lives to protect what they have claimed. We shall succeed against these French devils and their heathen allies or die trying.

"I understand you left horses with Ward's company, a splendid contribution, my good man. Those animals will be a big help to him and profitable for you, I would imag—"

A thunderous pounding at the door shook them to their feet. Rachel dropped her sewing, her crimson cheeks fading to ivory. The swells above her stays rose and fell as all waited for the servant to announce their loud visitor.

"Sit, dear niece." Campbell guided her back to the plush chair. "Dawson will get the smelling salts after he sees who is here."

The servant appeared in the doorway, his eyes full of concern and locked on Rachel. He opened his mouth to speak.

Andrew Milliken, one of Patterson's rangers, whom Stewart had just seen several days ago, brushed past, bringing with him the musty smell of the forest. "Pardon the intrusion, but the matter at hand leaves no time for decorum." He doffed his hat and nodded at Rachel. "Mistress." He noticed Stewart and nodded again. "Buchanan."

"Let us not distress the fairer sex among us." Campbell smiled at Rachel, then pulled Milliken out of the room. He returned a short while later, his alarm feebly cloaked. "I am sorry to cut our visit short, but I must go to Colonel Armstrong at once. Dawson, bring the mistress her smelling salts. No time to explain, Buchanan." To Rachel, he said, "Do not worry, darling. It is nothing serious."

But it was serious, serious enough for Campbell to abandon propriety and leave Stewart standing there, inappropriately alone with Rachel. She dabbed her eyes, and Stewart wondered whether he should comfort her. Would she welcome it?

She was as delicate as the first skift of ice on a pond. He supposed an uncle's indulgence and a cosseted life were responsible for her fragility. Girls exposed to hardship grew into resilient women. Unexpected news did not topple them; it spurred them into action. They reached for powderhorns and guns, not smelling salts.

He wondered how Catrina Davis would react in the same situation. Had the state of affairs not seemed so ominous, he would laugh at the thought of her fighting Campbell for the rifle.

The tick of a clock on a Chippendale table punctuated the awkward and lengthening silence as Stewart fumbled for a way to exit gracefully. In the end, he simply bowed and left Rachel to Dawson's care. The servant stood in the entrance hall waiting to bolt the door, a fowler resting against his shoulder and two more leaning against a table. Campbell had seen to his niece's safety, although if real trouble came, the lieutenant would surely take his niece *and* his servant to the fort.

The streets of Carlisle buzzed like a downed hornet's nest. Women shoved children through doorways into their houses. Dogs barked at nothing. Men ran with muskets for the open gate of the stockade, their powderhorns, leather flasks, and pouches slapping their sides. The contagion even infected the horses. Herds of them thundered inside corrals, raising the dust.

Stewart found Rose dragging Thomas across High Street. The boy swung wildly at her outstretched arms. By the time Stewart reached them, Thomas sat in the middle of the street crying and rubbing a rosy imprint of Rose's hand on his cheek.

"What happened?" he asked her.

Thomas wailed like a toddler.

"Another massacre in Tuscarora Valley," Rose replied.

The hairs lifted on Stewart's neck. "Whose farm? Shut up, Thomas!"

"I do not know. Help me get this lunatic home."

Thomas kicked at them when they tried to lift him off the ground. "Let me be. I want to work on our fort. I want to work on our fort! You'll be sorry when the Injuns come and get ye."

They lugged him down High Street and through the doorway of their house.

Stewart shoved the boy into a chair. "Stop it!" He handed a loaded fowler to Rose. "Stay here until I see what happened. We might need to go to the fort. Keep him inside until I come back."

He shook Thomas's shoulders, forcing the teen to look away from the cornhusk doll he now shredded. "Thomas, bide wi' Rose. Do ye understand me, lad? I have to go to the fort. Ye must bide here."

Thomas's scowl gave way to delight. "I have a fort. Ye wanna see it?" When he smiled, he looked so much like Mary.

"When I get back. If ye stay here and be good, I'll bring ye a surprise."

"I like surprises." Thomas skipped the frayed doll across his thigh.

Outside, Stewart nearly collided with Elias Hoffman.

"Vat have you heard?" the German asked.

"There's been a massacre in Tuscarora Valley."

"Then you know as much as I. Benjamin Tremble brought the news. They say he is outside Smythe's tavern."

They found Benjamin besieged by a crowd. He had not witnessed the scene of the massacre, but spoke with a man who had—Joseph Redcoat, one of the friendly Indians staying in Sherman's Valley with Andrew Montour.

Stewart pushed his way through the mob, his heart in his throat. "Which farm was it this time?"

"The horse farm."

"Jacob Meyer's?"

"Aye, the very one. Meyer's dead," Tremble said.

Stewart's legs threatened to collapse under him. "God help them. What of the women and the wain?"

Tremble shook his head. "No sign of 'em. Stock was all gone except for one dead mare with a foal ripped clean out of her belly."

The crowd uttered a collective gasp.

"Too burdensome to drive off," Joseph Duncan said. Joseph was one of two coopers in Carlisle.

"Aye," Tremble said, "so they cut off her hindquarters and carried *them* off. Redcoat got himself and Meyer's corpse to Robinson's fort before nightfall, but he nearly killed the horse under him in doing so. He reckons the enemy will move on Fort Bigham or Fort Granville next."

Duncan muttered, "Thank heaven Sam Bigham had the good sense to move back to York."

Hoffman whispered to Stewart, "Sam Bigham could *afford* to leave. Vat about those poor souls who could not, the ones sheltering at Bigham's fort?"

"Good question," Stewart replied.

Hoffman had tears in his eyes. "Vat is to become of them? How long can they last? There is no garrison, just a handful of backwoods farmers viss no military skill. They do not have enough provisions for a lengthy siege. Someone must do something." He scratched under his large hat and stared at the ground. "I vill write Joseph Armstrong. He *must* convince the Assembly to do something, and soon, or there vill not be a man left alive on the other side of the mountains."

~ ~ ~

Stewart lit a candle and blew out his lantern. Replacing the spring screw on a fowler required bright light and a steady hand, neither of which he possessed at the moment. Though Armstrong's scouts reported no fresh signs of Indians near the town, Stewart's anxiety had yet to subside.

He carried the candlestick toward the door separating his shop from the main room of his house, then paused to listen as Rose schooled Thomas on the proper way to prick biscuits.

They were safe for now. So, why did he feel so rotten?

Catrina.

Joseph Redcoat found no women among the devastation at the Meyer farm, which meant they either went to the fort or Indians took them captive.

God help the dumb brute who thinks he can handle Catrina Davis.

He smiled, then bit his lip as truth twisted his amusement into shame. There was nothing funny about captivity. Jacob's death and the mangling of the pregnant mare meant Catrina Davis already witnessed a small measure of the enemy's cruelty. It hurt his heart to imagine her clinging to Marie and Hans while stumbling over limbs and sharp rocks. Hopefully, they knew to keep Hans quiet. If he sniveled, the Indians would swing him by his heels and silence him against a tree.

Stewart would not wish such atrocities on his worst enemy, let alone people he liked. With Meyer dead, no one would search for Catrina and Marie. They were probably divided by now, one heading west to Ohio and the other north to Canada. They would assimilate into the tribes, if they lived long enough. That was what bothered Stewart the most, he reckoned—Catrina's poor odds of survival. She was certainly strong enough to withstand the malnutrition and backbreaking toil heaped upon captives, but the indomitable spirit he found so alluring would ultimately mark her downfall. She was just the sort of prisoner Shingas used as an example to exact obedience from the rest. Catrina would try—and fail—to escape. Her crime would earn her a gruesome, public death meted out over the course of days.

Unless . . .

He returned to his stool, then set the candle down on his workbench. Its flame lengthened the sensuous sway of shadows on the walls.

If only she had taken his advice and gone to the fort.

Mayhap, she had.

Wishful thinking, and he knew it.

Still . . .

It was *maddening* to wonder. Nothing but fresh news from Bigham's fort could cure his misery. He wouldn't have any until someone came to Carlisle for provisions. Armstrong could spare no men to go over the mountains; he'd even denied Andrew Milliken's request to return to Fort Patterson.

The isolated settlers in the Tuscarora valley were on their own until Captain Ward brought Stewart's horses. That might not happen for a fortnight, when the harvest was ready. The people at Bigham's fort could not hold out until then. Someone there would eventually risk a trip to Carlisle for supplies. Stewart would learn Catrina's fate then.

Or . . .

The unfinished thought circled like an osprey waiting to dive with outstretched talons.

He glanced at the fowler resting in his vise and wished the light had held. He would be busy now, his mind distracted by delicate work, not fretting over the plight of an Irish-hating woman who was decidedly *not* his responsibility.

Even if she *had* gone to Bigham's fort, her troubles were far from over. He recalled the filth at Granville, five times the size of the blockhouse Sam Bigham built and then abandoned. Granville held a garrison; Bigham's fort didn't. If Catrina fled there, she grieved with too many others behind a hastily constructed stockade. He imagined her trembling in the darkness—isolated, hungry, traumatized. Stuck.

At some late hour, the unanswered question of Catrina's fate became intolerable, leaving him two choices only: cross the mountains or go mad.

He would not go mad.

Chapter 6

Gunshots echoed down the creek. Catrina recoiled, falling onto her backside. She slid down the bank into the creek, then wobbled to her feet, nearly losing her balance again on the slippery creek bed.

Where are my shoes?

She could not recall losing them. Indeed, she could not recall wearing them.

Creek water wicked up her skirts and tugged her toward the channel. She gathered up the dripping fabric, then splashed upstream to a flat rock. Shivering, she sat upon it to catch her breath.

Where did those shots come from?

She cocked an ear, hearing only the falls of the creek and an unconcerned woodpecker.

Sunbeams pierced the treetops and glinted off the water. Shielding her eyes, she checked the sun's location. Angela had wandered miles past the fort, she knew now. Catrina originally went east. A few hours ago, she realized her error and turned around. With no hint of the fort in sight, she wondered now if it might have been better to press on to Patterson's.

She hugged herself, assessing her stores of strength. Could she reach the far side of the ridge where the afternoon sun still blanched the trees? She needed its heat; a night in wet clothes would prove lethal.

With twigs jabbing her soles and thorns snagging her hands and heavy garments, she climbed, crawling spider-like at times. Partway to the summit, a grouse flushed. She gasped . . . and fainted.

~ ~ ~

Catrina lay on plush moss serenaded by countless birds. Wind tickled lush foliage and nudged branches against a cloudless sky. Butterflies wheeled through shafts of light that brightened the umber trunks of ancient trees.

Nature had parted the curtains to reveal its finest room, an exquisite death chamber, Catrina reckoned. She closed her eyes and savored the warmth of peace, tempting death to claim her.

Hans. He must be so frightened.

Robbed of tranquility, she arose and pressed on, her joints creaking like new rope and her eyesight faltering under the burden of an unbearable headache. Still, she battled the incline, plonking one foot in front of the other until at last, she reached the summit.

Hope drifted in on a whiff of smoke.

She scoured the endless patchwork of vegetation stretched out below.

There.

A charcoal plume rose up from a dark square. *Pines.* Sam Bigham's lands lay in the middle of an evergreen forest. She distinctly remembered Hans and Benjamin McIlroy throwing pinecones at each other last year when they'd gone to pick up salt Jacob ordered from Carlisle.

Judging by the smoke's color and thickness, the settlers inside the stockade felt safe enough to roast a fat bear. The earlier shots had been theirs, she knew now. They would cook the liver first, a rich organ she needed for restoring her blood. She hurried, unwilling to miss her portion, sliding down the sunny face of the ridge and adding more cuts to her soles.

With no time to waste, she rested only when dizziness threatened to overcome her. Her skull throbbed and her feet bled, but she battled on, counting each step a victory.

When the terrain leveled out, soft leaves gave way to the prick of sloughed needles. Smoke hung in layers at eye level, hazing the forest. The thought of liver made her mouth water. She pictured Robert and Jane Cochran rushing through the stockade gate to seize her. Francis and Margery Innis would be there, too, and Susan Giles, heavily pregnant with her first child. The women would tend her wounds. The brave men would retrieve Marie and Hans.

She could barely see now, and not just because of the smoke. Color flashed like the northern lights, distorting her vision. Her legs faltered.

Not now. Not when she was so close!

She shut her eyes and lurched ahead, bumping into trees and adding more rips to the skirts trailing behind her.

The brightness of unfiltered daylight made her wince. She covered her eyes with hands that still seeped from burns.

Sam's field.

Hot furrows caved beneath her feet as she limped across the plowed turf, smoke stinging her nostrils. It was so thick! How many bears had they shot? She was close enough now to hear the snap of flames. Surely, they would turn away from their butchering and notice her soon.

"Help," she whispered, though she meant to scream the word.

She was dizzy, so dizzy. Would her eyes allow her one second of vision? Her circumstances warranted the risk of nausea, she thought.

She dropped her hands.

A mutilated man lay in a rut beside her.

Ahead, flames engulfed Bigham's fort.

Anguish turned her legs to limber blades of grass. She faltered, her gaze locking on a woman hunched against the burning logs of the stockade. *Susan.* Fear for the pregnant woman kicked her onward. *She'll burn up, and the babe with her!*

"Susan, come away." Catrina staggered across the field through intense heat, refreshing her burns and puffing steam from her tattered gown. At the stockade wall, she stooped to push Susan upright. A babe, still attached to its cord, lay among Susan's intestines. Both had been scalped.

Catrina vomited. She reeled backwards, then fainted.

Chapter 7

The horse Stewart borrowed from Hugh Gallagher was holding up well in spite of its narrow shoes. Like most traders, Hugh could no longer afford a blacksmith's services. To save on cost, he trimmed his horses' hooves to fit shoes he owned. It was better than no shoes at all, Stewart supposed, but another six months of the careless practice would lead to a stable full of lame horses.

He would have preferred his own horse, but Ace needed rest, and Gallagher owed him a favor.

The borrowed horse snorted as it climbed. Settlers and traders called this track "New Path" though the trail was anything but modern. Innumerable feet, first Indian and now European, used the trace since the dawn of time. It started at the Susquehanna River, then scored rich fields and cut across pristine waterways in Sherman's Valley. On Tuscarora Mountain, it wound around spines of rock and massive trees, then snaked down into the fertile Tuscarora valley through Bigham's Gap, a boulder-littered fissure carved into the mountain by Laurel Run.

It was just before this gap when Stewart caught movement. He yanked on his reins, then dismounted quietly.

Something blue passed between tree trunks.

Stewart's heart drummed. A man could expect shades of azure above the canopy and along the waterways, where bluebells formed thick carpets, but at eye level, a patch of blue meant one thing: man. And in the backcountry, man meant the possibility of danger.

He pulled the horse onto a bed of moss behind the dense boughs of a hemlock tree. Taking care to avoid stepping on twigs, he tied the reins, then crept to a limestone outcrop to observe his company.

On the trail ahead, the blue checked shirt moved west, dipped low, then returned. The man wearing it repeated the process three times. On the fourth, Stewart guessed why.

Horse threw his packs.

Spilled packs were never fun, especially in pouring rain or in dangerous territory. The fellow could probably use some help, but Stewart wanted to get a good look at him before offering any. The traveler could be French or worse— and only one of many lurking nearby.

Using a fallen chestnut tree for cover, he scuttled closer, cursing under his breath when the barrel of his gun rustled a grapevine. He leaned against the rotting log, held his breath, and waited.

A minute passed before he heard the man shuffling through leaves again. Stewart blew out his breath and peered over the log.

Just off the path, John Gray hoisted a pack saddle toward a sorrel gelding. At his feet, a jumble of goods lay dangerously close to fresh manure.

Stewart shouldered his rifle, stepped out from behind the tree, and coughed.

The saddle thudded back to the ground. Gray lunged for a fowler leaning against a rock.

"John Gray," Stewart said. "Do nae shoot."

"God's grace, Buchanan." Gray covered his heart with his hand. He set the fowler down again. "You cleaned the dung right out of me. I might have shot you for an Indian."

"If I *was* an Indian, your hair would be hanging from my belt now. Been watching ye for a solid two minutes. Ye by yoursel'?"

"I am *now*. Me and Innis was coming back from Carlisle when a sow and two cubs crossed the trail." He bent to retrieve the hapless saddle, then flopped it across the gelding's back. "This miserable horse spooked and took off. Scattered everything. Took me over two hours to find this much of it. Still missing a spice box I bought for Hannah." He scowled at the gelding. "Miserable horse."

It was a terrible loss. Spices were expensive.

Stewart scanned the ridgeline while holding the saddle so Gray could tighten a cinch. "Innis still looking for the spices?"

Gray shook his head. "Told him to go on without me." He tossed a string of casks over the horse's back. "Hated to leave our families, but we've been short on salt and flour at the fort for weeks."

Stewart's breath caught in his throat. "The fort? Bigham's fort?"

A sack puffed dust as Gray tossed it onto the horse's back. "Nowhere else to go. Hannah's folk went back to England. Mine are dead."

"Is Jacob Meyer's family at the fort?"

Gray halted mid-tie on a knot, his expression grave. "Have you not heard?"

"I heard Meyer's dead. Passed his grave this morn' at Robinson's. I was hoping his women made it to Bigham's."

"I wish I could tell you, but I know not. We was in Carlisle when the atrocity happened, which is why Innis went on ahead. Worried about our families, you see."

Stewart understood. "I went through Tuscarora Valley only a few days ago. Saw some moccasin prints along the river by Granville and a wee band of warriors on this side of Fort Shirley, but naught else."

"I am relieved to hear it." Gray returned his attention to the rope, which he knotted angrily. "Though I begin to think our enemy capable of dissolving at will. They appear from nowhere to strike and then vanish like smoke. The Assembly *must* equip us and soon. We are not trained soldiers. Hell's fiery gates, man, we aren't really farmers, either, are we? We're just trying to get by. Me and Innis went to see Colonel Armstrong yesterday, but his aide-de-camp said he would not be available until today. We missed our appointment, because when word reached us about Meyer, we set out at once." He donned his worn hat, then tapped it down. "I would be there now if those bears had not crossed our path. Just my rotten luck. This miserable horse."

Stewart sought to reassure him. "If Innis found trouble, he would be back by now."

"I pray you are right." Gray untied his horse's lead rope while looking at the trail behind them. "Surely, you're not on foot."

"Horse is behind yon hemlock. I'll get him and walk along wi' ye. Ye're welcome to ride, if ye want. My arse is wild sore."

"I will accept your kind offer. We marched through the night. Didn't even stop at Robinson's. Relieved to see it standing, though."

Stewart retrieved his horse, then handed his reins to Gray.

The exhausted settler climbed into the saddle. "It's good to sit for a spell, I tell you. I am much obliged. Shall we?" He squeezed the borrowed horse into action without waiting for a reply.

Stewart led Gray's packhorse onward.

"What brings you out this way?" Gray asked.

"Expecting deerskins at Patterson's." It sounded plausible. He hoped Gray would not question him further.

"Must not be many, what with only one horse."

Heat swept across Stewart's cheeks. He hadn't thought of that. "A man's got to take what he can get these days."

He hoped he sounded convincing. "Not many furs and skins making their way east since the Delawares went on the warpath. Speaking of which, we better move as quietly as possible. I would like to keep my hair."

That ought to shut him up.

With Laurel Run babbling beside them, they wound down the mountain. Gray dozed in the saddle, one hand loosely holding his reins and the other locked—even in sleep—on his fowler. Peril gifted men with such talents.

An hour later, the June heat turned oppressive. The horses sweated foam. They tossed their heads and swatted their tails at flies drawn to their discomfort.

Stewart fanned himself with his hat, then untied his sash.

When a shadowy veil sullied the forest, Gray awoke. "Whoa." He stood in the stirrups to stretch. "Looks like a storm's coming."

Stewart eased down to rest on a cool rock. "I shall be glad of it. It's hotter than the devil's shoe buckles." He pointed to a flour sack on the packhorse, now stained by sweat. "Bread's gonny taste like shite for a while."

Gray tensed, still standing in the stirrups. "Merciful God."

"Och, come now, it's only a sack of . . ." Stewart's words trailed off when he saw the real reason for Gray's panic: mushrooming smoke in the valley below.

"It's the fort! Something's happened!" Gray kicked the gelding's sides. "Yah!"

The animal sprang forward, scooping up and tossing pebbles and clods of ruddy earth with its ill-fitting shoes.

"John, wait!" Stewart leapt to his feet.

Hugh Gallagher's horse cleared a fallen log and disappeared with Gray.

"Of all the dumb ideas," Stewart muttered. If Gray survived the careless ride, he would get himself killed at the fort, where the godless devils were probably still reveling in their debauchery.

There was no time to dally. He sliced through the ropes on Gray's packs, sending the frontiersman's precious goods to the forest floor again. With his rifle in one hand and the packhorse's lead rope in the other, he jumped onto the rock, then threw a leg over the horse's back. Its hot sweat instantly soaked his breeches.

"Yah!"

The sorrel horse reared, then careened down the treacherous decline at a terrifying pace, clearing logs and skidding on loose stones. Stewart clenched his thighs and seized both rope and mane, fearing the strike of a low branch at every turn.

At the foot of the mountain, the trail leveled out and left the forest. He caught sight of blue and kicked his horse's flanks.

The horse belted toward the smoke fanning out against low storm clouds.

With no reins, Stewart maintained his balance by prayer and muscle alone. He cocked his gun.

His horse splashed through a creek, then raced across a meadow.

Just past a newly plowed field, where moccasin prints speckled the loam and dead men sprawled in furrows, Bigham's fort smoldered. Deep ruts from driven livestock led from the stockade to the pine forest.

Gallagher's horse, now riderless, panted at a fence rail.

"Hannah! Jane!" Gray wheeled toward the stockade, its entrance now secured by extreme heat. He cupped his hands around his mouth and shouted through the open gate. "Hannah!"

Stewart hastily scanned the scene as he dismounted the breathless packhorse. His legs burned from the toil of riding bareback as he dashed to Gray. "John, pipe doon. The fiends canny be far awa'." He gripped the distraught man's shoulders, but John's eyes looked through him to the corpses strewn about the field.

John sank to his knees, then hid his face in his hands. "Pray, look for me. I cannot."

Stewart laid a hand on John's quivering shoulder. "Aye, John. Bide here. I'll look. Just stay quiet."

Bigham's roof gave way, sending slates clattering into the belly of the blockhouse. Embers soared on a column of soot. There was no point in looking inside. The small amount of powder the settlers kept in the blockhouse must have exploded. No one could survive the inferno.

In the field, he found John Cochran and Thomas McKinney dead and scalped beside a butchered milk cow. There was no sign of Francis Innis or his family. The father of three probably thought himself fortunate when the bear scattered John Gray's packs and not his. Now, he was either captured or burned to death inside the blockhouse.

Stewart closed Thomas McKinney's eyes, then stole around the stockade and found Susan Giles blistering against the charred stockade wall. The state of her corpse made him clutch his belly.

"Blessed Jaysus, lover of my soul . . ."

He looked away, lightheaded, bile rising in his throat.

A second woman lay in a furrow among twenty or more severed chicken heads. As Stewart knelt beside her, he saw signs of previous injury. He stared at the bandages wound around her skull and considered the unfairness of surviving one attack only to fall prey to another. Her lifeless face was too swollen and grimy to identify.

If it's Hannah, John will go mad.

He cast a sympathetic glance at the sorrowful man staring vacuously at the ruins.

Stewart went to his horse, then returned with his canteen. Clean features might help him positively identify Hannah Gray.

He knelt to pour water on her face, feeling uneasy about disturbing the dead.

She moaned.

"Mercy!" He fell onto his bruised rear, losing the canteen, then crawled back to her. "Hannah? Hannah Gray?"

She moaned and blinked at the water pooling in her eyes.

He dabbed her face with his sleeve. "Hannah, can ye hear me?"

"*Lass m-mich s-sterben*," she slurred. "*Du irischer Teufel.*"

He covered a gasp, smearing dirt across his mouth, then sifted through the few German words he knew. "Frau Davis. Catrina, *sind sie das?*"

~ ~ ~

Garish sunlight outlined bold thunderclouds.

A man's unnatural keening gored Catrina's soul. She recognized the animalistic sound, and it brought tears to her eyes.

"My little girl," the man wailed. "Oh, my Janie."

Catrina turned her face toward the sound of sorrow.

He rocked on his knees, a silhouette made by fire.

. . . shall cast them into the furnace of fire: there shall be wailing and gnashing of teeth.

Hell. She was in it.

The devil loomed over the grieving man, saying, "I will nae let ye go, John."

The devil was Irish. Of course he was.

The sad man wanted to look for his family.

The devil refused to let him.

"We have to get this woman o'er the mountains, John. She'll die wi'oot our help."

An arm slid under her neck to force her up.

Hell plummeted into darkness.

~ ~ ~

She didn't have to open her eyes to know she straddled a horse. A man rode behind her with his arm crushing her against his him. *Papa?* She had much to tell him. "Papa," she muttered.

"Hush, woman."

His homespun shirt smelled of wood smoke and linseed oil, the hallmark scents of a gunsmith.

Oh, Papa. Her eyes fluttered open, revealing an unfamiliar powderhorn tied to her wrist.

The animal under them was a gaunt thing with burrs and beggarticks tangled in its mane.

Whose nag is this? Papa would not own a horse so hideous. He wouldn't press himself against her, either. Why, the man behind her had his thighs against hers! And he held her so fiercely her bosom threatened to escape her stays!

The violation unnerved her. "Who . . ."

"Hush, now. Almost there."

She remembered she needed help. "Marie. Need—"

"She's going to get us killed."

John Gray? Was *he* riding behind her?

Suddenly, she didn't care. It was enough to be alive.

~ ~ ~

Stewart failed to convince John Gray that pursuing the enemy was suicide.

John helped him get Catrina as far as Bigham's Gap, then hid his packs and headed northwest with the powder and lead brought from Carlisle. He needed them now more than ever, he said.

Stewart rode on without him, his arms aching from holding Catrina upright in the saddle. They passed Thomas Mitchell's sleeping place, a sagging shack three logs high. He considered stopping there for the night, but the storm dogging them pushed him on. Now, as lightning flashed and the first drops of rain splattered against his arms, he saw the soundness of his decision. This would be no mild shower. Mitchell's shack leaked; Robinson's blockhouse didn't. It lay a few miles ahead in Sherman's Valley. He would find shelter and help there.

The poor creature under them was beginning to share their misery. It threw a shoe on the south side of the mountain, a clench taking at least some hoof with it. Stewart could afford no time to retrieve the iron or examine the limping gelding. Hopefully, the crack wasn't too bad. He could pay for a shoe, but not a horse.

Wind howled down from the ridges and rippled fields of nearly ripe grain. In the deepening gloom, they passed the abandoned homesteads of Hugh Alexander, John Byers, John Hamilton, and John Wilson, Irish to a man. Like Stewart, they traded Ireland's high rents and taxes for the hope of prosperity. Some indentured themselves in exchange for passage across the sea. Others sold everything they owned in order to afford full fare. Each endured eight appalling weeks or more in the putrid belly of a brig.

Desperation pushed them past civilization into the wilderness, where dreams of success made ceaseless hardship a just sacrifice. They felled trees for cabins and carved fields out of the forest. Blood, sweat, and seeping blisters joined the rain in watering their seeds. What was their reward? Existence. Existence under constant threat of attack with acres of nearly ripe grain they could only observe from a hastily constructed blockhouse.

Stewart hoped Captain Ward would soon bring men to guard the reapers. Any loss now would be keenly felt by his countrymen, both financially *and* emotionally. Many would never recover. The hardy Presbyterians deserved a harvest in their Promised Land. They were poised to reap one beyond imagining . . . if only the enemy would let them.

Under torrential rain, the silhouette of Robinson's fort rose up against the dimming sky. There was danger in entering one fort when another lay in ruin. If Captain Jacobs had yet to satisfy his bloodlust, Robinson's could be the chief's next target.

Stewart inspected Catrina's swollen face and considered the wisdom in pressing on to Montour's.

Her eyes rolled in their sockets as she tried to focus on him.

Nay, he decided. Another two hours in the saddle would kill her. He had no choice but to seek George Robinson's help.

Lightning ushered in fearsome claps of thunder and stinging sheets of rain.

"Who goes there?" a man shouted.

Stewart was not surprised the sentry saw him from a great distance. George Robinson had wisely situated his fort on a knoll with a commanding view of his lands and the surrounding countryside. Less than twenty feet from the stockade gate, a spring flowed even during droughts, which meant a natural moat and no want of fresh water.

"Who goes there?" the man demanded more forcefully.

"Whoa." Stewart gently covered Catrina's ears. "Buchanan!"

When he heard the squeal of the stockade gate, he tapped the horse's sides.

The animal splashed through the rising waters, then limped up the hill.

George Robinson met them halfway to the fort. The broad-chested man had the swagger of a Highland chief.

Never one for pleasantries, he fisted the horse's reins below the bit. "God Almichty, did the bloody savages get her?"

Stewart allowed Catrina to slip from the saddle.

Robinson let go of the leather to catch her in his thick arms. "Who is she?" he asked, heading for the fort.

"Catrina Davis." Stewart dismounted with a groan, then led the horse uphill. "I found her in the field at Bigham's fort." He tapped Robinson's meaty shoulder, turning him. "George."

Rain trickled past Robinson's temples. "Aye?"

"Bigham has fallen."

Robinson's piercing eyes sparked with alarm before turning resolute. "It's pishin'. Let's gae inby an' talk in peace."

Robinson's fort boasted no swivel guns, no barracks, and no regiment. Two walls of the blockhouse formed one corner of the stockade. Robinson built the structure near the gate so its second floor overshot the first. The clever design made it possible for defenders to shoot down upon any would-be attackers. Today, the overhang provided shelter for five Indians.

Stewart bristled.

Robinson sensed his nervousness. "Iroquois," he said, as they passed through the gate. "They're feart noo that Montour joined Croghan and Johnson in New York. Lost all faith in the governor back in January when John Harris got himsel' ambushed on the way to Shamokin. There's been some haver o' them leavin' the valley, or at the least, sending their women and wee'uns to McKee's storehoose o'er on the Susquehanna. I suppose when they hear your news, there'll be nae stopping 'em."

Stewart recognized Joseph Redcoat, a lean warrior wearing an outdated officer's coat, but the rest were foreign to him.

On the new shooting platform clinging to the interior walls of the palisade, two soaked men paced back and forth with greased skins of cows' knees covering their musket pans to keep their gunpowder dry.

Robinson draped Catrina over his shoulder, then strode to the blockhouse. "Unsneck the door, ye louts," he shouted.

A hole yawned above them. A ladder stuck out like a tongue.

Robinson climbed up as if he carried a pillow and no more.

Stewart followed him into a room reeking of sweat, shit, and tallow. A single grease lamp illuminated the walls, where settlers sat like salted kippers, some with as many as three children on their laps.

"Michty me!" A woman rushed to spread a colorful stroud on the floor. "Lay her here."

Robinson eased Catrina down to the waiting blanket.

Women lit every available lamp and candle, adding more heat to the sweltering room. They carried their lights to Catrina, surrounding her while men sought news from Stewart.

He gave them a full report.

A debate followed over how to respond to the attack on Bigham's fort. Some thought it best to hunker down and defend their own fort. Others wanted to range out and "slay the divils whar they sleep."

When the argument heated to the point of fisticuffs, George Robinson raised his hand to silence everyone. "We'll go noo whilst it's dark an' their fires can be seen at a safe distance. Not a one will expect us in this bleeter."

He sent Joseph Redcoat to warn the friendly Iroquois at Montour's. Stewart was to stay behind with Robert Miller. Miller would take the first watch. Stewart would take the second, after much-needed sleep.

With rain battering the shingles, Robinson's men carried the few guns they had out of the blockhouse. Others took knives, hatchets, and even hayforks. They ranged out in parties of three with instructions to return at dawn, when George Robinson would plan their next action based upon reconnaissance.

Stewart stripped out of his wet shirt. He lay down on a blanket, too tired to suffer shame at his state of undress.

The women were too busy to notice. They had stripped Catrina down to her shift and were busy assessing her injuries.

Rebecca Robinson dispensed orders. "I need warm water an' a jug of Wilson's *poteen*. Haud the lamp closer, Elizabeth. Not too close or ye'll licht the puir woman afire. Gi' me thon cloot so I can wash her hauns. Och, see here, she burned hersel', the puir wee thing."

At the edge of the scene, a girl swayed and held her belly.

"Ye fixin' to boke?" Rebecca handed her Catrina's limp garments. "Here's an excuse to take some air. Soak these wi' the rest of oor salt or she'll ne'er get 'em redd. They may be rags, but they're likely the only clays she has. We'll do oor best to repair them for her."

A woman cradled Catrina's neck as they sat her up. Another supported her back.

"Slip her shift up o'er her heed. Careful noo. Her face is michty swoll."

Stewart knew he should look away. Any decent man would.

"There we go," Rebecca cooed. "Bless her hairt, she sewed her coins intae her shift. They'd be lost noo if she had nae. Take care wi' those, Sarah. Knock up a wee coin bag oot of the deed man's clays."

Stewart had mentally undressed Catrina Davis a hundred times, but he saw now how terribly unjust he had been in his fantasies. She was not pretty; she was flawless. Her tapering legs lured his gaze upward to the peaks of her pelvis. Like guards, they flanked a patch of fine hairs arching inward to form a dark line over her gash. She had a flat belly and a curving waist like her father's guns. Her breasts were plump with nipples only a shade lighter than her hair. He stared at them, wondering what it would be like to lift one to his mouth, then judged himself vile for becoming aroused when she was suffering, most likely dying.

Only when Rebecca began the daunting task of removing bandages did the horror of Catrina's situation draw him back to decency.

"What a blessing she is nae conscious," Rebecca said.

Indeed, thought Stewart, shame scorching his face. Catrina could not judge him, but God surely would.

When Rebecca reached the final bandage, she issued a warning to her companions. "I've a mind this will nae be pleasant. There's nae shame in lookin' awa', if ye canny stick it. Mary an' me can do it by oorsel', and that's a fact."

Two women turned their backs on the scene. Four more whirled when the final bandage fell, their hands covering their mouths. One sank to her knees and retched.

All wept.

Only Rebecca, Mary, and an ironclad girl of about twelve stayed. They exchanged nods and determined looks.

"Right," Rebecca said, reaching for a jug. "That is nae so bad, noo, is it? Let's redd her up. The rest of ye pray. Do it noo, and do it fervently."

~ ~ ~

Rebecca shook Stewart awake. "Ye're on for the watch."

He sat up, surprised at the swift passage of hours. He reached for his shirt.

"Nay," Rebecca said. "Take what's left of Meyer's. It's dry. He was aboot your size. Has a wee hole noo. We needed part of it for patches and a coin bag."

Stewart stared at the garment and remembered the last time he'd seen the shirt. When he broke bread with Meyer, he expected the stubborn man's luck to run out eventually, but he never imagined it would happen so soon. Or that he'd end up wearing his shirt.

"It's been washed," Rebecca assured him, evidently misinterpreting his pensiveness as superstition.

Across the room, Catrina lay like an angel in fresh bandages and covered with a clean quilt.

"How is she?" Stewart asked.

"She'll make it. I'm guessin' by the way ye gawked at her, ye'll find the news welcome."

He turned away, desperate to hide his dishonor in shadow.

"She'll likely forgive ye onything when she finds oot ye saved her. It's a good thing ye tied the hair across the cut on her heed. Not many know that trick. If ye had nae done it, I'm feart she would hae bled to death."

"I did nae tie her hair."

She gave him a puzzled look. "Well, someone did, an' whoever did it saved her life."

Chapter 8

Catrina's cheek rested against something soft and warm. An arm. She sniffed. A man's arm.

They were on horseback . . . in a field, she thought, since she smelled grass and saw no trees. She admired the dizzying swath of stars.

It was difficult to hear over . . . what was it? Water. It was water, wasn't it? A creek. Yes, a swollen one, with crickets and frogs. Oh, and a screech owl.

Where am I? Why does my head hurt so much?

She moaned and reached for her aching skull.

Someone pinned her arms down. Who?

Her mouth tasted bad. She belched something horrid.

"Want . . . down. Sick." Why were her words so slow in coming?

"Ye're only drunk. Hush, now."

Drunk? Was he crazy? She tried to turn in the saddle to see the lunatic behind her, but he squeezed the breath out of her.

Catrina knew a surefire way of getting his—or any man's—attention. She slid a curiously bandaged hand behind her back to the hot mound between his legs.

His thighs turned to iron bookends. He trapped both of her wrists in one of his hands. His words blew fiery breaths against her ear. "Be still. Ye're injured. Your hand is burned."

How silly of him to think she was hurt when she only wanted down from his horse.

Something hard prodded her tailbone.

She giggled, confident he would now relent.

"Whoa," he muttered, lust straining his voice.

The horse halted, nickered, and then pawed at the ground.

She laughed in spite of her discomfort. "I knew you would—"

The spout of a jug silenced her. She tried to turn her face away, but her captor pinned the back of her head to his chest and gave her two choices: drink or drown.

She drank. The liquid burned her throat and set fire to her belly.

"There's a good lass," he said, pulling the jug away.

She coughed, and it worsened her headache. "Let . . . me go."

"Jaysus, I should have known ye'd be trouble."

"How dare you take the Lord's name in vain?"

"How dare *ye* tempt a man when he can do naught aboot it?" He clucked his tongue and twitched his firm thighs to make the horse walk on. "By the time we head into yon woods, ye'd better be asleep or I'm gonny gi' ye another whack at the jug."

She marveled at the indigo clouds edged by bright moonlight, determined to defy him by staying awake, but the foul drink weighed down her eyelids.

"*You* are an Irish bazderd," she slurred as they entered the forest.

"And *ye*, my dear Dutch lady, put your sanctimonious hands on my cock. Do it again and ye'd better be ready to pull it oot and use it."

"Pfft." She wanted to slap him or discharge a caustic reply, but her strength failed her. And then, as exhaustion reclaimed her, his vulgarity no longer mattered. Only sleep did.

~ ~ ~

She lay on a soft bed. Something hard touched her lips and spilled warm liquid into her mouth. *Broth.* She swallowed.

Venison broth. Her head and back hurt from lying too long.

The warm thing pressed against her lips again.

She opened her eyes.

An adolescent boy jumped off the bed and launched a spoon against the far wall. His expression had a puerile quality she found confusing. His chin quivered, and he looked from her to the door and back again.

Her concern for him overwhelmed all else. "Do not be afraid." She smiled in spite of her discomfort. "What is your name?"

"Thomas." He retrieved the spoon, then shook it at her as he spoke. "Ye're Catrina Davis. Ye got your brains bashed in by them bad ol' Injuns."

Simpletons said the oddest things. Was she in an asylum?

A conversation in an adjacent room sent Thomas scrambling to press his ear against the door. He didn't need to. The voices were loud enough for all to hear.

"Three today," a man said in a commanding voice. "The hammer is stuck on this one, and these will not fire no matter what I try. Be careful with the long one there. I poured an unholy amount of powder in the pan."

Someone else replied, "I'll fix them tonight. I leave for Philadelphia on the morrow."

"You have my thanks, sir. The woods from here to Sherman's Valley are crawling with the devil's minions. Colonel Armstrong would like us to be able to shoot them."

"Aye, I'll bring them by later tonight."

They mumbled farewells. One door slammed, and another opened . . . the bedchamber door.

Thomas beamed. "Rose! She's awake!"

A woman peered down at Catrina. She was young, but deeply tanned skin bore the lines of too many summers spent in the sun. Her hair was dark, her eyes darker.

An Indian.

Catrina screamed and tried to flee. She fell out of bed instead, landing hard on the planks.

The woman rushed to her.

"Run!" Catrina shouted at Thomas, who fluttered his hands and backed against the wall. "Run!" she squealed, kicking bare feet at the she-devil trying to pin her to the floor.

Thomas slapped a hand across his mouth and began to wail.

Footsteps hammered the floor. A man added his shouts to the chaos. "What happened?"

An Irishman.

Catrina curled up on the planks, dizzy, her head hot and sore. She covered her face with her hands, not wanting to see the boy slain.

"She's feared of ye, Rose," the Irishman said. "Go in the other room. Take Thomas wi' ye."

When the Irishman knelt beside her, Catrina felt the heat of him. He slipped one arm under her shoulders and the other behind her knees, then lifted her off the floor and carried her to the bed. He sat, holding her on his lap. "It's all right, Catrina."

He knows my name.

He patted her back. "Ye're safe in Carlisle. The woman ye just saw is only my hoosemaid. Ye've naught to fear from our Rose."

Catrina believed him. He sounded familiar. She opened her eyes. *Oh, no, the Indian peddler.* "Why . . . How did I . . . When did . . . Who is the boy?"

"It's a long story," Stewart Buchanan said.

She never saw him so well groomed. One might even call him handsome in his fine waistcoat, with his hair clean and smooth.

He lifted her off his lap, then laid her on the bed.

She tried to sit up. "What am I doing here?"

"Take it slow. Ye've suffered terrible wounds." He stuffed pillows behind her back. "What do ye remember?"

"Not much." He'd been at her table, she thought. She remembered the flash of mischief in his eyes. "I served you broth."

"Aye, ye did, surely." Stewart took her hand, and she wondered at his boldness. "Who else was there?"

She pictured a stern, young man. *Jacob.* A woman placed cabbage leaves on coals. *Marie.*

"*Gott im Himmel!*" she wailed. Panic sucked her back to the attack. Horses screamed. Jacob's head exploded. Indians dragged Marie and Hans through smoke and burning shingles. They landed on the ground next to a corpse. Jacob's corpse.

"Marie!" Catrina tried to sit up, but Buchanan pinned her to the bed. She writhed and beat her fists against his back. "Unhand me, *du dreckiger Tier*! Marie and Hans are yet alive!"

Against her ear, Buchanan whispered, "They were taken captive, Catrina."

"But we may yet catch up to them!"

"Ye've been in this bed for a week."

"A week!"

"Aye."

Something cold broke open at her core and spread outward to freeze her limbs. She fell limp, willing the bed to swallow her. "Oh, *mein Gott*, I will never see them again."

When Buchanan sat up, there were tears in his eyes. "I am sorry, Catrina. If there was anything I could do to get them back, I would gladly do it."

She reached for his hands, then crushed them against her broken heart, feeling him tense. "Go after them," she cried. "I beg you."

His shoulders sagged. "I canny, Catrina, as much as I want to. Things are bad, very bad. Bigham's fort has fallen.

The French brought men to destroy Fort Shirley, but they got lost and attacked Bigham's fort by mistake. I found ye there. Do ye mind?"

She remembered the blazing fort . . . and Susan Giles, her babe dead and scalped on her lap. "Please, you must help us. Those brutes have my family. Marie will not survive this, Stewart. Oh, and Hans. Poor Hans. He must be so frightened."

"I can offer only my heartfelt sympathy . . . and a place to stay for as long as ye need it."

She sobbed, hoping the pain in her head would kill her.

He pulled his hands away, then slid them behind her back to lift her into a warm embrace. "I'm sorry. I'm so sorry."

Utterly deflated, she said nothing of his boldness. She was too weak to fight him, too sorrowful to care about propriety.

There must be something he can do. Ja, there is!

"Are you not a trader?" she said against his neck, shocked by the sudden calm in her voice.

"Ye know I am."

"A trader could surely travel safely if he had something the Indians wanted. A man with something valuable to trade could get a look."

He settled her back on the pillows, then sat upright. "Woman, be sensible. The men who destroyed Bigham's fort were *trying* to find Fort Shirley because they wanted to kill George Croghan, the most notorious trader in the province. They did nae know he's in New York. If the King of the Traders is unsafe, why would any man think he can travel aboot unharmed?"

"Ja, but mayhap they are only angry at Croghan because of his political dealings. It might not be the same with you."

"And yet, it might."

She threw off the covers, aware she wore nothing but her shift. "I will go after them myself."

He glanced at her bosom, then turned his head to rub his forehead. "Catrina—"

"Surely, you have things to trade, things they want, like . . . rum."

His mouth became a taut line, his eyes fierce. "Why? Because I'm Irish? Not every Irishman is a drunkard, ye know." He stood.

"I did not intend to—"

He headed for the door, leaving her no choice but to use her last, most precious weapon in her arsenal.

"Wait." She bit her lip.

Shock and torment twisted his features as she untied the knot at her throat. She slid her shift off her shoulders. "Mayhap *I* have something *you* want."

His surprise turned to pity. He whirled on his heels, then left the room.

Catrina wept, unaware Rose had returned until she felt a hand rubbing her arm.

"I am sorry," Rose said. "I did not mean to frighten you."

"Please forgive me," Catrina replied. "I treated you harshly."

"There is nothing to forgive. You were not yourself, mistress."

"Call me Catrina."

Rose squeezed her hand.

"No one will go after my loved ones," Catrina said.

"Stewart would do it at once, if he thought he could."

I'll do it myself. "Where is he? I owe him an apology."

"Gone, mistress.

"Where are my clothes?"

Rose went to a small trunk. She returned with a fine short gown and petticoat.

"These are not mine," Catrina said.

"They are now. Stewart wants you to have them."

She didn't care what Stewart wanted. Not now. Not ever.

"I will wear my own garments, thank you."

"He thought you might say so." Rose retrieved a second stack of clothes. "The Robinson women washed and repaired these for you. Stewart said there were many bloodstains. They scrubbed a long time in pouring rain and with the last of their salt." Rose handed her a bag. "They wanted to make sure you got this."

Catrina took it, then tugged on the drawstrings. "My shillings." Could she *pay* someone to take her to the Indian village?

Rose helped her swing her legs out of bed.

Catrina touched her aching head, feeling bandages there. "What is this?"

"Like Stewart said, you were badly injured. Do you not remember?"

Catrina saw again the club-wielding brute. She remembered throwing herself onto Angela's back and riding past Jacob's corpse. There had been a creek, and nettles.

She brushed her fingers across the fabric heaped on her lap, feeling the seams of patches sewn by women who had much to fear. "I need to see."

"I reckon anybody would want to. You should prepare yourself for the worst."

Rose brought a looking glass.

Catrina held it while Rose carefully unwound the bandages. She barely recognized her own reflection. Opaque shadows hung below her eyes like bunting. A bruise the color of new willow leaves adorned her hairline.

Willow.

She swallowed hard at the thought of the pregnant mare, now lost.

Scabs speckled every region of her gaunt face.

"It looks better than it did," Rose said, as the final bandage fell free. "It will not be the worst anyone's seen."

"Why does it feel cool?"

"The physician cut away some of your hair to expose the wound."

Catrina tilted the looking glass. "I can see nothing." She reached for her crown.

Rose caught her hand. "We are not to touch it except to dab it with vinegar and garlic. Come, there is a larger glass in the other room." She helped Catrina to her feet.

"Oh . . ." Catrina wobbled.

Rose slid under her arm. "Stand still until it passes. Find your feet. Take it nice and slow. Think of your loved ones. They will give you strength."

She did and found Rose correct. She imagined every tentative step taking her closer to Marie and Hans. Eventually, they conveyed her out of the bedchamber and into the main room of the house.

She braced herself against a wall in front of a framed looking glass while Rose brought a stool.

Moments later, she saw. "Look what that fiend did to me."

Her crown had been shaved to reveal a swollen, purple area the size of a man's palm. At its center, a brown scab framed a glistening, egg-sized wound. No hair would ever grow there again.

Rage shook the looking glass she held.

Rose slid her fingers underneath Catrina's lowest locks and gently lifted them. "When it is healed, we will pin your curls over the scar. No one will see it. Even so, there is always a cap."

No wonder Stewart found her temptation disagreeable. A week ago, he might have taken her offer. Now, he had no interest in her. Who could blame him? She was gruesome, a monster, not a woman.

She stared at her own fevered expression, glad that revenge, at least, required no beauty. She remembered threatening to kill Captain Jacobs with her bare hands if he harmed her family. He had not taken her seriously. She would see him sorry for that. And dead.

"I can guess what you are thinking," Rose said, "but you must not—"

"Do you? Do you *really*?" She glared at Stewart's housemaid, cut from the same cloth as the man who maimed her.

Rose took the looking glass, then placed her hands on Catrina's shoulders. "I do, mistress."

Catrina wanted to strike her. "You think you do. Just you wait until *you* lose a child. *Then* you'll know what desperation and sorrow feel like."

When Rose winced and averted her eyes, Catrina understood: Rose already knew.

Chapter 9

On the new road heading east, Stewart pulled hard on the reins, but his horse refused to slow down. The animal was overly fresh, a consequence of boredom and too much corn at dawn.

The gelding snorted under him, its rear threatening to pass its front, resulting in an uncomfortable, sideways struggle.

"Fine, ye rotten arse." He released the reins and kicked the gelding into a canter, jangling the coins in his bag. His powderhorn slapped his ribs, and the knife and tomahawk in his belt whacked his thigh.

Ten minutes later, the animal slowed to a trot, not its smoothest gait.

Stewart posted in the saddle, keeping perfect rhythm with the horse's movement. It was better than trying to sit out the jarring trot, but his thighs would burn when he reached Lancaster.

As the miles passed, he imagined the satisfaction of handing payment to Gratz. He was delivering a respectable sum, thanks to gun repairs and express deliveries. There was more to come, he would tell Gratz, and probably payment in full when Ward returned with his horses in August or September.

He would avoid debtor's gaol.

At last, the sweating horse tired. It slowed to a walk, froth dripping from its mouth.

"Ye done noo?" he asked Ace. They'd covered a lot of

ground, and it wasn't yet midday. He would go another mile or two, then allow his mount a rest and some grass.

The road slicing through the flat forestland here was so new it still had stumps in it. They were cut low enough to allow the passage of regimental wagons supplying Governor Morris's new frontier forts, but they remained impediments Ace had no interest in winding around. The horse kept to the ancient Indian path, reduced now to a groove in the center of the road.

Stewart came upon no other travelers or interesting wildlife on the monotonous road. Solitude and boredom made him consider what the land had looked like when the first European had set foot upon it. Surely, it had been both astonishing and frightening. Before the suspension of trade, he'd visited the unbroken forests of the western frontier. They were nothing short of daunting.

In all likelihood, little Hans Meyer was in those forests now, dressed in deerskin and dyed with walnut juice. By now, all but a shock of his light hair would be plucked from his head. His scalp would hurt, though not as fiercely as did poor Catrina's.

Hans was young enough to adjust to his new reality, and soon, his troubles would turn to grand adventure. Oh, his darker peers would mistreat him for a time, but only until he learned to defend himself. His German blood would see him redeemed early. It would broaden his shoulders and stretch him taller than any man in his tribe. He would command respect while his mates remained weedy. In the end, he would find contentment and probably, renown.

His mother . . . well, Marie was another matter. She would be hard used, as all captured women were, and if she had one drop of Catrina's blood in her, she would die trying to recover her son.

Catrina Davis was right to feel desperate for her loved ones, for their plight was dire.

He thought again of her proposed trade, the hundredth time today, and felt his cheeks burn. She'd offered her body, but it was really her dignity she laid bare, the last, most valuable thing left to her. Only a rogue would accept that.

One question circled him like a mosquito: what was he going to do with her? No one ever considered the respectability of keeping a roof over Rose's head, but Rose was very clearly a housemaid, and so plain as to be unattractive.

Catrina Davis was the opposite of unattractive. Once her wounds healed, her lingering residence in Stewart's house would call propriety into question, an untimely problem for a man pursuing marriage.

It would have been different if she'd come to Carlisle with her family. Such an event would be easily explained, since refugees streamed in from the harangued frontier every day to seek shelter in any available corner. Most came as couples or families. They moved on after a few days' rest.

Surely, one of Jacob Meyer's relatives in Chester County could take Catrina in. Stewart would help her contact them. If none had room for her, there was always the hope of finding work and lodging for her in Philadelphia. She would be miserable in the city, but women had little choice, and childless widows had none.

Though the harshness of her reality troubled him, Catrina Davis was not his responsibility. He had to make arrangements for her quickly. Rachel Campbell might admire him now for housing an injured widow, but when Catrina's bruises faded and her scabs fell away, Rachel's opinion would change.

Rachel was definitely warming to him and even looked disappointed last night when he announced his plans to leave town for a few weeks. She'd worn a silk gown of the palest yellow, cinched tight to lift her breasts as high as decorum would allow. Stewart had been the lieutenant's sole dinner invitee. With no other man present but the lowly servant attending to the meal, it meant Rachel purposely selected the gown to tempt Stewart. She *wanted* him to notice the untouched swells above her bodice.

Notice he did, and he would have savored the sight of them if another woman's breasts hadn't already blinded him. He remained unable to shake the image of Catrina's exquisite figure from his mind. Rachel was but a girl. Catrina was mature in body *and* mind.

If he had not glimpsed the rapture awaiting a man or felt the warmth of her hand on his cock in that damnable meadow . . . well, then, Catrina might be easier to forget. But he *had* seen her voluptuous body. She *had* touched him in the moonlight.

He shifted in his saddle. *Damn it.* She did it again.

His cock strained against the fabric of his breeches. Misery spread from his aching balls into his groin and down the tendons of his inner thighs.

At a shady stream, he halted the horse, then dismounted. While it grazed and swatted its tail at flies, he stripped out of his clothes and sat in the creek, seeking relief in the cool water, certain God was punishing him for ogling Catrina Davis without permission.

Chapter 10

Stewart browsed the shelves at Prentis on Arch Street, a lavender-scented shop stocked floor to ceiling with women's sundries. He'd been lucky enough to find work on the docks. Most of his wages went toward a second payment to Isaac Gratz. Enough remained to buy a few what-nots and a hot meal on his way home.

He pressed a sack of tea purchased earlier against his chest. It was a valuable commodity rarely seen in the backcountry nowadays. If Rachel Campbell found no merit in the extravagant gift, her guardian certainly would, and *his* opinion mattered more. Nevertheless, Stewart thought he should add some frippery a girl might find exciting. In the colonies, that meant a ribbon.

"This is a lovely shade." A woman well past her prime plucked a yellow ribbon from a rack on the counter. "She can wear it in her hat or use it to hang a bauble."

He shook his head. "I am looking for one the color of fresh butter." It had to match Rachel's silk gown. She would find his remembrance of the color significant.

Rose's ribbon had been easy to select. Green. The color of Henry Mosebey's provincial coat.

"This one, perhaps?" The clerk draped the perfect shade over an age-spotted wrist.

"Aye, that's the one. I'll take it."

He had a present for Thomas, too—a tiny ship found in a secondhand store.

It seemed rude to return home with gifts for everyone except Catrina, but he could not buy her a ribbon. Women like Catrina were practical to a fault. She would see a ribbon as both unsuitable *and* wasteful. He scanned the caps instead, knowing Catrina wore Rose's old one, hopelessly stained by now.

Smelling a sale, the clerk held up the most expensive cap on her table, a sturdy one edged with delicate lace. "This is of superior quality."

"Indeed, but a bit excessive for the lady I have in mind." In truth, he worried the lace would draw attention to Catrina's head, something he guessed she would very much like to avoid. "Do ye have something plain?"

"Of course." She showed him a serviceable cap identical to the one Catrina used to wear.

"I'll take it."

With his purchases made, Stewart left the shop. Outside, Philadelphia's cobbled streets teemed with strangers in town for market day. Two ships from Rotterdam added to the melee by belching a few hundred new immigrants onto the docks. Those poor souls wobbled on sea legs toward the market house, where they hoped to find a kind master and a light indenture.

The number of Germans scrambling off the gangplanks raised concern among the British inhabitants who were quickly becoming the minority in their own colonies. In Philadelphia, many establishments now displayed signs in German only. Stewart encountered one of these on Haverford Road. There, a hanging placard featured a German word and a painted spoon. He guessed the place served food.

Upon entering, he saw and smelled that he was right. He sat at a central table. With the last of his wages, he ordered a bowl of hearty stew and a jug of switchel.

To his left, two sailors whispered over a flagon. At his right, a group of muddy Germans laughed and gulped beer. Stewart guessed they were farmers. Germans usually were, and America's finest. One of them caught him inspecting them. He smiled and held up a tankard. *"Möchtest du ein Bier?"*

"I'm sorry." Stewart shook his head. "I do nae understand."

"Ein Bier." He pointed at his tankard, then held it out toward Stewart. *"Möchtest du ein Bier?"*

Stewart finally comprehended the offer. "Och." He held up a palm. *"Nein. Danke."* He was happy with the switchel, which had the added benefit of boosting a man's energy. He would need it for the long ride home.

A redheaded sailor shot up from the bench. "Why'd you go and do that?"

Stewart wasn't sure the sailor addressed him. "Eh?"

"You heard me, you filthy bog trotter. Why'd you answer them in Dutch?"

Stewart caught the powerful smell of rum. "Nae harm in it, lad."

The sailor braced himself against the table. "No 'arm in it? If everybody sees no 'arm in it, pretty soon, it's all we'll 'ear. If folk want to come 'ere"—he thumped his finger on the table—"I say they better learn to speak 'is Majesty's English, I do. I'm fed up tryin' to understand the nonsense spoke and writ around 'ere."

Tankards banged the table in front of the Germans, their beer and jolliness gone. The largest of them rose to a towering height. He had broad shoulders and a thick neck made leathery by long days in the sun. He looked past Stewart, his eyes small and penetrating. "Ich will nicht zu kämpfen."

"You're in America," the sailor seethed. "Specked zee English!"

The German laughed at the sailor's mutilation of his language.

"Fink that's funny, do you?" The sailor trembled with rage. "I'll show you what's funny. Come on, Will!"

The sailors scrambled up onto the table, their fists balled.

Stewart jumped up, too. "Come, now, lads, these men worked a long day, same as the rest of us."

At the hearth, the tavern keeper wrung his hands.

Stewart gestured to him. "Must that man see his tavern toppled o'er a misunderstanding? What say ye to a walk? Let us take some air together. Where ye lads from?"

The sailor roared and punched Stewart's eye.

Stewart dropped to the table, then rolled onto the floor on his hands and knees.

The sailors landed beside him. The redhead shouted, "Keep your Oirish nose out of it, you son of a whore."

Stewart leapt to his feet. He grabbed the redhead by the neck and shoved him into the one named Will. Their heads cracked together.

Will fell.

The redhead lunged.

Stewart cocked his fist.

An enormous fist came from somewhere behind him. It struck the sailor on the nose, spattering blood.

The sailor landed against the far wall, unconscious.

Stewart turned.

The German giant behind him patted his shoulder, then handed him a beer.

This time, Stewart accepted.

Chapter 11

An influx of new refugees meant bystanders in every corner of Carlisle. As Catrina raced along Bedford Street, she felt the blistering heat of their stares.

She focused on her feet, now shod with moccasins from Stewart's warehouse. Looking down avoided inquisitive eyes, but it also presented onlookers with a clear view of her stained cap.

"She's the one," they whispered. "That's her . . . the widow . . . Bigham's fort . . . maimed . . . scarred for life."

Let them look. She would not allow their revulsion to confine her for one more day. It was bad enough to lose three weeks by hiding in her room while Rose and even Thomas changed her bandages and dabbed her scalp with vinegar.

As her body regained its strength, her spirit weakened. Grief lay on her demeanor like a centuries-old grave slab. She cried herself to sleep each night only to be tortured by nightmares. Night after night, Captain Jacobs swung his club.

The thought of his arrogance putrefied her hatred of him. A cure existed for that deep infection. It lay on the other side of the mountains in a place called Revenge.

She passed a village of wagons and tents, where the displaced leaned against their belongings. Most were Irish, a race she no longer hated. She was different now, and not just because she abandoned her bigotry toward Stewart's people. The Catrina of old found it difficult to swat a wasp. New Catrina thought of little else but slaughter. She didn't just want Captain Jacobs to die. She wanted him to see it coming, and by her hand. In her dreams, he *always* recognized her at the precise moment her knife slit his throat.

That's right. Take the memory of my face into hell with you, she would say to him. His surprised outrage would delight her. Today, it even made her laugh out loud, an action that drew strange looks, since she walked alone.

What a lovely day for murder, she thought, ignoring the stares of bystanders. She took a deep breath of air that should have been fresh but wasn't. Carlisle was bursting at the seams, utterly unprepared for the surge of humanity and livestock. The place stank.

There were fifty men inside the fort now, which had a completed stockade, at last. She could see and hear the drills of men not fit for service. Stewart should have been among them, but he had yet to return from Philadelphia.

It was business as usual at the taverns, the lime kiln, and the shops springing up along Carlisle's muddy streets. At the log courthouse, a man drooped from the stocks.

She found the corral, where the horsey scent of home threatened to strangle her with emotion. She ripped a fistful of grass from a tussock, intending to feed it to the lone horse limping inside the fence. The animal eyed her doubtfully as she climbed under the fence rail.

"I'd stay away from him if I was you," a man shouted. He leaned out of a barn's uppermost window. "He's meaner than cat shit."

"I will be all right."

The man dismissed her with a wave, then vanished.

She sighed at the horse's condition. Were her people alone in their knowledge of proper equine maintenance? It seemed so in this dreadful place, where non-Germans used up their animals, then bought more. It was the same with land. Germans built their barns before their houses, ensuring the collection of manure to nourish their fields. The Irish and

English did it the other way around. They built their houses first. By the time they built their barns, their pastures were sour and their livestock weak or dead from exposure.

Catrina held out the grass.

The lame horse pinned back its ears.

"Come, now. You have nothing to fear."

It stretched out its neck and ripped the treat from her hand.

She froze while the horse chewed. Eventually, curiosity made it sniff every inch of her. When it smelled her crown, it snorted and recoiled.

The horses know.

She saw her reflection in its measuring eye. "*Guter Junge.*" She lightly stroked its neck.

The horse signaled its trust with a nicker.

She carefully ran her hands along its side, then down its hind leg. *Bowed tendon.* She wished she had the money to buy him. Maybe he was Stewart's.

Stewart.

No one knew how long he would be gone. He had refused to help her, but someone else might go after Marie and Hans. Maybe even Colonel Armstrong. She planned to see him today, though the thought of crossing the busy square made her wince. Could she withstand the revulsion and whispers?

Indeed, she could. What was embarrassment when compared with Marie's plight?

~ ~ ~

Lieutenant Colonel John Armstrong's aide-de-camp was a thin man with wire spectacles perched at the tip of a beak-like nose. He looked up from his papers. "As I said, mistress, the colonel is indisposed."

The entrance hall of Armstrong's grand house contained three painted doors. The colonel surely sat within earshot behind one of them.

"I suffered unbearable shame to get here, and I will not leave until I am heard, sir!" Catrina shouted.

He eyed her stained cap. "Mistress, your shouts will only give you a headache. The colonel is not here. I have the greatest sympathy for your plight, as does he, but he is, at the moment, too busy for one woman's worries."

"One woman's worries?" She thought her cheeks would burst. "Do you honestly think I alone suffer in this province? My plight is common to hundreds, if not *thousands* of women! There is no peace for *any* woman in this Godless land, Ensign Baker. What is the colonel doing about it? What is Governor Morris doing about it? What is your great king doing about it?"

He stiffened.

"I tell you plainly, sir, if the matter was left to women, we would have it well sorted by now."

Baker slid his spectacles up to the bridge of his nose, then offered her a seat.

She took it.

"Mistress Davis, the colonel's own cousin, the illustrious *Joseph* Armstrong, is, as we speak, in Philadelphia trying to muster support for all of us. You must understand. Only one man in twenty here has a gun, and of those, most are smoothbores, not the superior rifled weapons supplied to our enemy by the French.

"The problem lies not in raising men, although you would not know it by the pitiful numbers answering the call for a picket guard. The problem is few here are sufficiently armed.

"We need weapons, Mistress Davis, and to buy them, we need money. The Assembly controls the provincial purse strings, and, as most Assemblymen are Quakers, they are wholly opposed to war. They are at constant odds with the governor and council, who wear themselves out pleading for our aid."

Catrina trembled, enraged, but she knew Baker spoke the truth. *It is useless.* Sighing, she broke eye contact.

Baker stood, offered her his arm, then led her to the door. "We have some hope in a third faction arising in Philadelphia, one led by a man named Benjamin Franklin. He opposes the governor on many things, but he is wholly sympathetic to our cause. I implore you to take heart in that, mistress. And now, I bid you good day."

She left feeling defeated and forlorn.

Across Bedford Street, several men chewed grass stems and leaned against barrels. They were dressed in buckskin breeches and pullover shirts with drooping neck stocks. Two wore cocked hats. The third was hatless. She guessed them to be idle traders.

"Good day," she said to them.

The ones wearing hats touched them. "Mistress."

"Are any of you looking for work?" she asked.

They stiffened as though she'd shoved ramrods up their backsides.

The hatless one stepped forward to offer a slight bow. "Sam McClure, mistress." He was tall and meaty, with a round face, thick eyebrows, and an open-legged stance suggesting confidence. "What do ye have in mind?" A crooked mouth and twinkling eyes gave him an air of mischief.

"I'm Catrina Davis."

"I know." He looked her straight in the eyes, a kindness she appreciated.

"My daughter and grandson were taken captive by Captain Jacobs."

"I know that, too."

"I want them back. One of you must surely know how I can get them."

"Mmm." The leanest of them popped his grass stem back into his mouth. "Impossible."

"Indeed," another replied. "Impossible."

McClure cocked his head. "Not entirely. If she offered a high enough ransom, Captain Jacobs might let them go."

The thin man shook his head. "Ye're mad in the heed, McClure. It's what, a month since Bigham fell? If they're e'en alive, her folk are split apart noo and taken west or up to Canada, mayhap e'en on their way to France." He looked at the ground. "My apologies, mistress. I know it must pain ye to hear the cruel truth."

"Will you walk with me, sir?" she asked McClure. She turned, but not before seeing him wink at his mates.

They moved to the privacy of a shade tree.

"What would it take to make Captain Jacobs release my family?" she asked.

"Other than a ball to the heed?"

"You said I might offer a ransom."

"Aye, it's been done afore by wealthy folk." He bit his lip. "Are ye wealthy folk?"

"I am not destitute."

It wasn't exactly a lie. She had five shillings, more in the ashes of her bedchamber. If she could get to them . . . would they be enough? "How much would it take?" she asked.

"A hundred pounds at least, mistress."

Her heart sank. She did not have a hundred pounds, but she knew someone who did.

~ ~ ~

The candle sputtered as Catrina dipped a quill in Stewart's ink to scrawl her plea across the foolscap. She tried to recall the last time she saw her stepmother, who, if she was yet alive, would be in her sixties.

Anna—

I am certain you did not expect to receive a letter on this day or any other from the person you hate most in the world. Indeed, I did not imagine sending one, nor does it bring me pleasure to do so.

You will rightly guess that I do not dip a quill to convey my love and concern for you. My feelings for you remain as unchanged as yours for me. Let us find harmony in the truth of our mutual loathing.

I write because my only child, born of the abusive marriage you arranged, has been taken captive in this savage land. She has with her a child of five years, my grandson. Some believe a ransom will recover them, and for that, I write to beg for your assistance.

I implore you to set aside hatred for the sake of your late husband's kin. My father was a good husband to you. You owe this to him, if not to me. He would want you to save Marie and Hans, the last of his line.

My last five shillings will pay for posting this letter to you. I pray that God, from whom all blessings flow, will stir your heart enough to send me one hundred pounds in return.

Catrina Davis, Carlisle

Chapter 12

In the earliest days of August, the people of Carlisle received word by petrified courier that Captain Jacobs was renewing terror in the valleys. He brought a considerable force of warriors to the mouth of the Juniata River, where they murdered Robert Baskins and carried off his family. A day later, they attacked the Carroll homestead, took the entire family captive, and burned both house and crops.

By nightfall on the sixth day of August, a half-dead horse delivered a rider and the unwelcome news of Fort Granville's destruction. The man was sent by Captain Ward, now sheltering at Fort Patterson.

Ward had been guarding reapers in Sherman's Valley with Stewart's horses and half the garrison when the attack occurred. According to the only survivor, a wounded frontiersman fished out of the Juniata River, over one hundred French soldiers and Delaware warriors surrounded the fort and demanded surrender. Young Edward Armstrong, left in command by Ward, refused to capitulate. He and his crude regiment held out for two stifling days until the enemy set the fort ablaze.

Through a hole made by the flames, a Frenchman shot and killed Armstrong, leaving John Turner in command.

When a French officer promised quarter to all who peacefully surrendered, Turner opened the gates.

In return, the enemy killed or captured every man, woman, and child.

Catrina paced the main room of Stewart's house, her

refreshed anxiety as uncontrolled as a spooked team on a downhill slope.

In the far bedchamber, Rose keened loudly, her beau's passionate letter pressed to her bosom.

Thomas cried alongside her, although he did not know why.

Catrina trembled. All this worry! All this sorrow! And what were the men of the province doing about it?

She wished Stewart was home. He would know how to deal with Rose, whose undignified laments and contortions mystified her. He'd been gone three weeks exactly. Some said he rotted in debtor's gaol. Catrina thought it more likely he was simply avoiding her. He had not spoken to her since the night she offered her body in trade. Had he thought her too upstanding for such a proposal? Well, let him judge her. She would surrender everything to the first man capable of helping her.

Rose's wailing poured salt on her wounded spirit. It would take days or even weeks for a casualty list to arrive in Carlisle. Until then, poor Rose could only wonder if her sweetheart was dead or alive. The only known casualty was Edward Armstrong. Catrina secretly hoped the young officer's death would inspire his brother to defy orders and seek revenge.

John Armstrong.

His name resounded throughout Carlisle. The citizens loved their frontier nobleman. Because *he* mourned, *they* mourned. Catrina might feel sorrier for him if he had spared five minutes to hear her concerns. Three times, she braved humiliation to seek his help. Three times, he'd been too busy for a distressed widow.

Seeing him tonight would require no appointment. According to the town crier, a mourning Armstrong would receive visitors after seven. Catrina planned to attend, though she would offer no sympathy. Only the low would rebuke a grieving man, but circumstances left her no choice. If Armstrong had only offered false assurances or even a gentle denial of her request, she could share the respect of Carlisle's residents. But he *hadn't* offered her anything. In fact, he'd ignored her. Now, as she wrung her hands and wore out the floor of Stewart's house, she vowed to become the voice of every widow and grieving mother on the frontier, even if she had to wait in the receiving line until dawn.

The mantel clock chimed.

Half six. It was time.

On her way to the door, she paused at the looking glass, ignoring the familiar stab of revulsion. Pink scars speckled her cheeks and forehead. Her sunken eyes betrayed her perpetual anguish. Her borrowed cap would never come clean. She longed to fling the garment to the planks, but doing so would expose something far more hideous.

She smoothed her patched petticoat, sighed, and left the house.

Armstrong's men turned out in force to support their commander, their uniforms painting the town square green and scarlet. Chatting soldiers shook their heads and mumbled disbelief in hushed tones. They looked grave and ineffective in spite of their blades and brawn.

Amid stares and whispers, Catrina took her place in the line stretching from the church to John Armstrong's mansion.

Hours later, with men waving at moths circling their lanterns, she set foot on Armstrong's porch. Soldiers loitered there, and she wondered whether the fort had any men left in it at all. She followed the line through the doorway and into the entrance hall, now brightly lit and heated to an uncomfortable temperature by lanterns and candles. High-ranking officers with shiny gorgets at their breasts held silver cups and dabbed sweat from their brows near the place where the aide-de-camp's desk usually sat. A hall table by the door held a pitcher of water and a vase of lilies adding a funereal fragrance to the scent of unwashed bodies in proximity.

The three doors previously closed to her were now open. One led to a drawing room, where she saw the hawk-faced aide-de-camp whisper something serious to an officer fanning himself with his hat. The second door opened into a hallway, where a looking glass on the wall had been properly covered with cloth. At the hallway's far end, departing visitors streamed out a rear exit into welcome fresh air. The third door led to a dining hall, likely cleared of furniture to accommodate a receiving line. From within, a man's voice boomed. "Ensign Baker!"

The aide-de-camp rushed out of the drawing room and into the dining hall. Moments later, he reappeared and raced for the front door, his face cherry red.

Catrina braced herself on the table. Had something happened?

His eyes met hers only for a moment as he passed, long enough for her to detect concern.

She hoped whatever happened wouldn't undermine her plans. If she stood here all night for nothing, she'd go mad.

By the time she crossed the dining hall's threshold—and confirmed the furniture had indeed been removed—she was faint from heat and anxiety. At the end of the receiving line, Armstrong stood dressed in his resplendent uniform. He possessed the towering presence and assured demeanor of his reiver ancestors. One of his large, ink-stained hands held a goblet of wine. The other rubbed his forehead.

She stared at the gilded buttons of his coat. They matched the lace and gorget at his chest. He wore a white wig, probably the only one in town, maybe even in Cumberland County. She thought he must be hot enough to melt, yet he did not appear to sweat.

When she was two men away from him, she rehearsed her tirade.

The townsmen in front of her offered quick condolences and moved on.

Her hands turned clammy. She wasn't ready!

Armstrong offered a pained expression no amount of finery could hide.

She stepped forward, then curtsied, tears springing to her eyes as she presented him with her most unpleasant feature.

"Mistress Davis."

She recognized his voice. He'd been the one to summon Ensign Baker, and he seemed to know her. How odd.

"Have we met before?" she asked. Why wasn't she already hurling the practiced insults? *Tell him, you fool!*

"We have not. I only guessed by . . ." His gaze slid up to her crown.

"Ja, of course."

"My dear woman, I am profoundly saddened by your loss. Indeed, I can think of no other who could possibly relate to the frustration and anger gripping me on this dreadful night."

She blinked at him, surprised he would say such a thing.

"I knew your father. He was a good man. Did they ever catch the scoundrel who killed him?"

"Nein."

"I am sorry to hear it. As to your present misfortune, I hope you do not mind, but I took the liberty of writing my cousin in Philadelphia the moment I heard your unhappy news."

Catrina's hand flew to her chest.

"Sir, I am . . . Thank you, sir. I tried to see you, but your man would not disturb you or set an appointment."

He inhaled deeply, then let the breath out through his nose while his cheeks turned crimson. "Four others claimed the same tonight, including a man called John Gray. You know him, I believe."

"We lived in the same valley until . . .."

"I am truly sorry. To put it plainly, my aide-de-camp has grown too big for his breeches. Nothing a reassignment to Fort Shirley won't cure, I assure you."

The man next in line coughed his impatience.

Armstrong said to him, "Patience, Erasmus. This is Mistress Catrina Davis. She survived the attack on the Meyer farm last month."

The man dropped his gaze to his shoes. "Apologies, Colonel. Mistress."

Catrina said, "Sir, Captain Jacobs took *men* captive this time, some of them soldiers from Fort Granville. Should you not attack now, whilst we have men in the brute's own village?"

He made no attempt to hide his astonishment. "Mistress Davis, you make me quite sorry women cannot enlist." His voice flattened as he leaned next to her ear. "In truth, it will be a miracle if even one of the men taken from Fort Granville saw another sunrise."

His eyes turned intense. "Understand me now, mistress. I will destroy Kittanning and every warrior in it the moment I have the men and munitions. I plead so often to Philadelphia I fear my fingers will never come clean." He held up the ink stains to prove it. "My cousin Joseph is an Assemblyman, as you may know. He reports some headway with those tightfisted Quakers enjoying their safety in Philadelphia. He advises me to be ready to move in a month."

Catrina hung her head. "My family does not have a month. Sir," she said to her shoes, "are the women of this province to do nothing but bake and sew whilst our loved ones are carried off and our harvests rot in the fields?"

He took one of her hands, then patted it. "I am sorry, my

dear lady. I wish I could offer you more. Please know I am doing my very best."

She looked up at him, then nodded, certain he spoke the truth. "I came here tonight to cut you down with a very sharp tongue."

An impassive smile did nothing to brighten his eyes. "I do not blame you."

"I am glad I didn't." She curtsied again. "I have taken up enough of your time." She looked at the man called Erasmus. "And yours, sir."

She gifted Armstrong with honesty. "I am truly sorry for your loss."

"And I for yours."

She left then, confident of two things: John Armstrong was indeed a good man, and she would have to rescue her family all by herself.

~ ~ ~

The night air was cool on her sweat-soaked clothes.

A month. How could Marie and Hans endure another month?

Despair kicked her up High Street, now almost empty of bystanders. At the Sign of the Sword, a shadowy figure staggered away from a group of pipe smokers to halt her.

"Bit late to be oot alone, innit?" Sam McClure reeked of whiskey.

"I had to wait a long time to see Colonel Armstrong. I am on my way home now." She brushed past him.

He reeled alongside her. "Ye mean *Buchanan's* hame."

"Ja, Buchanan's home."

"He back yet?"

"Not yet." She picked up the pace.

"Nor will he be anytime soon." He lurched in front of her.

She stepped sideways, but he matched her move and lowered his voice. "Could be he's in debtor's gaol."

"Pray, sir, let me pass."

He slid a finger down her chin. "Mayhap there's something I could do for ye whilst he's gone."

"Be gone, you drunken fool, or I will kick your bag up to the back of your throat." She looked around for help, but the other smokers had gone inside the tavern.

He grabbed her arm and pulled her to him. "If ye're nice to me, I'll be nice to ye."

She shoved him.

He stumbled, then came at her again, laughing. "I like a spirited lass . . ."

She kicked him. Hard.

His hands flew to his crotch. He doubled over, groaning. "Jaysus, ye did nae have to . . ." He dropped to his knees, then vomited and spat. "Och, my baws."

"I hope you choke, du Arschloch," Catrina shouted as she raced away.

Chapter 13

Catrina no longer trusted Sam McClure. She would travel to Kittanning by herself even *if* Anna sent ransom money. For that, she needed a map.

"How long does it take you to make one?" she asked the carver, running her fingers over a surname etched into a cow's horn.

He stood, nearly hitting his head on the powderhorns dangling from his stall roof's overhang. "A week, at least."

"That long?" Her disappointment was unfounded, given her lack of funds.

The carver brushed dust off his apron. "It usually takes a few days, but I have provincial orders to fill. Those come first."

"Of course. How much for a map to Kittanning?"

"Just the map, or must the horn hold powder?"

Powder. She would need gunpowder. And lead.

"It will have to hold powder."

"Then add another day or two for me to fit a base and spout. Whole thing'll cost you a pound." He narrowed his eyes. "Why do you need it anyhow? Armstrong don't allow camp followers, you know."

"My cousin is a private in Captain Hamilton's company. If Armstrong marches, I want to make sure Elias can find his way home."

Using the name Anna Hechwalder, she placed the order, not knowing how she would afford it.

It felt good to be out of the house and on the south side of town, a lonely plain with few prying eyes. Thomas played in the marsh here. She looked for him, but noticed only signs of a dying summer. Full tassels crowned cornstalks. The breeze lifted seeds from exhausted plants. Clouds of migrating birds darkened corners of the sky.

Winter would be upon them soon, and with it, misery for the exposed.

Marie.

Had she managed to don her gown on the night of the attack? She recalled Marie's battle with her stays, her face contorted by fear. What about shoes? Catrina focused on the deerskin popping in and out below her hemline as she walked. *Do Marie and Hans wear moccasins now, too?* She smiled at the memory of Hans's chubby toes. How she missed him . . .

"Oh!" She collided with a man. "John?"

John Gray looked confused . . . and ten years older. His clothes were torn and filthy. Grime smudged his drawn features and formed crescents under his fingernails. A measure of vacancy left his eyes as he recognized her. "Catrina? Catrina Davis?"

"Ja, John. My, but it is good to see you. Are you staying in the town?"

"Not for long. I only came to check if there's been news of Hannah or Jane." He rubbed at scratches crisscrossing his face. "Been out looking for them ever since . . ."

She touched his arm and felt the bone and sinew of a malnourished man. "I heard. I am sorry."

"And I for you." The lines in his forehead deepened. "I am relieved to see you. I have news of your family."

Lightning struck her bowels. Her legs faltered. "What?"

John grabbed her before she sank to the dirt. He held her steady until she recovered her strength.

His next words echoed as though spoken into an empty barrel. "I was on the Kittanning path when I met a wounded boy named Cornelius Potter near Frankstown. I nearly shot him for an Indian until I saw his blue eyes. He'd been taken from his farm near Penn's Creek last fall. He was pretty bad off. I patched him up as good as I could. A day later, his captors came looking for him. We hid in thick laurel. God must have been on our side. The warriors found my horse, but Cornelius and I escaped.

"He told me he had been kept a prisoner in Kittanning. Each time new captives arrived, they were forced to run the gauntlet. Those who survived were either murdered or divided up like stolen treasure. After Bigham's fort fell, a Shawnee warrior claimed a woman and her girl and took them to Canada. I believe them to be my Hannah and Jane."

"Oh, John." She covered her mouth with her hand. Her sympathy turned to dread. Was he about to tell her Marie and Hans were in Canada, too?

"I asked Cornelius if he could recall the names of his fellow captives. He could not, because they were never allowed to use them. Anyone caught speaking English or German is beaten severely. He described those he could remember, though. I am sure he knew your Marie. He mentioned a timid, German woman with hair like golden ringlets, who arrived with a fair son of Hans's age."

Catrina thought she might vomit.

"You're shaking," he said. "Let us find a place to sit." He led her to a fallen log. "There is more. Do you want to know?"

She bent over her lap and gathered up fistfuls of her petticoat. "Please." She sobbed into the fabric. "Tell me."

"It is unpleasant."

She prepared for the worst. "I must know."

John's trembling hand pressed against her back.

"A woman named Alsoomse claimed Hans. Cornelius said he is spoiled and does not mind his new life. Marie, on the other hand . . . Life is hard for her. She is a slave to the women of the tribe, tormented and treated worse than the village dogs. They say she deserves it, because even a dog will defend itself when beaten. You know how meek she is, Catrina. It is an admirable quality in our culture, but considered repugnant in theirs."

Catrina sat up and sniffled. "She will endure. I know it. She will do anything to stay alive, to stay near Hans. Do you think if she remains quiet and does a good job for them, they will tire of abusing her?"

John shook his head. "Unless she stands up for herself, she will never rise above her current place. To gain their respect, she must defend herself, and yet, to fight back means risking death. She is in a terrible predicament.

"If there is any good news, it is that Captain Jacobs's son shows Marie special favor. This probably saves her life, but Cornelius said it also hones the resentment of every woman in the village."

Catrina knew it was actually the women of a tribe who devised the cruel methods of murder carried out by its warriors. It was a gruesome competition of sorts, a game to concoct the most imaginative way to kill someone.

"How will I ever sleep again, John?"

Gray rubbed her back. "I wish I knew how to help you. I was there, you know . . . the day Bigham's fort fell."

She was suddenly in the valley again, where a man sobbed on his knees. "That was you . . . in the field." Not wanting to embarrass him, she stopped short of mentioning his undignified lament before the blazing fort. How could she forget it—and him—until now?

She wiped her eyes, then saw he'd been crying, too.

He had a faraway look. "I was there with Buchanan . . . for a time. I was not myself. I helped him get you to Bigham's Gap. I am ashamed to admit I abandoned you there. Time was not on my side. I had to go after my family—"

"Of course, John." She pardoned his offense without hesitation. "Anyone would have done the same."

He looked at the top of her head. "Does it pain you much?"

"This hurts far worse," she said, laying a hand over her heart.

He wiped his nose on his sleeve. "I know what you mean. Rape is unknown to the Indians, but my wife and daughter could now be in the hands of Frenchmen. I imagine the unthinkable. My little girl . . ."

"Oh, John, let us pray it has not come to such an outcome."

"Why ye bawling?" Thomas's voice startled them. He stood with two freckled boys, the Monroe twins.

"Thomas, you frightened me." Catrina wiped her eyes. "We cry because we miss our families."

One of the twins scowled at Gray. "Men are nae supposed to bawl."

John tousled the boy's fiery hair. "True, so I shall stop." To Catrina, he said, "I'll head to my camp now. I pray your loved ones are returned to you."

"And yours to you, neighbor. God go with you. Thank you for telling me about Marie and Hans."

She watched him go, his shoulders hunched, wondering if she would ever see him again.

Thomas tugged on her sleeve. "Ye wanna see my fort?"

"Not today, Thomas. I am sure it is splendid."

"Oh, it is."

Stewart was a saint to keep Thomas employed. He had a marvelous proclivity toward collecting the lost and unwanted. First Rose, then Thomas, and now her. She still owed him an apology for insulting him on the day of the attack, and now . . . well, now, she owed him a great deal more. She would see him repaid . . . if he ever returned.

Thomas lashed a willow whip at the squealing boys running in a circle around him.

An idea took shape. "Thomas," she said.

"Aye?"

"I went to see Colonel Armstrong last night."

"His brother is dead."

"That's right, he is. Do you know what Colonel Armstrong said to me?"

"That his brother is dead? Rose was sweet on a fellow in his regiment, ye know. He's prolly dead, too."

"I know, but he said something far greater. He said to me, Mistress Davis, I heard Stewart Buchanan's servant is a builder of fine forts."

Thomas dropped his whip. "Did he really? Armstrong really said that?"

"He did. He commented on your grand talent, then he said, 'Wouldn't it be something if young Thomas could also fix firelocks?'"

"What did ye say to him, then?"

"I said if you could fix firelocks *and* build forts, you would be the most valuable man in the province, maybe even more important than John Armstrong himself!"

"Jaysus."

Catrina ignored the oath.

He ambled closer, his innocent eyes wide and twinkling. "I *can* fix firelocks."

She feigned awe. "You jest, sir."

"Really, I can." He jabbed an elbow into his friend's ribcage. "Tell her, Alex."

"I ne'er seed ye fix nae firelocks."

Thomas scowled and gave the boy a shove. "I can so." He took Catrina's hand to drag her toward the town. "Come on, I'll show ye."

~ ~ ~

Catrina didn't know what was worse: people staring at her cap, or people glowering because a she—a woman—hammered iron at Stewart's forge.

By the time the sun set, her head throbbed, and she could barely stay awake. Keeping Thomas on task proved more exhausting than the labor of childbirth, but the boy turned out to be brilliant at repairs. The trick was in making it a game, a ploy he fell for every time.

"See?" He held up a newly repaired and polished gun.

"I do not believe it. You fixed the sights on it already?" She hopped off her stool to admire the weapon. It was a Tanner-made longrifle of superior quality. "Thomas, this confirms it. You *are* the most valuable man in the province."

He grinned widely. "Told ye so. Will ye say so to Alex Monroe?"

"Of course. In fact, I may have the town crier announce it."

He giggled.

"Come on." She picked up the candle, a bout of dizziness turning the room to a brig on stormy seas. "It is late, and I smell stew."

Chapter 14

Stewart shambled beside his gelding on the road linking Harris's Ferry with Carlisle. Days in the saddle meant a numb arse and legs slow to regain their feeling.

An abandoned wagon sat in the weeds, its useful parts stripped and carried off.

Thirteen.

He'd been counting discarded carts since Lancaster. They belonged to the dispirited, men with neither money nor heart left to fix them. Once transporters of dreams, the wagons now served as gravestones, ghoulish markers of places where all hope died.

Fourteen.

To his right, Blue Mountain loomed against a clear sky, its level top broken only by a narrow crevice. Travelers named the mountain gap after George Croghan, the area's first settler. For three years, it funneled land-hungry settlers into the valleys between the washboard-like ridges of the Northern Appalachians. Last year, it spat them out again, first singly, and then in panicked droves.

They burst forth from the forest and raced across the sloping fields, thanking God they still had their health and their hair. Most did not stop until they reached the level plain where Croghan's Path intersected the main road.

Here, at a shady spring known as The Five Oaks, Stewart found Sam McClure with two horses, one his usual mount, and the other a well-bred draft animal.

Sam stood to brush mud off his backside. "Reckoned

I would nae see ye back in these parts anytime soon. What happened to your eye?"

Stewart cupped a hand over his bruise. "Sailors."

Though the swelling had gone down, his eye still smarted. He dreaded Catrina's reaction to the blemish. She would, of course, assume he earned it in a drunken brawl . . . whilst women starved. Laughable, since he'd kept his "binge" to a single, watery beer.

"Ye were gone long enough. Trouble find ye?" Sam asked.

Stewart crossed his arms. He disliked McClure. "Ye mean did I end up in debtor's gaol? Nay, sir, I did nae. I found work on the docks." He gestured toward the draft horse. "New horse?"

"Found it next to the creek on my way back from Patterson's."

"Tuscarora Creek?"

"Aye."

It had to be one of Meyer's, which meant it rightfully belonged to Catrina.

Sam reached into his saddlebag. "Ward sent this for ye." He handed a letter to Stewart. "Suppose ye heard the news aboot Fort Granville."

"Yesterday in Lancaster. Grim times, though ye would nae know it in Philadelphia. Folk there go on like there's naught wrong in the world. Any trouble in Carlisle?"

"Only the stink of the place."

"Lancaster's the same."

"Folk are cryin' o'er two things, the lack of flour and young Armstrong's death. Terrible loss."

"Indeed." Stewart was devastated by the news of Edward's death. He'd genuinely liked the young officer.

"Is there a list of the dead yet?" he asked. If Henry Mosebey died, he didn't know what he'd say to Rose.

"Not that I know of."

"They get Armstrong's body back?"

Sam shook his head. "Sounds like Ward will be the one to go after him." He gestured toward the letter. "Mayhap he mentions something in there?"

Stewart broke the seal. The letter contained assurances concerning the welfare of his horses, which were in Sherman's Valley when the enemy attacked Fort Granville. Ward closed by saying he was taking the animals and the remnants of his regiment to Fort Shirley to await further instructions from his commander.

"Any word?" Sam asked.

"Says he's heading to Fort Shirley. Suppose he'll bury Armstrong along the way."

"If he is nae burnt up." Sam patted the big horse's flank. "I reckon this here is one of Jacob Meyer's beasts."

"I reckon the same." Stewart refolded Ward's letter, then slipped it into his pocket. "It's a miracle Captain Jacobs and his men did nae find it."

"She has a mighty scrape." Sam pushed the mare's haunch, and it turned, revealing a wide scab along its side. He rubbed under the animal's mane. "Scrape or no, she'll earn me a wife."

Stewart bristled. "That horse belongs to Catrina Davis. It should go back to her."

"And it will." Sam winked over his shoulder. "When I take her to wife."

"Ha! Good luck! She'll cut your baws off afore ye're done askin'."

Sam cracked his knuckles. "When a woman walks alone wi' a man, she's looking for more than directions."

"And I suppose the widow Davis walked alone wi' ye."

"Twice, as a matter of fact."

Stewart tugged at his neck cloth. It was soaked with his sweat. "God forgive your lies, ye ballocks."

"Nay, sir, I tell the truth. Both times, she approached *me* to do it." He cocked his head arrogantly. "A woman who does that is interested in more than idle talk aboot the weather."

"Ye're daft, McClure. Catrina Davis is interested in nae man."

Sam whacked his thumb against his chest. "She'll be interested in *this* one if she wants her horse back."

A scowl worsened the ache in Stewart's eye. "You're lower than snake shite in a wagon track, McClure."

"Some might say my affairs are none of your business. Far as I can tell, Catrina Davis is free to make up her own mind. I might nae be the best-looking man in Carlisle, but I am nae the ugliest neither. Besides, I would think ye'd be glad to be rid of her. The whole town knows ye have your sights set on the Campbell lassie. Looked bad enough when ye had only a savage living wi' ye." He side-eyed Stewart. "Ye tuppin' her? I always said ye would nae, but now that I think on it, I suppose if a man got hard up, he could—"

Stewart thought of good and faithful Rose, no doubt sick over her lover's fate. His blood boiled. "That's enough."

"Ye tup the widow, too?" Sam asked. "She paying her rent wi' her fancy bits?"

Stewart took a step closer. "I'm warning ye. This is no way to talk."

Sam turned to fiddle with his tack. "I mean, sure, she got an ugly mess on top of her heed, but a man would hardly notice it while he's got his plow stuck in her furrow." He tightened his saddle's cinch. "Bet she's as pretty down there as a stained glass window on a Presbyterian church."

"Sam, I'm warning ye!" Stewart balled up his fists.

"Reckon her legs are something else. Woman's spent a lifetime straddling her papa's big horses. Soon as she says, 'I do,' I'm gonny slide masel' between—"

Stewart lunged.

Sam whirled in time to throw a punch that glanced across Stewart's unbruised eye socket.

Stewart bent his knees and threw an uppercut from his waist, lifting McClure off his feet and dropping him next to his horse.

He didn't stay to make sure McClure was all right. He tied Catrina's horse to his saddle, then headed for Carlisle.

What was Catrina *thinking*, walking alone with Sam McClure? Worse, what would Lieutenant Campbell think of it?

He recalled the sight of her shift slipping from her shoulders. He'd judged her desperate at the time, but what if her injury damaged her wits or left her wanton?

Heavens.

The last thing he needed was a promiscuous woman under his roof.

He rubbed his newly injured eye and passed another abandoned wagon.

Fifteen.

~ ~ ~

By the time Stewart finished tending the horses, he was furious. How could Catrina be so careless? She probably only *walked* with Sam, but a competitor for Rachel's hand might use the impropriety to sully Stewart's reputation. He would need to set Catrina straight, and right away.

He slammed the corral gate and stormed up Bedford Street to High. By all things holy, the woman owed him a modicum of decency! Why did McClure interest her anyway? He was a dirty old 'possum, with only a rocky patch of unbroken property to his name and that on contested lands. He couldn't even access his tract, let alone settle a wife there.

Stewart put his head down to race past Campbell's

house. God help him, if Rachel looked up from her sewing, she would see him at his filthiest.

Inside the fort's stockade, Edward Clancy waved. He returned the gesture, but hurried on, ignoring the townsmen smoking outside the Sign of the Sword.

He threw open the door of his house so hard it bounced off the wall.

Catrina jumped back from the dough board, flinging yellow meal. Her cheeks were flushed from kneading in the muggy room. Brown strands of escaped hair framed her face.

A proper woman revealed her locks to her husband only. He grunted his displeasure.

"Stewart! You are home!" She beamed.

What was this? She was glad to see him?

He blasted a snort, murdering her smile. "Where is Rose?"

Her confusion was palpable, her struggle to comprehend his hostility evident. "She went for a walk with Thomas."

He undid the belt on his sweat-soaked coat. "How refreshing to hear at least one woman under my roof knows not to walk alone in the town. She probably keeps her hair well covered, too."

Catrina tucked her hair back inside her cap. "As I said, she went with Thomas. God's mercy, Stewart, have you heard the news? Fort Granville has fallen. Rose is beside herself about—"

"Good and decent Rose. Reared by wolves, yet she knows how to behave." He shrugged his coat off his shoulders.

"Why are you so—"

He slammed the garment across the back of a chair.

She flinched.

"Woman, ye owe me an explanation!"

She straightened like a cattail shaft. Her eyebrows pinched the bridge of her nose, forming two vertical lines. "An explanation for what? Stewart, why are you so angry?"

His powderhorn and possibles bag clattered as he tossed them onto their pegs. "I ran into Sam McClure on my way hame."

"That no-good scoundrel. Pray, what manure sprayed from *his* mouth?"

A bawdy image of the pair popped into his head. He gripped the mantelpiece and stared at the ashes in the hearth while heat swept up the back of his neck. This wasn't about jealousy, he told himself. It was about Catrina's impropriety and its potential for ruining his plans.

He turned to see her approaching while wiping her hands on her apron. "Stewart, I—"

"Who else ye been walking wi'?"

She halted as though struck. "Just what are you . . . No one. Well, John Gray, right enough, but he's an old neighbor, and I . . ."

Stewart shook his head. So, it *had* been more than one man. "Were ye alone?"

"Ja, but—"

"Can a man leave his hoose unattended wi'oot scandal?"

"Scandal! What are you *talking* about?"

He flopped into a chair to strip off his leggings. "Sam McClure says ye walked alone wi' him."

Her voice turned sharp. "He is a liar! There were two other men present when I first spoke to him. I asked all of them for help in getting my family back and no more."

"Sam saw it differently." He cast his leggings aside.

"I do not care how he saw it. The man is disgusting."

"Walking wi' him once could be o'erlooked, but twice?"

Despair poured into her eyes. "He attacked me as I walked home from Colonel Armstrong's house!"

"Were ye alone at the time?"

Her silence answered for her.

"After dark?"

"It could not be helped, Stewart! The line to see Colonel Armstrong was so long."

His heart softened at her trembling voice. Her discolored cap reminded him of her grievous loss and made him feel like a monster. A distant voice begged him to stop yelling at her. It implored him to forget this nonsense and greet her with a tender embrace. He lowered his voice. "Walking alone leads to trouble. Ye should be more careful."

"Are you saying my actions were worse than Sam McClure's, that if he touched me unsuitably, I somehow deserved it?"

"Not at all."

She slammed her hands on her hips, fury seeming to overtake all else. She raised her chin and shot him a malevolent look. "A man with two black eyes has some nerve lecturing me about civility. Have you been out satisfying your lust for violence?" She stormed back to the table and pounded the dough with renewed vigor. "Men are no better than barn cats. I talked to Sam McClure about getting my family back and no more! If you want to believe it went beyond talk, then perhaps *you* are the depraved one. I and God know the truth." She thrusted a dough-covered finger at him. "*You* may think what you like."

Stewart leaned back in his chair, fighting the amusement borne of her ire. "I'll thank ye to confine yourself to women's work and leave the rest to the men of this province."

She pounded the dough. "Ja. They've been champions thus far."

They fell silent until he announced he was heading to the creek for a bath. He paused at the door. "I would be grateful if ye considered how your repute affects mine. I am courting a young lady, and canny have—"

"Ja, the babe barely off the breast ihrer Mutter."

He stiffened. "She may be young, but ye could learn a thing or two from her."

She kneaded the dough as though intending to drive it through the board. "You will have no more trouble from me. I will limit myself to sewing and cooking." She feigned a smile. "Since women are good for nothing else."

~ ~ ~

Rachel's jaw dropped when she sniffed the paper sack. "Uncle, look!" She held it up. "Tea! Real tea!"

Campbell made no attempt to disguise his astonishment. "What a luxury! You have our thanks, Buchanan."

"And a ribbon!" Rachel squealed.

"Why, darling,"—Campbell winked at Stewart—"it matches your silk gown perfectly."

She draped the ribbon across her lap and ran her unblemished fingers along the length of it. "Thank you, Mister Buchanan." True appreciation glittered in her eyes. "You are most kind."

Campbell flattened his hand on hers. "Why don't you sew now whilst the men talk?"

"Of course, Uncle."

There. That was it. *That* was what Catrina Davis lacked: amenability, malleability, propriety, refinement, obedience. And yet, as Rachel set the gifts aside to take up her needlework, Stewart could not stop thinking about the widow. He hadn't asked about her health or her loved ones. He merely tore out her heart like a feral dog and stormed away.

What if Sam *had* touched her without permission? The thought galled him. And yet, was he any better than McClure? Hadn't he relished Catrina's nakedness without her knowledge *or* consent? The memory of her perfection set fire to his groin. He shifted to avoid discovery.

". . . could it possibly mean?" Campbell was asking.

"Sorry?" Stewart asked.

"The letter. The French missive found tacked to the tree near Fort Granville. It confounds me."

Stewart had no idea what he was talking about.

Campbell laughed. "You seem far away."

Stewart pointed to his black eyes. "The journey hame was nae wi'oot its challenges. I fear exhaustion makes me an unseemly guest." He stood, and his hosts stood with him.

"You must return when you are rested," Campbell said. "Perhaps, for a cup of tea."

"I shall look forward to it."

Stewart bowed to Rachel, who curtseyed.

In a significant gesture, Campbell did not call for the servant. He showed Stewart to the door himself.

Though Stewart left the house confident of his improved standing, passion discharged no butterflies in his belly. He wore no silly grin. Infatuation did not lift him off the cobbles of Campbell's walkway. Instead, regret stooped him over and sapped all pleasure from his victory. He could think of nothing but Catrina. He saw again her delight at his return, the wane of her smile, the anguish when he crushed her.

Just past the fort, he saw her for real. She chased Thomas along High Street looking no worse for his tirade.

Thomas skipped around her on weedy legs, giggling as she pretended to lunge for him. She pressed her hands against her temples as if pained, pausing to close her eyes before lunging again. She clearly felt unwell, but Thomas—dear, simple Thomas—was blind to all discomfort but his own. He could be persistent, and Catrina, apparently too kind for her own good.

A man shouted from the open stockade gate. "Buchanan!"

Ensign William Blythe was the last person he wanted to see. The handsome officer frequented the Campbell residence too often for comfort. Worse, Stewart had yet to repair Blythe's musket, brought to him nearly a month ago. He sought an excuse Blythe might find acceptable.

"What magic did you sprinkle down the barrel of my fowler?" Blythe asked over the drone of drilling soldiers. "It shoots better than ever."

Confusion twisted Stewart's smile into something akin to a grimace.

"Aye, I'm coming," Blythe shouted over his shoulder to someone inside the stockade. To Stewart, he yelled, "I'll talk to you later if you're about."

Stewart was still mulling over the odd exchange when Randall McGinley strode out of the Sign of the Sword. His damaged rifle stood in a corner of Stewart's shop along with three others sent for repair before Stewart left for Philadelphia. He walked faster, hoping McGinley wouldn't recognize him.

"Buchanan, hold on." The breathless frontiersman caught up to him, his pipe in his hand. He looked content for a man whose gun lay in pieces in Stewart's shop.

"McGinley, how are ye? Listen, I, uh—"

"I'm better now that my Tanner's back under my own roof."

Stunned, Stewart rubbed the back of his neck. "What did ye say?"

"I said I'm better now that I have my Tanner back. You know. My rifle?" McGinley puffed on his pipe and looked up High Street, where Catrina still played with Thomas outside Stewart's front door. "Reckon folk thought ye an eejit when ye took her in." His elbow jabbed Stewart's ribs. "Ye're smarter than they thought, aye?"

Stewart gaped, utterly lost.

"Every man in town's got his heart set on the Campbell lassie, but"—McGinley pointed his pipe stem up the street— "right there's a woman a man could treasure. Why, if I was nae a married man, I'd give it a go. She seems to have a way wi' your indolent servant, too."

Thomas squealed and threw his arms around Catrina, who laughed and patted his back.

Her smile vanished when she noticed Stewart. She muttered something to Thomas, then both of them went inside the house.

McGinley blasted smoke. "Looks like she's none too fond of one of us, sir." He spat a speck of tobacco. "Did a fine job on my Tanner, I'll tell ye."

Stewart looked at McGinley so fast he sprained his neck. "*She* repaired your rifle?"

"Ye did nae know? Mercy, man, I thought ye set her up to it. Aye, she fixed it, all right. Had your laddie working the forge, too."

Stewart looked back to the place where Catrina had been, all words lost to him.

McGinley knocked his pipe against his hip, dumping tobacco ash onto the street. "I suppose ye stick Hans Schneider's daughter in a gunsmith's shop, and she's gonny touch a thing or two. Folk say after her maw died, it was just him and her for a few years. Reckon she learned a thing or two from her papa." His voice turned contemplative. "As I said, sir, she's a woman a man could treasure."

~ ~ ~

Behind him, Thomas hopped from one leg to the other. "We saw ye. We saw ye. We saw ye coming oot of that lassie's hoose wearing your fine weskit." He peeked around Stewart's arm. His breath stank from a feast of wild onions. "How come ye're wearing your fancy weskit and got your hair all slicked back?"

"Thomas, go on awa'. Your breath is boufin'." Stewart stood just outside Catrina's door, his hand poised to knock.

"Cat says ye're sweet on that lassie wi' curls like a dirty old sheep. I do nae like her. She looks like a drownded worm, all washed oot and limp." He made a gagging noise.

Stewart turned to face him. "She wears the latest hairstyle, Thomas. It is called a *tête de mouton*, and it is *supposed* to look like a sheep."

"Why would anyone want to look like a dirty old sheep?"

Stewart wondered the same, but women's fashion rarely made sense to him. "Where is Rose?"

"Pounding corn over at the Jenkins hoose. Been there all day."

Rose pounded the shite out of corn when upset.

Stewart pulled the green ribbon from his pocket. "Ye want to gi' her a surprise?"

"A ribbon? Really? Ye'll let me to gi' it to her?"

"Aye, if ye can find her."

"Oh, I can find her no bother, but she told me to stay awa' from her today."

Bless her, Rose probably wanted to spare him. Thomas absorbed emotion and made it his own. If Rose cried, he would cry harder.

"I'll bet she'll want to see me now!" Thomas snatched the ribbon and sprinted out of the house.

Stewart rapped on Catrina's door.

"Come in, dearest."

As he entered, she flinched, then reached for her cap. "Forgive me. I thought you were Thomas." She quickly covered her hair.

Stewart went to her. "Let me see it."

"Nein." She turned away.

He decided not to push her. "May I sit?"

"It is your bed."

His belly fluttered with butterflies that should have belonged to Rachel Campbell. They made no sense.

Ignoring the urge to flee, he sat. "We have been at odds for some time. I wish to make peace and begin anew."

She pressed a hand to her chest. "Oh, Stewart, I would like that very much."

His mouth felt dry. "Catrina—"

"Stewart, let me say something first, please, something that has weighed heavily on my mind since that awful day in the valley." She looked toward a corner of the room, now dimming in the waning light, as if lost in memory. "I was unkind to you then. Marie even told me so, but I ignored her. I am truly sorry for what I said. You know, about . . . the Irish. You probably will not believe this, but I was actually thinking of you that very night when the horses began to . . . scream. And then, there was the misunderstanding between us when I awoke here and mentioned you might have rum." She rubbed her arm as if chilled, though the room was quite warm. "I only mentioned rum because you are a trader, not because you are Irish. But, of course, you knitted the two together because of my earlier offense."

Stewart abandoned respectability and took her hand in his. Her knuckles felt like a young girl's. He resisted the temptation to run his thumb over them.

Her countenance turned earnest. "As for Sam McClure, I promise you—"

He squeezed her fingers. "I know ye have too much sense to throw yourself at yon eejit."

"Still, Stewart, I did walk alone in town at times. I never gave a moment's thought to how it might affect your chances with that . . . lovely girl."

He bit back a smile at her choice of words.

She noticed and laughed, sending sparks to her eyes.

He wondered if she knew how utterly beautiful she was.

She slipped her hand from his.

He instantly felt its absence.

"We saw you coming out of the Campbell house today," she said. "You looked quite handsome, even with two black eyes. Did your visit go well?"

"Aye, I believe it did."

Handsome. She thinks me handsome.

The idea excited and frightened him. He rubbed his sweaty palms on his thighs. "Heard a few odd things in town, though."

"Oh?"

"Imagine my shock when men thanked me for repairs I did nae make."

"I meant to tell you, but you came rumbling into the house like a thunderstorm and gave me no chance."

"Apparently, ye did a fine job."

"I wanted to be of use, to repay you somehow for taking me in. I cannot take all the credit. Thomas was a great help."

"*My* Thomas? The Thomas who plays with cornhusk dolls and builds forts in the marsh with boys a fraction of his age?"

She chuckled. "The very one."

"Do ye keep magic in your pockets, woman?"

She shook her head. "If you order Thomas to do something, he will do the opposite. I know, because . . . let us just say I was not the most pliable child."

He faked a gasp. "Madam, ye jest."

She nudged his shoulder. "Stop, or I will get mad at you again. Seriously, though, Papa had his hands full after *mein Mutter* died. He could not build guns and watch me at the same time, so he lured me into his shop by making work more fun than running wild with the Conestogas who lived near us."

Stewart's eyebrows shot up. "Ye ran wi' Indians?"

"Of course, I did. It was great fun until Reverend Stroup found me in the woods wearing nothing but a loin cloth. I caused quite a scandal *that* year."

"I cannot imagine the shock."

"It was all very innocent. I was but a child, after all. Only my hair betrayed my sex. It was much lighter in my youth." She turned wistful. "My best friend was a boy named Yellow

Bear. He died of the pox a year later, when I was nine. I spent all of my time with Papa after that. Until he remarried and my stepmother deemed smithing unbecoming of a lady."

"Was she unkind?"

Catrina nodded, her fingers pressed to her lips.

"Enough of this gloomy talk." Stewart stood. "I have a surprise."

"For me?"

"Nay, for the mouse in your pocket, ye eejit. Of course, for ye."

"Why would you have a surprise for me?"

"Just come." He worried she might think he found her family. "Do nae set your expectations too high." He pulled her up from the bed, then led her into the house's main room.

Thomas flung open the front door and hauled a breathless Rose across the threshold. "I found her."

"Stewart." Rose rushed to him, the ribbon trailing from her hand. "I am glad you are home. Thank you for the ribbon. It reminds me of . . . I suppose you know what it reminds me of."

He embraced her. "I looked for ye earlier. Any word of his fate?"

"Not yet." She pushed away, then held up the ribbon. "If he is dead, I shall cherish this all the more. I shall always have it . . . and his words."

"Indeed, Rose." He would never tell Rose who really penned the beautiful words she held dear. His heart sank at the thought of young Edward Armstrong's fate.

He took the lantern from the mantel. "We were aboot to go for a walk. Would ye care to join us? We can stop at the tavern and see if there's any word on Henry."

She shook her head. "Already asked. I have been out all day. Trying to stay busy, you see. If you do not mind seeing to your own supper, I would like to lie down and pray."

Catrina said, "Think no more on supper, Rose. I shall see to the meal. Go, and lie down. I will bring you something to eat later."

Rose nodded, then went to her room.

Stewart could not walk alone with Catrina, and not just because it was improper. He grabbed an apple from a bowl on the table and turned to Thomas. "Ye wanna go for a walk wi' us, ye wee gulpin?"

Thomas beamed at the false insult. "Aye." He never seemed to tire.

A bright moon made the lantern unnecessary. Stewart sent Thomas back into the house with it.

When the boy returned, they walked along High Street. Inside Carlisle's softly lit houses, men read Bibles or bounced children on their knees.

Just past the fort, the shadow of Campbell's imposing house blackened the street. Rachel would be at her dinner now. Closed shutters prevented him from seeing who dined with her.

At Armstrong's mansion, they turned onto Bedford Street, where long lines of campfires gave a false sense of celebration. There was nothing festive about the fires. They were for comfort only, put to use by the exiled families watching them pass.

Someone plucked a jaw harp. Pots and pans clanked. Dogs barked. Children cried. A man pounded at something broken on his wagon.

As they left the town, the chorus of night creatures picked up where the clamor of humanity left off. Feverish crickets and katydids trilled in a late summer crescendo. Frogs croaked. Owls hooted.

Stewart directed Catrina to the corral, crowded tonight with the horses of those making their way back east. The draft horse was nowhere to be seen, a pleasing happenstance.

"Watch," he said. "Ye ready?"

"Ready for what?"

"Just watch." He imitated a chickadee's call. *Chick-a-dee-dee-dee*.

Ace abandoned a hay pile and trotted up to the fence.

Stewart handed the animal his apple.

Catrina said, "Smart. I suppose if you are hiding, you cannot simply call his name, can you?"

"Not if I want to keep my hair." Stewart regretted the statement the moment it left his lips.

She gave no outward sign of offense. "He seems a good horse."

Thomas ripped grass from a clump growing beside the road, then handed it to Stewart's gelding.

Saliva dripped as Ace ground up the treats.

"He's not as fine as your horses were," Stewart said, "but what he lacks in looks, he makes up for in brains."

"Did he carry us back from the valley?"

The memory of her warm hand on his cock made his balls churn. *Damn it.* He shifted from one leg to the other, sorry he hadn't visited a whore in Philadelphia. "That was Hugh Gallagher's horse."

"Can I go to the barn?" Thomas asked.

Soft light glowed from the window in the hay loft. Reeves and Johnson were probably drinking and playing card games.

"All right, Thomas, but take one sip of poteen and I'll skelp your arse, ye hear me?"

"Aye, I hear ye."

"Do nae be gone long either. We have nae eaten yet."

"I know. There's pork and cabbage at hame. I helped Cat make the bread. I'll be back fast. Ye'll see."

He turned and loped away.

Darkness swallowed him up.

When Stewart heard the barn door squeal, he asked Catrina, "Did ye have a particular way of calling your horses?"

"I whistled for them."

"Show me."

"Oh, Stewart, I cannot bear to."

He caught the glimmer of sadness in her eyes. "Please, Catrina. I would like to know."

"It is too painful."

"Try."

"I do not know if I can even . . ." She sighed and gave a half-hearted whistle. "Something like that."

Hoofbeats turned her toward the moonlit corral.

The draft horse cantered out of shadows and leaped with surprising agility over a hay pile, scattering a group of whinnying mares. It trotted up to the fence, then used its bulk to shove Ace aside.

If it hadn't been for the fence, Catrina would have collapsed. She braced herself on the top rail, then touched the horse's muzzle with trembling fingers. "Maple? *Sind Sie das*?"

Close to tears himself, Stewart reached for her, withdrawing his hand as she whirled to face him. "Are ye pleased?" he asked.

"Pleased? Stewart . . ." Joy and grief collided at once. She wept and laughed and looked as though she was about to say something. Instead, she threw her arms around his neck.

He felt her breasts crush against him. The memory of their sensual beauty kicked his cock to life so brutally he bit back a groan. He pushed her away, concerned she might feel his hardness.

The moonlight glanced off her damp cheeks and accentuated the shadow of her cleavage. Her eyes were wide and searching, innocent in spite of her years, as though her deepest regions remained untouched by a man. She was like a bride on her wedding night, frightened, yet curious.

He trembled, unable to suppress his desire for her. The deep inferno at his groin annoyed him unmercifully.

"God, forgive me."

A single step erased the distance between them. He pressed his lips to hers.

She squeaked into his mouth as he lost all sense and crushed her against the fence rails.

Her body tensed for a moment, then yielded in soft surrender. She slid her hands up his sides and around his back.

Her submission set him ablaze and turned his kisses cruel. His lips forced hers apart, and he met her tongue in a slippery dance that made his hardness throb. He *had* to have her. Had to. He clawed at her, clumsy and groping, all movement heavy with desperation. His hands cupped her face much harder than he intended to, sending her cap tumbling from her head and into the night.

Her freed hair tickled his arms. He swiped it away from her neck to plant a sucking kiss behind her ear.

She groaned and threw back her head, exposing her throat.

He burned a trail of hot kisses up her neck and across her cheek, finding her mouth again and punishing her lips with his.

The barn door squealed.

Mercy, Thomas. Not noo.

He broke away from her kiss to hold her, panting against her ear. "Catrina." The heat of his words ricocheted back to scorch his mouth. He gripped her wrists and lifted them to his heart.

She looked up at him, her mouth open and lips full, her eyes drowsy with rampant desire.

He tenderly cupped her face. "We canny."

Hurt crossed her face, then anger. She slipped out of his grasp, then crawled between the fence rails to retrieve her cap. "Go."

"Catrina . . ." Her sudden coldness confused him. He longed to pursue her, but Thomas was coming.

With her cap settled onto her head, she turned to him. Her hands rolled into fists. "I said go!"

Not knowing what else to do, he kicked a fencepost, then whirled away, leaving her standing inside the fence with her face hidden in her horse's mane. Two strides later, he stepped in a fresh pile of manure.

"Damn it!"

Thomas met him where the path from the barn intersected the road. Moonlight illuminated excitement in his childlike face. Apparently, he had important details to share about his grand adventure to the barn. "Stewart, guess what? There's a dead chicken in there. Oy, smells like ye stepped in shite!"

"Aye." Stewart fumed and wiped his soles on a tuft of grass.

"What's wrong wi' ye?" Thomas asked.

"Naught, Thomas. Will ye walk Catrina hame?"

"Ye gonny go see the lassie who looks like a drownded worm again?"

"I need a dip in the creek."

"Aw, but it is nae e'en hot, Stewart. Besides, ye have horse shite on your shoes."

"Thomas, do as I ask, and get Catrina safely hame."

The boy stuffed his hands in his pockets. "All right, all right. Ye can count on me, Stewart. Colonel Armstrong himsel' could nae walk her hame better'n I can."

Chapter 15

Catrina sat on the edge of the bed. She touched her eyes, still puffy from last night's tears. How humiliating . . . How could she face Stewart after . . . What was it, exactly?

Passion. It was passion. Her first experience with it, and at her age!

Her face burned. She recalled Marie's gossip on their last day together.

Rebekah Todd once told me some wives find their duty tolerable. Pleasurable*, even. Can you imagine, Mama?*

She could now.

So, *this* was the secret guarded by matrons, the thing known and never discussed. How was *she* to know such marvelous ecstasy existed when her marriage had been a cruel experience, satisfying only to Matthew.

Pleasure was sinful. *She* was sinful. Her son-in-law was dead, her family taken captive, their home burned to the ground. What sort of person—a mother, no less!—fell prey to lust during such a time?

"Gott, forgive me," she uttered.

Was it lust? Some, certainly, but not all of it. Much of it had to do with the sanctuary offered by Stewart's strong but gentle arms. His tenderness unbarred the door to her deepest chamber, a dank room long protected by contempt. Oh, how she longed to air out that room, to refurbish the parts of her soul stored there like broken furniture.

She inhaled deeply to allay her mounting despair. Her head, already pounding from too much crying, could stand no more. Her stomach reminded her of the morning meal, yet to be prepared. Rose, who was up half the night helping to deliver a baby at the Wertman residence, would not be up to it. The task of feeding the household would fall to Catrina alone. She could not hide any longer. She must face Stewart . . . and her disgrace.

She pressed an ear to the wall. Reassured by silence, she opened the door.

"Morning, Cat."

She flinched at the sound of Thomas's voice.

He sat on the floor, playing with his new ship near Stewart's chair, thankfully empty.

"Do you ever sleep, child?"

He grinned, revealing stained teeth.

Alarm replaced all else. "What did you eat?"

He turned to hide his face in his folded arms.

"Thomas, what did you eat?"

"Portable soup."

She went to the cupboard and found the empty waxed paper. "Oh, Thomas, what if Stewart decides to go away soon? He will have nothing for his broth."

"I could nae help it, Cat. I was hungry. Rose was supposed to make more, but she's been pounding corn for days." He started to cry.

"Rose is not herself, dearest." She went to him, then rubbed his back. "There, there. Dry your tears. We shall make more."

"But it takes so long to make it."

"Then we better get started right away." She lowered her voice. "Is Stewart up yet?"

"He left afore sunrise. I wanted to go along, but he would nae let me."

Catrina gave him a sideways glance. "So you ate his portable soup?"

His lip twitched.

"Come on." She tapped his shoulder. "Go and get me a piece of venison from the smokehouse. We'll need to start right away."

The front door opened before Thomas could rise.

In the doorway, Stewart held a small sack.

Catrina's heart leapt to her throat. She rushed back to the cupboard, where she pulled out the corn meal, glad for an excuse to turn her back to him. "I'll start some Johnnycakes."

She heard him cross the room to his chair. "Thomas," he said, sitting, "light a fire."

"Aye."

"Not a big one, mind, or ye'll roast the eyeballs oot of our heeds." His voice sounded flat.

She looked up from her stirring.

His leg jittered as he watched Thomas arrange kindling in the hearth. He leaned forward to pick up a dropped stick, accentuating the brawn beneath his shirt.

She remembered the hardness of those arms. They were like thick branches around her, a welcome refuge. His kiss conquered her troubles—all of them—lost family, her bitterness, and the ceaseless pain in her head and heart. For one glorious moment, she had had peace, the first since Papa's death. Stewart had wanted her. Not her horses, not her father's knowledge or wealth. *Her*. Until her cap fell, and her disfigurement ruined all. Not even Stewart Buchanan, collector of the lost and unwanted, could see past *that* ugliness.

It was for the best. Good heavens, if they'd . . . well, it certainly would have ruined his scheme to marry the Campbell girl. His financial predicament surely required an advantageous marriage. An affair with a homeless widow wouldn't carry him too far down the path to fiscal recovery, would it?

So, why would he jeopardize his plans?

She decided his behavior could be explained quite simply. He'd visited his chaste sweetheart yesterday, which probably left him as frustrated as a young stallion. The fault was Catrina's alone. Had she not given in to her emotions by hugging him after seeing Maple, none of it would have happened.

His reaction was predictable and wholly defensible. Unlike women, men were *expected* to fall prey to their carnal urges. Fornication was a punishable crime, but few were nailed to the pillory for it. Men understood and forgave the frustration rattling males of every species. Why, hadn't Heinrich lost all sense and destroyed his stall when a settler rode by on a mare in season?

Desire turned males stupid. Last night, Stewart went stupid. She should be *glad* her cap fell. Only God knew what the wreckage would look like now if it hadn't. Still, she had some explaining to do. Yesterday, her worst offense had been walking alone with a man. That misconduct paled in comparison with the events of last night. What must he *think* of her, throwing her arms around him like a brazen hussy?

"How are ye this morn', Catrina?" he asked.

She stared at his lips, those deliciously cruel purveyors of passion. "I . . . My . . ." She blinked, confused by the mixture of fright and delight at his concern for her.

An escaped strand of dark hair curved toward his strong jawline. Thomas's fire reflected in his eyes. He looked feral, like Heinrich after he'd broken up his stall.

"My head hurts a little." She stirred the batter, already well mixed. *My heart hurts worse.*

"Do ye want me to help ye stir—"

"Nein," she half-shouted. "Danke." She couldn't bear to have him near her, not with his musky, manly scent so fresh in her mind.

What would Marie think?

Catrina smiled. Marie would laugh and tease her about falling for a man she once detested. She would swoon and ask, "*Don't you just love the way he talks?*"

"I'll be leaving for Fort Morris this morning."

"Oh?" She hid her disappointment by whirling her spoon through the world's best-stirred batter.

"Aye, the smith down there packed it in."

"He gonny go back to England?" Thomas asked.

"Scotland. There's no one left to make repairs, an unfortunate happenstance, since the regiment just got a shipment of faulty guns from Philadelphia."

Catrina's middle turned to ice. How did Stewart know this so early in the morning? Had he been to Lieutenant Campbell's house? Did he see his young sweetheart already this morning? She had no right to be jealous, yet the thought of him bowing to touch the tip of his nose to the back of her pristine hand made her stomach roil.

"That batter ready yet?" Thomas asked.

She felt Stewart's scrutiny as she carried the batter and Rose's crock of fat to the hearth. Thomas had disobeyed him by building a too-large fire. They would suffer the heat long after the flames died.

As a Johnnycake spattered in the pan, Stewart said, "Catrina, I nearly forgot. I brought ye something from Philadelphia."

She flipped the cake, then faced him. "Really? Why?"

His smile nearly knocked her down. "Because I wanted to." He had straight teeth and stubble that matched his hair. Marie was right. She saw it now. Stewart Buchanan *was* handsome.

"I'll bet it's a ribbon," Thomas said. "Is it a ribbon, Stewart? Stewart, is it a ribbon?"

Mercy, what if it *was* a ribbon? He would expect her to wear it in her hair, which meant taking off her cap, and . . . that was impossible.

She concentrated on the frying cake, determined not to let her anxiety show in her grip.

"Thomas, mind the cakes so Catrina can open her present." He gestured to another chair. "Sit."

She eased onto it, her heart thudding.

He handed her the limp sack. "It is nae a ribbon."

She flattened her hand on her belly.

"Open it." Stewart leaned closer, his elbows on his knees.

Catrina took a deep breath, reached into the sack, and pulled out a new cap.

A new cap.

She stared at the garment.

A new cap.

Her throat constricted as she laid Stewart's gift on her lap.

A new cap.

She wished now for a ribbon. A ribbon would have meant he was blind to her hideousness. A cap meant he expected her to hide it.

"Och, Stewart, what a grand present." Thomas crawled closer to inspect the gift. "She can get rid of her stained one. Is it not grand, Cat?"

A wave of lightheadedness turned his words tinny. She focused on the cap, knowing she must soon say *something*.

"Do ye like it?" Stewart's voice was soft and uncertain.

Her tight throat prevented any reply. Without taking her eyes off the present, she pressed her fingers to her lips and nodded.

"I thought it looked like the one ye had . . . afore."

She swallowed hard, hoping he would misinterpret her reaction as gratitude. "Indeed, it . . . is the very same." She pretended to admire the quality of the gift by running her finger along its edge. "I do not know what to say, Stewart. It was very kind of you to think of me. Danke."

She looked at him, at last, confident her contrived smile hid her mortification.

He sat back, fooled and obviously relieved.

"Now, then." She stood and retrieved the pan from Thomas, her head spinning with the need to weep. "Let me finish our cakes."

~ ~ ~

With Stewart on his way to Fort Morris, Catrina went to her room. She closed the door and leaned her forehead against it, her gift still clutched in her hand. Alone at last, she allowed the tears to come.

Rose woke her hours later, her new ribbon presenting a polished clamshell at her throat. "A letter came for you."

She saw, as she followed Rose into the sweltering main room, that the letter was from Anna. "Do you want me to make you something to eat?"

Rose shook her head. "I had a leftover Johnnycake. I'm helping Abigail McMasters pound last year's corn. It helps, pounding samp. Gets rid of a lot of vexation over things one cannot control. Would you care to join us? Just to beat the living thunder out of something?"

It seemed an altogether agreeable task, but Catrina declined. She wanted to stay and read Anna's letter. It didn't feel thick enough to contain money, but it might hold the promise of it.

When Rose left, Catrina broke the seal. She knew instantly by the harsh scrawl that Anna denied her plea. The jagged peaks and valleys of her stepmother's handwriting looked as though they'd been cut into the foolscap.

Catrina,

The dowry I paid to secure your marriage was my last charitable act where you are concerned. If love failed to blossom under your roof, that is your fault, not mine.

As for the loss of your child, have you forgotten my own dear sons moulder in the ground because you saw fit to infect them with the pox?

Catrina balled up the letter and threw it into the hearth. She would read no more of Anna's venom.

Did Anna honestly think Catrina did not mourn the loss of her dear half-brothers? She *still* saw them in her dreams, where those lithe little rascals never aged. They'd been like colorful butterflies floating on the breeze in a field of brown.

A knock at the door startled her.

A lanky boy about Hans's age looked up at her. "Mistress Hechwalder?"

The carver's boy.

"Ja?"

"My master says to tell ye the horn will be done in two days' time."

Catrina glanced up and down the street. A crowd of men with serious looks on their faces gathered outside the Sign of the Sword. They were too far away to hear. One of them halted three soldiers making their way to the fort.

"Has something happened?" she asked the boy.

"Folk say Armstrong's getting ready to move on Kittanning."

"Same old tune again." She nearly rolled her eyes. John Armstrong had been *getting ready to move on Kittanning* since her arrival in Carlisle. She wasn't about to put her trust in *that* perpetual rumor.

"Please tell your master I will see him first thing Wednesday morning."

"Aye, mistress."

She closed the door, then watched Anna's letter writhe in a corner of the hearth, still warm from the morning fire. She hoped it burst into flames. She hoped Anna burst into flames, too.

"Well, then," she said to the empty room. "The hag left me no choice."

If John Armstrong *did* finally launch his expedition against Kittanning, he would arrive to find Catrina dancing on Captain Jacobs's corpse. She smiled at the thought, but her good humor faded quickly. It was wrong to experience joy when Marie had none.

No matter, she thought, going to her bedchamber. Marie would smile soon enough. First, Catrina needed the horn, and obtaining that required money, money buried beneath a charred cabin.

She tidied her room, then stood in the doorway to inspect it. Her gaze fell to the bed, where Stewart sat to take her hands. Would she ever see the mattress again—or him? Ja. She had to. Otherwise . . . *Marie.*

The cornhusk doll resting on her pillow made her wince. Thomas would worry about her, and Rose, too. Would Stewart, if he returned from Fort Morris to find her gone? She guessed not. Like all men, Stewart would skip concern and head straight for fury. Her belly fluttered as she imagined his tirade, a rant she would instantly forgive, since a childless man could never comprehend the depth of a mother's devotion to her babe.

~ ~ ~

Catrina did not wish to borrow new tack from Stewart's warehouse. Using it would render it unmarketable, and thus add to his financial burden. She found an ancient bit and bridle hanging low on the back wall. The leather was old, covered in blue mold, and made for a riding horse, not an animal of Maple's size.

At dusk, while Rose still pounded corn and Thomas made mischief in the swamp with the Monroe twins, Catrina carried everything to the corral.

The mare ground her teeth on the ill-fitting bit, a situation she regretted. There was nothing she could do about it now. Thankfully, Maple was neck-reined and responded well to voice commands, making discomfort unlikely.

Laughter directed her gaze upward, where soft light glowed in the barn window. The stable hand had company. They were probably playing cards or drinking whiskey. Maybe both. She led Maple out of the corral, then closed the gate without anyone hearing it.

Once mounted, she found the shadow of Blue Mountain looming against the horizon. She exhaled, ridding herself of Carlisle's rancid air, then twitched her thighs.

Maple flinched, then moved under her.

They were off.

Chapter 16

The stockade at Fort Morris had bastions at each corner and a gate facing the town. It enclosed a draw well and a clay oven that infused the fort with the aroma of baking bread. Nine log huts served as barracks, magazine, storehouse, guardhouse, and officers' quarters. Most were empty now, the majority of Captain Hamilton's regiment having already marched for Fort Shirley.

Stewart inspected the pole shed where his predecessor had tossed his tools and announced his intention to return to Scotland. The outraged Scot left behind a decent forge, bellows, and an anvil mounted on a stump. The arrangement was primitive, but sufficient.

According to the private who'd greeted him at the guardhouse, the faulty weapons sent from Philadelphia had been the final sparks in their smithy's powder keg; Watson declared he would not spend another minute blistering his skin for a government that armed men *"wi' useless sticks of polished shite."*

Stewart stretched his back, stiff from a bad night on a buggy mattress. Sleep finally claimed him near daybreak, but an erotic dream about Catrina Davis woke him and left him in torment.

The matter of their growing attraction must be addressed, and soon. Asking her to leave would solve the problem, but where would she go? Could he toss her out onto the street—or worse, into the arms of a man like Sam McClure? Nay, he could not, same as he hadn't tossed out Rose or Thomas.

Hopefully, the rumors of an impending march on Kittanning were true. Once Armstrong destroyed the enemy's stronghold, Catrina could return to her farm. Neighbors would help her rebuild a functional cabin, and if they didn't, Stewart would.

In the meantime, he planned to avoid her as much as possible. That shouldn't be difficult, given the rising number of drills and the demand for gunsmithing at the outlying posts.

He surveyed the yard where men cooked breakfast at lonely fires. They were the remnants of Captain Hamilton's company, the unfortunates ordered to stay behind and guard the town. Beyond them, Ensign Thomas Hutchins and a lanky private emerged from the magazine carrying guns like sticks of firewood. They brought the munitions to Stewart's forge, a task usually reserved for men of low rank, but today, Hutchins did the job himself.

"There's the first load." He slid the faulty weapons butt-first into a barrel. "Hope you fare better than Watson did." He shook his head as the private's load clattered into the barrel next to his. "Our enemy shoots rifled guns at us, and what does the Commission send us? Smoothbores incapable of hitting a two by six board."

He kicked the container, rattling the weapons and making the private flinch. "*If* the damnable things fire at all."

Stewart lifted a gun with a splayed barrel. "This one fired, surely."

"Aye, and the private who pulled the trigger is down to one eye. How are we to fight with such fickle weapons?"

Stewart swiped his predecessor's wood shavings off a table. "I intend to find oot. Are ye sure the powder's good?"

"Aye. Fires just fine in the few guns we had. Watson thought there might be a problem with the frizzen springs." Hutchins stared wistfully at the stockade gate. "Gone back to

Scotland, they say. Who could blame him?" He clasped his hands behind his back and rocked on his heels. "I must ask the impossible question. How long do you think it will take to make them ready?"

"Depends if I have or can make the parts."

The ensign paused as though carefully selecting his words. "I need every gun as quickly as possible. I have orders, Buchanan. I can say no more."

He didn't need to. The rumor of an imminent expedition followed him like a hungry dog from Carlisle to Shippensburg. The desperate few holding out at their farms knew Captains Hamilton and Steel had already joined Captains Ward and Mercer at Fort Shirley. It was a good sign, they said, one that assured Armstrong intended to march the balance of his battalion over the mountains soon.

He had to admit it seemed probable, and the thought of being left behind irritated him. If there was to be a raid, he wanted to march with Armstrong's company, not with the fragments of Hamilton's, which would bring up the rear. There was no chance of impressing Lieutenant Campbell from there. Marching with Campbell meant repairing the guns and getting back to Carlisle as quickly as possible.

"I'll work until I drop," he assured Hutchins.

The ensign's bloodshot eyes flickered. "I shall look about the town at once for a woman to help you."

Stewart jerked his head back. "Why would I need a woman to . . ." *Catrina.* "Very funny."

Hutchins snickered. "Ensign Blythe claims she did a fine job on his fowling piece."

"She does a fine job on lots of things not her concern," he said, thinking of his muddled heart. "Wish Armstrong would get off his arse and move on Kittanning so she can go hame and do a fine job there."

Hutchins winked. "Then you had better get to those guns

right away."

~ ~ ~

Storm clouds bruised the western sky.

Sick of rain, Stewart kicked the gelding into a trot. He wanted to reach Carlisle before the skies opened up.

The horse was tired. So was he. Repairing fifty guns in four days had a way of pulling the stuffing out of a man. He hadn't slept in two days. His last meal had been a slice of bread slathered with salty pork gravy at daybreak. He was parched and ready for a hot meal, a barrel bath, and a long night's sleep.

"Come on, Ace." He urged the frothing animal onward. "We're almost there."

At the walnut bottom southwest of town, now swaying with the first of the storm's winds, he slowed Ace to a walk. Putting a horse away hot led to colic. The long line of refugee encampments began here and stretched all the way into Carlisle. Today, the usually somber place buzzed with excitement.

"What happened?" Stewart asked a grimy man standing next to a wagon.

"Regiments are going over the mountains to Fort Shirley. Folk are saying there's to be a raid on Kittanning."

Stewart tensed. "Has Armstrong gone, too?" If he missed the march, he would lose his mind.

The man nodded toward the long line of wagons. "Ye think if he had, any of these folk would still be here? We're prepared to fight wi' our bare hands, if we have to, in order to take back what is ours."

Thunder rolled in a distant corner of the sky. Ace pawed at the ground.

"Looks like they'll have to fight off a storm first," Stewart said.

"Aye, another one. Better get where ye're going."

The man ducked under a piece of canvas fastened to his wagon. "Hope to see ye oot there." He nodded toward Blue Mountain. "And soon, by Jaysus."

~ ~ ~

Rose rushed from her room. "Stewart, thank goodness you are home. Catrina left."

Stewart dropped his possibles bag and powderhorn onto his chair. "What do ye mean she left? Left for where?"

"I know not." Rose raced to the table, then returned with a charred piece of foolscap. "I found this in the hearth. Mistress Jenkins read what remains. It sounds like Catrina wrote to a relative for money, and the relative refused."

Stewart unfolded the partially burned letter, signed by someone named Anna.

Rose said, "I do not know who this Anna is, but she sounds terribly cruel. Stewart, you don't think . . . You don't think Catrina would be stupid enough to go to Kittanning by herself, do you?"

He held up his fingers to silence her so he could read in peace. When he finished, he refolded the letter, leaving smudges of ash on his fingers.

"I'll check if her horse is at the corral." He headed for the door.

"Weren't you just there?"

"Aye, but I did nae look around. Wanted to get hame afore the rain hit." He opened the door, nearly colliding with Thomas, who arrived with a flash of lightning.

Stewart smelled poteen.

"Thomas!"

Thomas raced past him. He fell over the ash scuttle, then lay giggling on the floor.

Rose stared at him, her hands covering her heart. "Mercy, he's drunk."

Stewart slammed the door. He dashed across the room,

then fisted Thomas's shirt to haul the boy to his feet. "What would your mother say, God rest her?" His chest burned as he recalled Mary lying on the ground near the spring, her ebony hair glued by her blood to the moss.

Thomas hiccupped. "I did nae try it, Zteward. I only went to loog after Gatrina's horse, bud when I did nae find it, Reeves said I should gum in tae the barn to blay a hand of gards." He hung his head and wept. "Reeves said he would dell me wha' happened to Gatrina's horse if I toog a dring of *poteen*. So, I did, and he said if I did nae dring more, he would tell on me."

Stewart didn't know whether to panic or fume. "How much did ye drink?"

Thomas held up his thumb and forefinger. "Tha' mudje in a tangard."

It wasn't enough to harm him, but he would certainly have a sore head in the morning. "I'll deal wi' Reeves right now." He went for his rifle.

Rose blocked his exit. "Wait until tomorrow, Stewart. You are too angry."

She was right. In his present state, he would murder the drunken stablehand. Besides, darkness was settling upon the town. The coming storm would be violent.

Damn her eyes, Catrina had more guts than sense. And Thomas . . . what was he going to do with the muddled boy?

"Thomas," he asked. "Did Reeves tell ye Catrina's horse was gone, or did ye see for yourself?"

"I looged. There are only riding horses in the gorral."

"She must have taken her mare," Stewart said. "Damn her!" He slammed the door, shutting out the wind. "How long has she been gone?"

"I last saw her yesterday around midday," Rose replied.

Catrina would know enough to avoid George Robinson, rightly anticipating that the Scotsman would try to talk her out of going to Kittanning and maybe even return her to

Carlisle. Avoiding Robinson's fort required a grueling trek through unbroken forest. She would find nuts and berries . . . and bears eating them.

He hoped she knew not to light a fire.

Wind rattled something against the door. Stewart could not trail her in such weather. Besides, he was dangerously tired. The other side of the mountain required vigilance. Hell, *this* side was beginning to require vigilance.

He went to Thomas, who soaked a chair with his tears. "Why'd she leave us, Zteward? Why?" The boy wiped snot on his sleeve. "She did nae e'en say goodbye. Go on and get her back, Zteward. I canny live wi'oot her."

Stewart had not seen Thomas this sorrowful since Mary's death. He abandoned his anger and gathered him in his arms. "Tomorrow, Thomas." He kissed the boy's hair, which smelled of sweat and bits of hay. "I'll look for her tomorrow."

Chapter 17

Traveling unnoticed meant avoiding established trails. This added miles to Catrina's journey and plunged her into the blackest of forests, where greedy conifers starved all vegetation but ferns. In those chilling thickets, she closed her eyes and lay flat against Maple's back, silently pleading with God and horse to deliver her safely to the other side.

Not wanting to destroy her only outfit, so carefully repaired by the Robinson women, she lifted her skirts at each patch of scrub, exposing her shins to thorns and pokeberry stains. After suffering the consequences of crossing a particularly harsh bottomland, thick with hawthorn and wild rose, she dismounted to fashion guards and ties out of birch bark.

All went well . . . until she reached the foot of the Conococheague, a milestone worth celebrating. But a circling buzzard there stole her joy. It lifted her gaze to a corner of the western sky, where clouds billowed as though strangled. An hour later, they unleashed a furious tempest.

Bowing her head against the rain, she pushed her mount onward, following a deer trace up the ridge and telling herself the storm might pass quickly.

Cracks of thunder chased lightning that branched across the sky. The mare balked, tossing its head and dancing under her, no doubt wondering when it would be stalled, or at the very least, offered shelter beneath a lean-to.

"Easy," Catrina muttered, not wanting to employ the ill-fitting bit. She tapped the mare's sides with her heels, coaxing it toward a dell ahead. The horse obeyed, squeezing its bulk between tree trunks that surely witnessed the dawn of time. When it bounded off a low bank, onto the dirt of the clearing, the storm became the least of Catrina's worries. Her heart pinged like a blacksmith's hammer, driving blood through her veins to warm her limbs. She stared open-mouthed at the glade. By pure accident—and rotten luck—she'd found the thing she'd been trying to avoid. *The main path*. Disappointment saturated what the storm could not. How did she end up here, in the open, in the most dangerous place in the world? *Or was it*?

"Whoa," she muttered, twisting to look behind her. Surely, no one else used the trail today, not in *this*. Raindrops stung her cheeks as she examined the lashing canopy. Only months ago, getting caught outside in the mildest storm would have triggered the need for smelling salts. Now? Well, when a mother lost her child, was there anything left to fear?

The trail was safe enough, she decided. After all, Captain Jacobs and his hellions had the luxury of waiting for clear nights to commit their atrocities. They would be at their fires now, deliciously warmed by fuel carried into their huts by sweet Marie. Catrina pictured her enemy nestling against his loved ones, his copper trinkets glinting. She fisted the reins and ground her teeth together. *Enjoy it whilst you can, Sie Teufel*.

As the adrenaline wore off, so did the warmth it provided. She would need to find a safe campsite before it grew any darker. The storm wasn't lifting, and Maple was due for some oats and a rest. When she slid off the mare's back, the weight of her sodden garments slammed her against the ground and broke her shin guards. With the help of a sapling, she rose again, then brushed mud away from a stinging cut on her shin. With her dripping petticoats balled in her arms, she limped off the trail, pulling the mare into a stand of hemlock saplings. The grove flanked the ridge crest, a limestone ledge exposed by time and weather. It was convenient to the path, thick with dense boughs and carpeted with sloughed needles to mute her footsteps. Catrina followed the outcrop away from the path, rejoicing when she found an overhang, mercifully dry underneath.

She slipped the borrowed bit from Maple's mouth, thankful it did no damage, then plucked thorns and burrs from the mare's berry-stained chest and legs.

Her wet gown and petticoat made the simplest tasks burdensome. She vowed to borrow a man's outfit for the trek to Kittanning. Tired of struggling against the weight of her garments, she stripped down to her shift. By the time she'd hobbled the horse and poured oats from a greased buckskin bag, her arms were like ice. Shivering, she checked her grain supply. Two days' worth. Surely, she wouldn't need more than two days to dig up her coins and return to Carlisle. She wanted to beat Stewart back from Fort Morris. If she didn't, she would lie and tell him she wanted to see the farm for herself.

As Maple devoured the grain, Catrina ducked under the overhang with her bed roll and an apple. She kicked off her soaked moccasins, then wrung out her hair, careful not to tug too hard.

In spite of its age, the oiled canvas wrapped around her bed roll did a fine job of keeping it dry. She untied the tumpline, then shook out the moth-eaten blanket borrowed from Stewart's warehouse. Once stripped of her shift, she whirled the brown wool about her shoulders, savoring its warmth while eating her apple. Her aching bones begged for a fire, but common sense refused to concede. Smoke was too risky.

Something splashed.

She paused mid-chew.

Mayhap a large raindrop—or hail—on a flat leaf.

She strained her ears, hearing only the hiss of rain.

Maple ceased chewing to look north, toward the path, her ears erect.

The horses know.

Catrina raced to the mare, the blanket fluttering behind her like a windblown cape. "Easy." She patted the mare's warm neck and jammed her apple core into its mouth.

Distracted by the rare treat, the mare traded concern for delight. It ground up the fruit, slobbering apple-scented slime while Catrina poured her entire bag of oats on the ground. A gluttonous horse was a quiet horse. Silence was more vital than oats at the moment, more vital than anything, though Maple would hunger tomorrow.

If we live until tomorrow.

Catrina whirled the blanket around her nakedness. Heavens, if a man caught her now . . . Using a deer trace, she skulked away from the sound she'd heard, sneaking downhill through the darkening hemlock forest. Careful not to sway any boughs, she crouched behind a forked tree overlooking the dusky path.

A lightning strike revealed the trail—and shadows of men on horseback. One of them coughed.

Who are they?

Another flash revealed crimson at their chests.

Uniforms.

It was too soon for relief. Natives dressed in the garments of dead soldiers. Even if they were soldiers of the province . . . The consequence of being found naked in the woods by any man made her shudder.

They traveled single file as weary men do, with rounded shoulders and firearms resting across their thighs. As they approached, she curled up on the wet ground beneath the blanket. An eternity seemed to pass. Something crawled across her hand. She hoped it wasn't a spider.

One of the soldiers' horses snorted.

Please, Maple, stay quiet. If the mare whinnied, Catrina would run and hope for the best.

The horse snorted again, probably winding her.

"Easy," a man whispered.

English.

At least, they weren't Indians. Or, worse, French.

She dared not move a muscle. Armstrong's men were trigger-happy, and trigger-happy men shot at anything that moved too quickly. They were probably scouts from Fort Patterson, evidence of truth in the town crier's decree that Colonel Armstrong ordered patrols between the forts. This one was heading south toward Robinson's, which meant another would travel north at dawn, passing right by the farm. If Catrina timed it right, she could follow them undetected, assured the way ahead was safe.

It was a stroke of good luck.

Convinced the men were out of earshot, she rose, then carried her wet blanket back to her shelter, determined to get a few hours of sleep before setting her plan in motion.

~ ~ ~

Lieutenant Campbell ordered the dining hall shutters closed to protect the windowpanes, an extravagance not easily replaced. Wind shrieked through cracks and agitated the tapers on the polished table. The wails reminded Stewart of his bed in Ireland, where his father often sat to tell him stories of banshees, those unwelcome spirits that keened shrill warnings of imminent death.

Was a banshee cautioning him now? If so, whose death did the hag foretell?

Catrina . . .

A boom of thunder shook him out of his reverie and rattled the dining table and everything on it.

Rachel slapped her hands to her chest. "Mercy, so close." A star-shaped trinket pulsed at her throat, where it dangled from her new, yellow ribbon. Her golden hair was arranged in ringlets cascading down her neck. Tiny roses nestled between ranks of curls framing her face.

On a delft plate in front of her, a roasted breast of dove lay next to a baked squash, both untouched.

Stewart dabbed the corners of his mouth, then dropped his napkin beside his empty plate. He should have eaten less. Clearing a plate so quickly marked him as gluttonous and ill-mannered. Perhaps the offense would be overlooked. Campbell surely knew he had had little time to eat or sleep since returning from Fort Morris. He swallowed the last bite of meat, tender and generously seasoned with guilt. It pained him to dine on superior fare while his exiled countrymen hungered in the walnut grove less than a mile away. He thought, too, of Catrina, and his soul winced. Rose thought she may have taken his portable soup, since the packet was empty, but Stewart thought Thomas a more likely culprit.

Wind banged the shutters.

"It's not fit for man or beast out there." Ensign Blythe sat as straight as a ship's mast, his elbows well off the table and his meal respectfully picked-at.

"Creeks will be high." Campbell held up his glass goblet, nearly empty now. "Buchanan, more wine?"

Mary's limp frame rolled across Stewart's thoughts, her skirts bloody and her arms outstretched. He shook the memory aside, then pressed a hand to his belly and proffered a seated bow. "Thank you, but no."

Campbell shrugged, then quaffed his wine. When his empty goblet struck the table, Rachel stood.

Blythe shot out of his chair.

Stewart stifled a groan as he wobbled up on legs aching from long hours at Captain Hamilton's forge.

"I shall see to the tea," Rachel said.

She meant she would see to the *servants* who would see to the tea. Women like Rachel did not make the tea. Not now.

Not ever. Her job as lady of the house was to give orders. And to look nice while doing it. The servants did the rest.

Doubt gnawed at Stewart's ambitions and put him in a foul mood. He often wondered whether he could keep Rachel content. A better question, he supposed now, as his eyes fell again to her untouched meal, was whether *he* would be happy with *her*. One calamitous marriage seemed plenty enough for a man.

She offered a curtsey. "Do not trouble yourself, gentlemen. Please, sit. I shall call you when I am ready."

Ye mean when the servants *are ready.*

Ensign Blythe smiled and watched her disappear amid a swish of silk.

They retook their seats.

Stewart suspected Blythe vied for Rachel's hand, but until tonight, he didn't know how successfully. The ensign's presence at dinner removed all uncertainty. Blythe possessed no wealth or title, but his bloodline stretched back to stiff Herefordshire stock. Everyone loved him, especially Colonel Armstrong, who called him *that feisty Hereford bull*. He seemed destined for a long, brilliant military career, something Campbell would admire, if not Rachel.

As rain flayed Campbell's house, Stewart assessed his young competitor. Blythe sat across from him, impeccably groomed and striking in the green and crimson uniform accentuating his broad build. He had smoothed back and secured all of his thick hair except for three perfect, brown curls stacked above each ear. Long lashes framed his eyes, which matched the color of polished chestnuts. He must have spent the entire day scrubbing his hands, for they were as clean as a lord's.

At the head of the table, Campbell leaned back with folded arms looking as sleekit as a mink in a chicken coop.

Annoyance turned to ire as Stewart comprehended the *real* reason he'd been invited to dinner. *Throw your best dogs into the pen to see which one comes oot on top, aye*? He scowled at Campbell, biting his cheek to prevent his rage from turning to words. He'd left poor Thomas sobbing for *this*.

On any other day, fatigued or not, Stewart would happily accept the challenge, but his promise to leave for Sherman's Valley at first light demanded an early bedtime. Blythe, an unattached man, had no such hindrance. He could stay until Campbell kicked him out. The good-looking ensign would win this battle.

Enjoy it while ye can, ye wee shite. I'll be back to win the war.

He would find Catrina—probably at Robinson's fort—and return to Carlisle, then recover lost ground with Campbell.

As if to stir the pot, Campbell asked Blythe, "Did you know we have Mister Buchanan to thank for the tea? He brought it from Philadelphia for Rachel."

"Indeed!" Blythe feigned awe, flashing his perfect teeth in a grand performance, though his eyes were cold and hard. "What a generous offering." He projected his voice toward the drawing room. "How very kind of Mistress Campbell to share her great gift with us." To Stewart, he said, "I have not had real tea since . . ." He scratched the curls above his left ear. "I cannot recall the last time I drank tea." He turned to Campbell. "Surely, it was at our drafty barracks in Herefordshire."

It was an admirable blow, one Stewart should have crushed with a sardonic reply, but something pinged against the shutters, slowly at first, then in wild percussion. He rushed to the window. "Do I hear ice?" Through a crack between shutters, he saw pea-sized hail bouncing off every surface.

Campbell swiveled in his chair. "Indeed, I believe it is. I would not relish a march in these conditions. We had similar weather at Fort Necessity two years ago. A July storm cut a swath through the forest and turned the trees to kindling. Never saw anything like it before or since."

Poor Catrina. Few things outdid the misery of spending the night in wet clothes. He supposed it was far worse for a woman. Years of trade taught him a thing or two about the insufferable weight of wet skirts.

"There is a bright side to this foul weather," Blythe said.

"How so?" Campbell asked.

"Our enemy will not venture out in this, not when they have the benefit of time to choose clear nights for their ambuscades. The men on their way to Fort Shirley can expect an unmolested march. They'll arrive drenched and perhaps a bit cold, but alive."

Stewart hoped Blythe was right, not only for the sake of the Second Battalion, but for Catrina's, too.

"I believe it may be easing now," Campbell said.

The storm disagreed by spraying the window with rain.

"The tea is ready." Rachel stood in the archway.

They followed her into the drawing room, where four plush chairs had been arranged around a tea table. A tea caddy rested on a matching tray there, along with an exquisite teapot and cups of bone china.

"The tea set was my late mother's." Rachel handed Stewart a warm cup and saucer.

Mercy, do nae drop it.

He carefully accepted the dainty cup and saucer, suddenly embarrassed by the roughness of his skin and the umber crescents under his nails. If only he'd had more time!

"Pray, sit." Rachel offered him a chair.

Blythe and Campbell had already taken their seats.

Blythe sipped loudly. "Delicious." He smiled up at Rachel, his lips moist and rosy from the tea. "Tea—and the presence of a fine lady such as yourself—are true indulgences in this lackluster wilderness." His cup clinked against its saucer.

All conversation fell away as they relished a treat rarely enjoyed on the frontier. Stewart wondered if Catrina had ever tasted it.

The table clock, conspicuously loud, hammered away at time. Stewart watched its minute hand drop toward half seven, the precise moment he planned to excuse himself for the night.

At 7:29, his young adversary thwarted his plans.

"Did you know Mister Buchanan has a *woman* living with him who can repair guns?" he asked Campbell.

Stewart's breath caught in his throat. He fumbled for a reply, but the ensign's brashness stunned him. He offered a feeble defense. "She insists on working to repay me for taking her in."

"Do you refer to the German widow?" Campbell's eyes flashed. "Or his dark housemaid? There are two living under his roof, are there not?"

Stewart's hands turned clammy. The evening was falling into the jakes of hell.

Blythe cocked a brow. "Aye, which is it, Buchanan? Your Seneca housemaid . . . or the striking German widow everyone's talking about?" He winked at Campbell.

Campbell leaned forward, clearly delighted by the first nip of the night.

Heat swept up the back of Stewart's neck. His muscles turned hard, and his heart drummed. He resisted the urge to grab Rachel's precious teapot and break it over the ensign's head. Instead, he narrowed his eyes and settled on honesty.

"It's nae secret I have two unattached women living under my roof. Make sport of it. Judge and condemn me, if ye must, but I will make nae apology for compassion."

Campbell could shove Rachel's dowry straight up his arse. Or hers, for all he cared.

He rose from his chair, his painful legs forgotten. "Kindness merits no ridicule, sirs." Carefully setting his cup and saucer down to prevent his trembling hands from doing something clumsy and irreparable, he prepared to leave with his tail tucked between his legs.

A miraculous thing happened then. Rachel set her cup and saucer on the tray, then looked up at him with enchanted eyes. "At a time when men are driven by greed, I find Mister Buchanan's beneficent nature most admirable." She spoke softly, but her message was loud and clear. "Correct me if I'm mistaken, Mister Buchanan, but you saved your housemaid from the Allegheny River, did you not?"

"Indeed, I did, Mistress."

"And I believe we all know the widow's story, may God preserve her." She pressed her delicate fingers against the bauble shimmering at her throat. "I cannot imagine the horror of what she has been through, or you in finding her and attending to her terrible wounds." She shot a reproachful glance at Blythe, who flushed and pretended to brush something off his lap.

Campbell stared at Rachel as if he did not recognize her.

Her dress rustled as she stood.

Blythe stood with her, but it was Stewart she addressed. "Then, there is the matter of your servant, whom you keep in your employ despite his addled mind. Clearly, Mister Buchanan, you are a man of high morals, one guided by a lofty conscience. I find it altogether deserving of praise, not censure or judgment."

She sank back down to her chair, her expression returned to its usual placidness. "Another cup of tea, Uncle?"

"No, thank you. I believe the storm is over," Campbell said.

Indeed, it was. And Ensign Blythe looked as though he'd been struck by lightning.

Chapter 18

Sunrise brought steam, birdsong, and morning rangers.

With her horse concealed in the hemlock grove, Catrina watched them pass, fifteen men in all.

An hour later, she led Maple onto the path, confident the men were too far away to hear her, yet close enough to assure safety ahead.

She mounted the mare and allowed it to lumber along at its own pace. Maple was bred for strength, not speed. Nonetheless, Catrina would reach the farm before nightfall. Avoiding discovery then would involve keeping Maple quiet until the next watch passed through the valley.

Her wet skirts and blanket lay across the mare's withers. They were covered with hair and reeked of horse sweat. There were worse things, she supposed. Once she reached the farm, the day's strong sun would dry her clothes in an hour. For now, she wore her damp shift alone. The birds certainly didn't seem to notice or care.

She expected to find at least part of the barn still standing. Her post-attack delirium made any recollection suspect, but she thought she remembered one corner of the building escaped the fire. Regardless, she would find shelter somewhere, even in the chicken coop, if she had to, and if it survived.

Maple swayed and frothed under her as they descended the mountain. At the foot of Tuscarora Mountain, she halted the horse on the crossroads to survey the path stretching toward the outpost now called Fort Shirley. Kittanning lay several days beyond the fort. She would trek there soon—on foot, she decided, realizing now the impossibility of a heavy horse traveling anywhere in secret. Maple left deep dents in the mud, a matter she could not change now. Her only hope was to veer into a meadow and pray the grass hid the proof of her passage.

As she passed Sam Bigham's ruined tract, she noticed weeds taking hold in the fields. Oh, how soft those furrows seemed on a day not so long ago. Men prepared the loam for buckwheat, not bodies. Her gaze fell upon the mounds east of the ruins. They held her neighbors now, John Cochran, Thomas McKinney, Susan Giles, and Susan's baby, a boy denied a single breath of life. The memory of that horrific scene made her cringe. Only the devil could do such things to an unborn child . . . Oh, how she longed to get her hands on the babe's murderer. *Soon.*

She shifted on the mare's back and tried to focus, but as time passed, her thoughts lingered on death. Someone buried Jacob near Robinson's fort, or so they said. She was glad. It was hard enough knowing poor Willow's rotting corpse remained above-ground, though buzzards surely picked it clean by now.

"Whoa."

She stared at the hillside. There it was, Jacob's pride and joy, the farm too important to abandon, now reduced to spilled ink on the surface of the world. A bull's-eye marked the remains of the cabin. One corner of the barn remained, its timbers reaching up like a dying man calling for his mother.

She kicked the mare's sides, sending the animal trotting uphill. They passed the gleaming bones of a horse. *Willow.* The chicken coop was eerily silent, its door open and askew. The axe she swung at her attackers leaned against the stump she'd used to mount Angela. Did Joseph Redcoat place it there?

She dismounted where Jacob lost his hair, then stared, strangely emotionless, at the spot where she too had fallen.

She floated beyond the confines of her body, numb, lost.

It was the apple tree that undid her, so heavy with fruit its limbs drooped to the ground. They'd brought it from Lancaster as a sapling. Oh, how lovingly Marie tended its grafts. They'd hoped and prayed for a healthy crop last year, and it yielded one apple, which Hans picked as Jacob hoisted him overhead. The tree's bounty this year—when no one was left to eat it—seemed a mockery.

Using the axe, she chopped a path into a single, unspoiled corner of the barn. The roof had caved in above it, but only to the second floor. Everything from there down looked as it had before the attack. A wooden fork and leather tack hung on the wall next to a bucket, mute witnesses to unspeakable horrors.

Miraculously, some hay had fallen from the loft and escaped the fire. Catrina forked it away from the wall, dropping her tool and nearly squealing when she discovered two intact grain barrels. Maple would eat well, after all.

She carried water in from the spring, then pulled the reluctant mare into the barn.

Upon discovering the oats and hay, the horse abandoned all fear. While it feasted, Catrina turned her attention to her wet clothes. Hanging them in the yard was too risky. She cut the clothesline from the poles, then retied it between two sun-drenched beams hidden inside the ruins.

There was just the matter of her coins now. By nightfall, she would have them.

Chapter 19

Catrina had not passed by Robinson's fort, but the rangers sheltering there reported unusual hoofprints on the far side of the Tuscarora.

"Size o' wagon wheels," one of them joked.

Stewart found the tracks hours later under gathering rainclouds and expected them to lead him southwest at the crossroads, toward Fort Shirley. Instead, they turned northeast and vanished at a meadow, where butterflies struggled against wind to land on orange flowers.

"Whoa."

Ace danced in place beneath him as he inspected the sky. Would it ever stop raining in this infernal place? He returned his gaze to the undulating meadow, knowing what lay on the other side of it: a swath of brambles and scrub, then a verdant copse of saplings, where ferns grew between moss-covered stumps. The young forest opened into another patch of briars and sumac, which yielded to an oak stand. On the other side of those woods, a spring flowed down from the ridge . . . right through Jacob Meyer's property.

God love and preserve her, she's going hame.

Did she believe by some miracle Marie would be there? Empathy slapped its cruel hands around his throat as he pictured her first glimpse of the scene awaiting her. Nothing could prepare her for the devastation. He remembered well the icicle that skewered his gut when he first saw Mary, the anguish that dropped him to his knees and left him like stone.

Poor Catrina. Would she bear up to it until he reached her?

God willing.

It was pouring rain and nearly dark when he left the forest and found the usually placid spring now a torrent boiling through the oaks. He followed the murky waterway, compassion riding with him. Meyer's farm appeared ahead.

"Whoa."

Summer always brought the risk of flash floods, and this one had been wetter than most. On Meyer's property, ebony veins pumped the earth's lifeblood across the blackened landscape. With little vegetation to subdue them, the arteries washed away topsoil and carved deep gullies to destroy Meyer's fields. Fragments of burned logs lay in the yard, probably dragged there by Captain Jacobs and his men, who often returned to the scenes of their massacres to sift through rubble for nails and other valuable bits of iron.

Nothing moved but swollen waterways and a few undulating branches on fire-scarred yard trees.

He leaned forward to inspect the mud for tracks, pouring a waterfall off the rim of his hat.

Naught.

There should have been *some* sign of her by now.

The deluge could have washed away her trail, or . . . He would not consider the alternative.

"Giddup."

There was a chance she went on to Patterson's. If the weather broke, he would send her back with the night rangers. Stewart would wait for them in a corner of the barn, which looked as though it might have survived the fire. He'd brought an oilcloth. Surely, the barn contained a beam he could use for a ridgepole. The floor might be wet for a while, but it wouldn't be the worst sleep he ever had.

He halted Ace near an apple tree. Water splattered from his hat and watchcoat as he slid off his horse. He bent over his rifle pan to protect it, then jogged with the gelding around the corner of the barn.

What a relief it would be to get out of the driving—

"Good evening, Stewart."

He pitched his gun, then clutched his chest. "Jaysus, lover of my soul . . ."

~ ~ ~

Catrina instantly regretted frightening Stewart.

His face gray, he retrieved his rifle, then leaned it against the wall next to the broad axe. He bent forward, panting, to brace himself on his knees.

She rushed to him, the damp braid falling from her cap smacking her back. "Stewart! Stewart! Are you unwell?" She'd only meant to prove her prowess, since, like most men, he thought a woman incapable of surviving on her own.

He shot upright, grabbed her sooty wrists, then gave her a mighty shake, sending her blanket to the hay and exposing her shift.

"I might have shot ye, ye eejit!" His fingers were like cold shackles. His still-black eyes gave him a ghoulish appearance. "Where are your claithes?"

"Unhand me." She yanked her wrists out of his grip, then backed away. "There." She pointed a smudged finger at her makeshift clothesline, now tied in the corner, where her garments hung for the second day in a row. "I got caught in the rain. I saw little prudence in spending the night in wet skirts."

"Prudence?" He erased the distance between them, shuffling through hay. "Prudence?" The word scorched her face. "Did ye think it *prudent* to leave the safety of Carlisle and come here? What in the world were ye *thinking*, woman? By all things holy, ye're covered in soot!"

"Ja, because I chopped through fallen beams to get the horse in here." Only partly true. Most of the soot came from excavating the cabin ruins. She'd done it naked to spare her shift, sobbing while using Willow's scapula as a spade. Without benefit of soap or vinegar, she had not come clean in the spring.

His voice softened slightly. "Ye cut yoursel'."

She twisted her arm to inspect a laceration near her elbow. "It is nothing."

It was the opposite of nothing. It was something, and it was a fairly deep something, thanks to an iron spike in a section of char wrenched from the heap. She added the valuable bit of iron to her belongings and considered the wound no more. How could she, when the removal of the hostile beam exposed the burnt floorboards? She hacked away at the planks with blood dripping off her fingertips. Not long after, she found the pot, cracked by heat, still holding her precious coins.

"Let me see it." Stewart lifted her arm. "I'm sorry I shook ye. I forget aboot your heed sometimes."

He was lying, of course. A man blind to her ugliness would not buy a cap to hide it.

"Do not trouble yourself." She withdrew her arm, then returned to her moth-eaten blanket, still spread out near the edge of the hay pile. "I will bind it later. There is a strip of clean linen in my bag."

"Ye mean in *my* bag." He uttered a heavy sigh. "I never took ye for a thief, Catrina."

She huffed. "I only *borrowed* your things. I fully intended to put them back. Pray, look. I took nothing new. Everything I brought is barely fit for use." She hoped he didn't inspect too closely, or he would find the coins.

He turned instead to his horse, which he unsaddled and hobbled next to Maple.

Her face burned as she watched him. To think he believed her capable of stealing from him or anyone else. It was unpardonable!

She rose again, hurried to the grain barrel, then scooped oats onto a shard of bark she'd been using as a feeding trough. "Here." She carried the meal to his steaming horse. "Surely, this grain partly repays you for your trouble. There is more in the barrels, praise God. Hay, too, as you can see."

"I brought my own grain."

"Not enough by the looks of your mount. I can see his ribs, the poor thing. Feed him well. There is no sense in wasting good grain. It is by God's grace alone the hay and grain survived the fire. I wish we had an empty sack to take it with us. I am tempted to use my petticoat."

Steady rain pushed them deeper into the hay-scented corner. As darkness fell, they sat in silence and watched their mismatched horses eat their fill.

"I canny remember a wetter year," Stewart said, his annoyance apparently cooled. "Have ye eaten?"

"Not much." She dared not risk a fire to cook the oats, and more apples would upset her constitution.

He sniffed. "I smell apples."

"I ate two and scrubbed with another. I thought it might remove the soot."

"It did nae."

"I know."

Rain dripped off the severed floor joists above them.

"Ye scared the dung oot of me."

"I apologize." She chuckled. "You must have thought me a specter."

"I do nae mean this e'en. I mean . . . When Rose said ye'd gone . . . Catrina, Thomas is inconsolable. Ye worried all of us. Why . . . *Why* did ye come here?"

"I had to."

"But *why*? Why *here*? Did ye think ye could rebuild the hoose on your ain, wi' your bare hands and naught but a dull axe? Wi' Captain Jacobs and the French skulking through the trees and provincial rangers only too happy to shoot at anything?"

She stared at the crumbling hillside, where a spirited Heinrich once pounded the ground. Had little Hans helped to kill and eat their magnificent stallion?

Stewart pressed his hand against her back. "Does it not *pain* ye to come here?"

"Of course it does." She grabbed a fistful of hay. "Jacob forked this hay in here a week before his death. See that wooden crate? Hans stood on top of it to scoop grain out of the barrel the day you gave him the bilbo catcher. And the axe next to your gun? I swung that thing at the devil who did this to me." She pointed at her head. "Do you honestly think it *pleases* me to come here?"

"Then why? Why come?"

She used the lie she'd practiced. "I had to see it for myself, to know what I am left with once the war is over."

"At this rate, ye'll see the end of this war from inside a wooden box." He untied his wet hair, then blew out a breath and raked his fingers through it. Even with the bruises at his eyes, he looked fetching with his dark locks loose and unkempt. She stared at the white streaks near his temples, remembering Marie's mention of them.

"I could have told ye what was here and saved us both the trouble of coming," he said.

"I did not ask you to come." She lowered her voice, barely uttering, "Why *did* you come?"

He looked away, rubbing the back of his neck. "Ye know why."

She did, though she would not make him say it. If he said it, she would hear it. If she heard it, she might leap into his arms. If she leapt into his arms, he would never marry Rachel Campbell. If he didn't marry Rachel Campbell, he would go bankrupt. He was too decent to suffer that fate.

"I thought I would get back to Carlisle before you did. I was going to make up a story you might believe, but the truth is, I came here because it is the last place I saw my family alive."

Another lie. Jacob's cabin was the last place she wanted to be. She felt awful including Marie and Hans in her ruse, but she could hardly tell Stewart she came to dig up her coins so she could leave him again in a few days.

His gaze drilled into her. He wasn't buying it.

She lit the wick on a much bigger gun. "I know it must make no sense to you, Stewart, but only because you are a man. Men know nothing of the bond between a mother and her child."

"Men love their wains, too."

"Mayhap, but until you have one of your own, you cannot comprehend the depths of a parent's love."

That part was true.

He looked away, too late to hide his pain. "Catrina," he said to the horses, "Thomas is nae my servant."

She stared at him, suddenly understanding why he tolerated the boy's sloth. "He is your son?"

"He is now."

She slid through the hay to kneel in front of him. "But I thought . . . I thought you were his *master*."

He took her hands in his, now warm. "So does everyone else, and I want to keep it that way." He rubbed his fingers over her knuckles, and the roughness of his skin added to his charm. This was no indulged nobleman, but a man who possessed the strength and cunning to blaze trails, and not just through America's remote forests; he could tame the wilderness of a woman's heart. The scars and callouses on his hands said he'd *lived*, was living still.

"The reason your opinion of the Irish cut me so deeply," he said, "is because . . . in my case, it is nae far from the truth."

She shook her head and squeezed his hands. "Stewart, it was unjust of me to—"

"Pray, let me finish. I want ye to know." He rubbed his eyes. "I came to America as a servant when I was but four-and-twenty. My master was an elderly gunsmith from Chester County who died partway through my term. His widow kept me on. I served my years, then one more in exchange for room and board. She was a kind old matron who treated me like a son, and I never once minded looking after her. In the weeks before her death, she begged me to marry her widowed niece, saying she could nae rest until I did so.

"The idea of taking Mary Murray to wife was nae unpleasant. She was a striking lass wi' raven hair and eyes like bluebells. I met her only once, but I remember thinking it a terrible crime to cover such loveliness with mourning garments. She was nearly twenty, wi' a son not yet walking.

"To please the old woman, I visited Mary, who lived wi' Thomas and her cousin John in a byre. I felt sorry for her, and Thomas, too. Wi'in days, my pity turned to infatuation."

"Did you marry her?"

He nodded. "Just after the old woman died. John inherited the property. Still lives there, as far as I know. I bought my master's tools at a fair price, then took them wi' my new family to Lancaster County, where Mary's late husband left unbroken property. The trouble began there. I was . . . there's just no delicate way to put it."

He pulled his hands away, then tucked them under his armpits.

"I was a virile man of three-and-thirty married to a beauty who fulfilled her marital duty wi' the vigor of a corpse. At first, I thought her modest or, perhaps, inexperienced. I vowed patience and treated her as gently as a man might an injured songbird. I thought her heart would soften. I hoped she would eventually reward my persistence wi' affection, but a woman canny surrender a heart owned by someone else."

"She never got over the death of her husband."

He shook his head. "A lad she left behind in Ireland."

"Oh."

"Thomas is *his* son. She confessed to her husband late in her condition, knowing the wain would be born much sooner than anyone expected, and . . ."

"He beat her."

"Aye, hit her in the belly wi' a board. Thomas came a month later. She thought him unscathed. It took a year or two before the truth became evident. He was too placid, too slow in learning."

"Poor Mary. Poor Thomas," she replied.

Stewart said, "I clung to the hope that Mary would one day love me, but my efforts to woo her fell like sparks to a puddle. She was capable of loving a man . . . quite deeply, as a matter of fact." His palm thumped against the hard muscles of his chest. "Just not this one."

"I am truly sorry." Catrina never knew men, too, sometimes endured loveless marriages.

His voice lost all emotion. "I grew bitter, turned awa', and sought comfort elsewhere. I found it in the arms of whores and jugs of poteen. I stopped smithing, dabbled instead in trade, left for long periods of time, got drunk wi' men of every race, color, and creed. Hell, I got drunk wi' fishes and fowl alike.

"One morning, I left Erie wi' nae goods and nae money. Och, I'd earned plenty on that trip, but I rode hame wi' empty pockets because I drank up all of my profits.

"I returned to a stick of a wife and a son wailing from hunger. Mary's cheeks were hollow and her limbs weak, but by Judas, she mustered up enough strength to throw the empty flour bin at me." He chuckled. "Tore the cupboard off the wall and threw *it* at me, too."

The amusement drained from his voice. "For six days, they had naught to eat but bitter dandelion leaves and two potatoes."

"Oh, my . . ."

"It woke me up. I gave her my jerky and portable soup at once, then grabbed my rifle. Even though I was exhausted from my long journey, I went hunting. I wanted them to have meat as soon as possible, and as I stalked through the woods, I swore to stop drinking and make it up to them.

"Whilst I was gone, Mary went looking for mushrooms to add to the broth. When I returned wi' a deer, I found her at our spring, stone dead."

"Blessed savior. What happened to her?"

"Clubbed and scalped. Bastards torched everything."

She ignored the oath, one too just for such an enemy.

"Robert McCain shot 'em one farm o'er, where they went wi' Thomas and my wife's hair. McCain brought both back to me the next morn', along wi' Ace, who wandered up to his place wi' the dead deer still strapped to his back.

"I'm sorry, Stewart. That is . . . horrible. And, I guess . . . Thomas is an orphan?"

"Aye, but I tell folk he's my servant to protect him. If I *own* him, nobody can haul him off to an asylum." His voice broke. "I will always . . . look after him and not just because he's Mary's son. I love the lad." His eyes turned intense and watery above flushed cheeks. "I tell ye all this so ye understand that some men *do* know what it's like to love a wain wi' all his heart."

She offered a loose hug. "It seems you do. Forgive me. It was unfair of me to assume you knew nothing of a parent's love for a child."

He slid his arms around her. "Turns oot ye were right aboot one thing, though. I *did* drink up my wages whilst my family starved. It's why your words cut so deep. I have nae been drunk since."

She longed to melt into his embrace, but instead, she pushed away. Giving in to desire would harm him, and her. She slid next to him, drawing her legs inside her shift to take advantage of her body heat. "If only we could go back in time with the knowledge we have now."

She would do things so much differently. First and foremost, she would discount no man because of his race. If Stewart Buchanan taught her anything, it was that.

"I find it exceedingly unfair that wisdom comes only wi' age," Stewart said, rubbing his knees. "Can ye still see the horses?"

She squinted. "Not very well."

"It strikes me how like us they are."

"What do you mean?"

"Maple is a German beauty. Ace is . . . well, Ace is like me, the product of an accidental breeding." He laughed. "He's stiff-jointed and past his prime, but by God, there's nae quit in him. They are two varieties of the same animal, just like us. Look at them o'er there, standing side by side, resting comfortably and feasting on their grub. And yet, we have nae got on since the day we first met."

"A matter I regret," she said. "I was wrong to judge all by a few. Let us agree here and now never to quarrel again."

She squirmed, knowing she just made an empty promise. He would fume when she left for Kittanning. Perhaps, he would declare her a lost cause and let her get on with it. She knew, too, he'd only called her a beauty out of politeness. Otherwise, he would have bought her a bauble or a packet of sweets in Philadelphia, not a cap to hide her disfigurement.

"We better get some sleep," he said. "Morning comes early. At least, this time, ye'll make the trip to Carlisle sitting up."

She flushed, vaguely remembering the night she palmed his . . . Did *he* remember? He wouldn't embarrass her by mentioning her most degrading moment, would he? She'd been drunk, after all.

"Come on." He gestured toward the top of the hay pile. "Climb on up there whilst I get another blanket."

As he went to his packs, she scrambled to the top of Jacob's hay, then nestled into it and covered herself with the shabby, borrowed blanket. "When I watched Jacob pile this hay, I had no idea what lay ahead."

Stewart soon settled next to her, bringing welcome heat and the scent of linseed oil. "You're shivering." He flipped the second blanket onto her.

"But now, you have no blanket."

"I'm a hardy buck." He chuckled.

"Danke. I'm nearly frozen."

"Slide closer. I'm hot enough for the both of us."

She backed against him, grateful.

He sniffed. "Ye still smell like an apple."

"Sorry."

"Ye will be when I wake in the middle of the night and take a bite oot of your shoulder."

She laughed, then regretted it. Marie wasn't laughing tonight. She was cold and hungry and serving abusive masters in relentless wind and rain.

"Ye thinking aboot Marie and Hans?"

"Ja."

"God willing, ye'll have them back soon enough. Armstrong is planning to move on Kittanning soon. It's one of the reasons we have to go back to Carlisle as soon as possible. I want to be ready to march."

Catrina sighed. "That rumor's been hanging around Carlisle since the day I arrived. The man needs to shit or get off the chamber pot."

"That's the first foul word I e'er heard ye use, Catrina Davis."

"Mayhap, you are wearing off on me." She recalled scolding Hans for saying *aye* instead of *ja* on the day of the attack. If she could only hold him again, she'd let him say whatever he wanted. Sorrow liquefied and slid from the corners of her eyes. She struggled in vain to suppress her tears.

"Och, pet. Ye crying?" Stewart threw an arm over her and drew her closer. He was warm and sturdy, and he made her feel safe.

Would it be terribly wrong to roll over and forget the mad world, if only for a few hours? Could she even tempt him into showing her exactly what Rebekah Todd meant when she told Marie some women found their duty tolerable?

The hardness prodding her backside said she could. She would not judge him for it. He held a scantily clad woman in the dark, and he was probably desperate for a woman, *any* woman.

What if she just asked?

"Stewart?" Her voice wavered.

"Aye?" He was trembling, and not from the chill.

She thought of Rachel, the highborn lady good and decent Stewart Buchanan deserved.

"Nothing. Good night."

He sighed. "Night, pet."

Chapter 20

Big Beak shoved Marie outside and into the driving rain. She needed more firewood. So did her friend, Trout Face. Those weren't their real names, of course. Their real names sounded like men clearing their throats.

Marie dared not protest, no matter how dire her hunger and fatigue. Hugging herself, she rushed away from her mistress's wigwam. Only when she was out of Big Beak's sight—and more importantly, beyond her reach—did she pause to consider the logistics of the task given her. Standing still was dangerous; even the shortest lull brought risk of a beating. Those watching from their doorways were foul of mood, thanks to hunger and jealousy. They would not hesitate in laying a stick to Marie to gain favor with Big Beak, whose matrilineal line stretched all the way back to the Great Waters.

Marie hunched her back to the rain and wove among birch bark huts that looked like overturned bowls. Oh, how she longed to see them upended and filled with a hearty stew.

She stepped across an ebony puddle, one of many idle firepits pockmarking the landscape. The women would revive the fires when Captain Jacobs and his men returned with game, or so they promised the little ones. Yesterday, the bitter cries of children bit into every heart. Today, they were ominously silent, a matter preoccupying her. Though she had not seen Hans since the day of their arrival, he remained in Kittanning, according to her mistress, who often taunted her with threats to slit his throat.

Marie rounded a wigwam and mouthed a prayer for Captain Jacobs's success, not only so Hans would have something to eat, but because a fruitful hunt would bring Cauldron Man back to the village. He had been nothing but kind since the dreadful night of the attack, often bringing food and firewood to the leaky wigwam she shared with Oldest Woman, the only resident willing to tolerate her.

Once, he brought her a plush bearskin, a lavish gift she immediately gave to Oldest Woman out of pity and gratitude. Seeing Marie's concern for her, Cauldron Man sent a boy to deliver a basket of round river stones. He claimed they would ease the old woman's pains if heated in the fire. This gift solidified Marie's good opinion of him. A grown man who cared about an arthritic elder could not be all bad, Indian or not.

When he brought hopniss, tubers Marie loved for their likeness to potatoes, she used the few Algonquian words she knew to invite him inside Oldest Woman's wigwam. She recalled the sudden flash in his eyes and later, the delight playing upon his full lips as he sat across the fire from her. He was handsome and fit. Had her grief not been so fresh, the radiant planes of his torso might have stirred the embers of passion, but sorrow and longing for her son left no room for desire.

She sighed and wrung out the hair that probably saved her life. Its color seemed to hold Cauldron Man rapt.

"Your hair like sun."

If only. She would spin through the village setting nearly everyone alight.

As Captain Jacobs's son, Cauldron Man was something of a prince. The women disapproved of his infatuation with Marie. She saw condemnation in their scowls and heard threats muttered across fires. Red Cheeks made no effort to disguise her enmity. She spat at Marie every time their paths crossed. She had her reasons, Marie supposed. Her shy daughter Looks Away was of marrying age and previously courted by Cauldron Man. According to Oldest Woman, he abandoned that budding romance when Marie and her golden locks arrived.

Cauldron Man's favor brought some protection from abuse, but now, he was away on the hunt. Now, Marie was fair game, and every woman in the village knew it.

She mouthed another prayer for his hasty success, then felt her soul shrivel at what she just requested—the likely murder of fellow Christians. She would beg for mercy later, when livestock ambled into the village with captives sure to follow. Her heart hurt at the thought of them, wrists bound and eyes wide in their battered faces. Captain Jacobs would make great sport of them. He would force them to run the gauntlet. Those who survived would be rewarded with torture. Who could forget the cries or the stench of John Turner, whose trust and compliance at Fort Granville earned him a three-hour roasting over a bent sapling? In her nightmares, young boys still pierced him with red-hot gun barrels, just as they had on the sultry night of his arrival.

She would never condone such evil, but she understood the war chief's motives a little more these days. When a man hungered to the point of madness, he became capable of anything. Everyone was counting on Captain Jacobs, called Tewea here, to provide them with sustenance. They could not hold out much longer, having stored no food to carry them through periods of famine, a European practice they deemed offensive. The green corn had yet to ripen. Powdery mold rotted the beans and squash. The clouds of pigeons had not come. Overhunting reduced the deer and elk herds to scattered pockets. Any game wily enough to survive one season grew skittish and difficult to stalk the next.

Oldest Woman spoke of better times, when finding nourishment was as simple as dismantling the village and drifting to a more bountiful place. She encouraged Cauldron

Man to talk with his father about doing it now. In her dotage, she did not comprehend that roaming anywhere in these modern times meant encroaching on lands of either white settlers or hostile tribes.

Marie surveyed the desolate village, now slick with rain. How was she to find sticks in a place too long inhabited and devoid of all but misery? The ground was so compressed it defied the rain and prevented seeds from taking hold. Nothing grew here. Not vegetables, not weeds, and certainly not trees. There was firewood aplenty in the vast woodland surrounding Kittanning, but their branches were off limits to Marie, whose mistress forbade her from walking past the longhouse.

Desperation forced her to the frightening riverbank, where the Allegheny roared threats to consume all. She watched upstream, praying for the waterway to deliver something burnable soon.

Scores of overturned canoes lay like suckling piglets here. This annoyed the Frenchmen staying in Kittanning. They came to see Shingas, the Delaware chief, whose village lay on the other side of the swollen river. No one would carry them across. Only a fool would venture out on the angry Allegheny. A fool or . . .

She stared at the boats. If she stole one, no one would pursue her. They would surrender her to the river's cruelty and return to their fires. The canoes were light enough to lift. Mama would have been brave enough to do it, and wasn't she her mother's daughter?

If only . . . She looked back at the sea of wigwams, wondering which one sheltered her son.

A branch raced past, severing her thoughts. She chased it, her moccasins sliding on mud. In a perilous swoop, she caught one end. The other swung around and smacked against the bank. She pulled the limb out of the churning water. Relieved she would not return to Big Beak empty-handed, she broke the limb into suitable lengths.

A fat branch bobbed past, just out of reach. Marie watched it go, sorry she had not waited to break up her first catch, which she could have used as a hook.

Though her deerskin shirt and wraparound skirt had surprising waterproof qualities, they did nothing to prevent her hair from funneling rain down her neck. She still felt indecent in her scant garments, even after so many weeks. Or had it been months? She measured time in meals instead of minutes now. Her last had been a handful of chestnuts and tea made from bracket fungi.

Ten days ago, Shingas's hunters killed two young bears and ten muskrats. The meat was not sufficient to feed the people on the sachem's side of the river. Regardless, he sent half of the kill across the river to Captain Jacobs, who divided it with the greatest equity. Even Marie got a share, thanks to Cauldron Man.

She had watery broth a few days before that, made from their last watchdog.

A second branch dragged from the river gave her more firewood than she could carry. She left half of it on a pile and headed for her mistress's wigwam with the rest. Just outside Big Beak's doorway, she slipped and fell to one knee. The wood clattered onto the ground.

Her mistress shrieked insults.

Panic speared Marie's empty belly. She retrieved the spilled sticks quickly, glad now for the rain that prevented Big Beak from carrying her hickory stick outside.

Marie bowed her head reverently and entered the wigwam, where Kicks Hard, Big Beak's mother, lounged on stacked deerskins. That wasn't *her* real name either.

Marie arranged the firewood slowly. She wanted to savor the heat as long as possible, but Kicks Hard shouted something about dripping all over the skins and booted her toward the doorway.

"Take some to Alsoomse," Big Beak demanded in the language Marie was only now grasping.

Trout Face, Cauldron Man's widowed sister.

Though Big Beak's fish-faced friend visited often, Marie did not know where she lived. "How I find?" she asked in broken Algonquian.

A hint of cunning sparked in Big Beak's eyes. "Along the river. Third cabin."

Marie had seen the cabins from a distance. She could not reach them without passing the longhouse. Cauldron Man lived in one of them. Was Big Beak trying to make her sad by thinking about him? Or, was she testing her? Is that why she looked so calculating?

"I no go longhouse."

Big Beak smirked. "You may today. But *only* today."

Excitement crushed all suspicion. Seeing a new part of the village would seem a small thing to most, but to Marie, any break in the monotony of her cruel life was a source of delight. She left quickly, no longer minding the cold rain, then retrieved a large armful of the wood she left stacked by the river. As she passed the longhouse, Red Cheeks raced out of her wigwam and up the hill, presumably eager to report Marie's crime to Big Beak.

Good. Let the dirty gossip get wet for nothing.

Marie found the cabins and passed the first two, wondering which belonged to Cauldron Man and his father. At the third, she did her best to call Trout Face by her given name.

"Alsoomse."

The oak door swung open, revealing a slender woman wearing a blue and white petticoat. Marie stared at the garment, recognizing it at once. It still bore scorch marks from the night of the attack and seams where someone repaired it. The last time she saw it, a Frenchman whirled it over Heinrich's head to blind him. Was their stallion in the village, too?

The sound of giggling caused her to turn and see Red Cheeks and Looks Away standing behind her. Refusing to reward them with an outward display of emotion, she locked her gaze on the wood in her arms.

"Come in," Trout Face said to all.

Marie bristled as Red Cheeks and Looks Away shoved her into a cabin too warm for one in supposed need of firewood. The scalps of many victims hung about the single room, no doubt placed there by Trout Face's dead husband, a renowned warrior. Trout Face possessed many colorful strouds and bearskin rugs. A solid table held two silver candlesticks, obviously European. Those lovely things reminded Marie of home, but she hardly noticed them. Neither the cabin nor its accoutrements made her heart soar, but the boy tossing sticks into the hearth did.

"Hans!" Wet firewood rattled to the floor. Marie ran to pick up her son, whose bewildered gaze darted past her to Trout Face. "My baby. Oh, my dearest child." She kissed the cheeks stained dark by walnut juice, then ran a hand across his scalp, plucked clean of hair except for a dyed tuft at his crown.

With his chin quivering, he examined her, uncertainty turning his amber eyes to deep gingerbread. Other captive boys had light eyes to betray their English or Irish lineage. Hans's brown ones made him a valuable prize, since outsiders would think him just another Indian. His adoption by Trout Face made perfect sense, since the childless widow's lineage entitled her to the best of everything.

Red Cheeks sprang into action. She ripped Hans from Marie's arms and demanded to know who she thought she was, trying to steal another woman's son.

Shaken, Marie backed against a wall, suddenly realizing she had taken the bait set for her. Stealing a child was punishable by death.

Was Trout Face in on the ruse?

Her haughty expression said she was.

Marie narrowed her eyes and addressed her in English, knowing the infraction no longer mattered. "I suppose when you learned of your brother's affection for me, you worried I might one day be too close for comfort." She ground her teeth together. "I never once encouraged him, you barren she-devil, but I hope when he learns of your treachery, he pounds you like your shitty samp." To Red Cheeks, she said, "May your ugly daughter climb into bed with a dirty Frenchman and spend the rest of her days popping blisters."

They glared as if they understood her.

Determined to make her crime worth the punishment, Marie bent forward and stretched out her arms. "Hans, come to Mama."

He ran to her.

She held him, savoring the scent of the child she brought into the world. "Be strong, my son," she whispered against his ear. "Remember me always. Do not cry, my child. I will always be with you."

She set him down again, then stood tall in the face of her enemies, ready to make the agonizing journey to heaven, where she would tell Mama she grew brave, at last.

~ ~ ~

Buzzing flies annoyed her cheeks, no doubt drawn there by her blood. Marie tasted it on lips cracked by days of sun her swollen eyes could no longer see.

She lay on her back, tied to the ground with her arms and legs outstretched. Sore ribs allowed only short, painful breaths. Her lungs were filling up with water. She was drowning in her own fluids.

When a cool shadow blocked the sun, she guessed the women came at last to finish her off, then thought it more likely they brought a hot poker or a dull blade.

"Marie?"

Cauldron Man.

She coughed, too weak to reply.

A rough hand stroked her head, where the hair he loved grew no more. Red Cheeks saw to its destruction, laughing maniacally while cutting it close enough to draw blood.

Cauldron Man babbled disjointed threats to tear the hair from every woman in the village. He cut through Marie's restraints, freeing her limbs.

She cried out as he pulled her arms to her sides.

He lifted her then and carried her through the scent of smoke and cooking meat to Oldest Woman's wigwam. There, the decrepit woman sobbed while patting Marie's cheek.

Hearty broth spilled into Marie's mouth. She gulped greedily while Cauldron Man roared outside the wigwam.

Female voices turned shrill and pleading.

A fist struck bone.

In spite of her pain, Marie smiled and whispered his real name for the first time. "Taspecawen."

Chapter 21

With Stewart away at Fort Lyttelton and Rose pounding corn, Catrina had plenty of time to rummage through the goods in the warehouse.

"What ye doin'?"

She flinched, nearly dropping her lantern. "Thomas!" She covered her heart with her hand. "You scared me."

He beamed. "Ye should know by now that I'm like a cat."

She had been the first to say so, a declaration she now regretted, for he liked the comparison very much; enough, in fact, to trade fort construction for espionage.

"What ye doin'?" he asked again, scanning the goods in her arms.

She couldn't tell him she was gathering supplies for yet another flight into the wilderness. "I'm playing dress-up."

He grinned and wiggled his fingers in the air. "Can I play, too?"

"Not today, Thomas." She did not want him underfoot. More importantly, she did not want him to bear witness to her deception.

He scowled. "I'm gonny tell Rose."

She set down the lantern, then rushed to him, her mind racing for a solution. "But, Thomas," she said, gripping his shoulders. "This game is like no other. The players of *this* game must be able to keep a secret. You are certainly sneaky enough; catlike, in fact, but we both know when it comes to secrets, you are not—"

"Am so." He crossed his arms and scowled.

"Oh, Thomas." He would tattle, but she saw no other option than to include him in her plan. "All right, if you promise not to tell anyone, I will let you play." The most she could hope for was his silence until she left town.

"I promise, Cat, I really do."

"If you tell, then I shall never play this game with you again. Do you understand?"

He nodded enthusiastically.

Catrina pretended to inspect the room for eavesdroppers. She whispered, "This game is a little harder than simple dress-up, because you not only choose items for dressing a particular character; you must also tally the value of those items in a book."

"Ohh," Thomas whispered. "That old Stewart plays this one all the time."

"All the more reason to keep our play secret. We shall practice until you can whoop him at his own game. Won't *he* be surprised?"

He beamed and looked to some faraway corner of his mind. "Aye . . ."

"Let us begin." She lifted the lantern, then led him to Stewart's ledger. "First, we need to pick a character. Whom shall we dress?" She tapped a finger on her chin. "A fine lady?"

Thomas wrinkled up his nose. "Naw, they're dumb. Have ye e'er seen the one Stewart's sweet on? She makes me wanna boke." His face brightened as an idea came to him. "I know! Let's dress an Injun chief!"

She pursed her lips. "Hmm, a fine idea, Thomas, but I do not think Stewart has wampum belts and turkey capes in here." She rifled through the stacks of shirts and hunting frocks. "Most of his goods are suitable only for a man on the trail." She moved to a table, where canteens and leather pouches leaned against loading blocks and fire starting kits."

I wonder what sort of man uses these?"

Trader, Thomas. A trader.

She scratched her head.

He scratched his, too.

"Mayhap, a gentleman?" she asked.

"Naw, a gentleman would wear silks and such, not homespun."

She lifted a bedroll and a bowl of fishing hooks. "I wish I knew who uses these things. For the life of me, I am mystified."

"I know." He snapped his fingers. "A trader."

She snapped her fingers, too. "You know, Thomas, I think you may be right. A trader it is. Let us commence play. I will list items a trader might need, and you can find and bring them to me. Together, we will tally their cost in the ledger."

He appeared to like the idea.

She muttered items as she listed them in a column of Stewart's ledger. "Tie wig . . . hat . . ."

Thomas rushed to bring her the finest of each.

"I nearly forgot to mention the most important rule. We have only ten pounds to spend, and everything we buy must fit the player listing the goods. Try to pick out things I could wear. If we overspend, we lose. This is why Stewart is so good at this game. He knows the price of things by heart."

"I'm gonny beat him at it one day."

"I do not doubt it for a moment."

Thomas "shopped" more sensibly, bringing her a brown wig and a round hat flattened by a horse.

"These are perfect," she said. "The wig is unkempt, but serviceable. The price of the hat has been reduced, I see. Good work. Let us tally the cost."

They recorded the items in Stewart's book, where Thomas demonstrated an uncanny talent for cyphering. As he went for additional items, Catrina could not resist flipping through the pages of the ledger, which displayed many lists of goods sold on credit. Only a handful of the totals had been satisfied. She wondered if Stewart prepaid for his inventory or if he, too, purchased his goods on credit. In either case, he certainly wasn't making a profit. She saw quite plainly why he needed to marry Rachel Campbell.

Guilt forced her eyes away from his private business. "I need breeches and a shirt," she called to Thomas.

He brought them quickly, laughing as he held up a shirt. "This one is Stewart's. He left it hanging on an old spinning wheel in the back."

"We cannot take Stewart's shirt."

"I canny see why not. It's been hanging there for a fortnight. We can buy it for next to naught since it has his stink all o'er it. Go on." He pointed at the book. "Write it doon."

She did, finding his thrift too endearing for argument. There seemed little harm in buying a shirt Stewart had not missed. It would hang on her like a feed bag, but malnourishment had most men wearing oversized shirts these days. "You are quite good at this game, Thomas. The shirt saved us a bundle. I need a waistcoat, stockings, and leggings." She would wear her own moccasins and fashion a neckerchief out of a scrap of cloth.

"What aboot a hunting frock?"

"Too warm. Besides, I think the balance of our funds would be better spent on supplies like a canteen, barley, hooks and line, an oilcloth and rope, a sack, and a hatchet." The list went on until they could buy nothing more without depleting Catrina's funds. The whole ten pounds could never buy a musket, but she planned to take Robert Johnson's fowler, repaired only minutes after he dropped it into her hands. If she returned safely, she would give it back to him. If not, then she would have to beg God's forgiveness for stealing it. The fowler lacked the accuracy and lethal distance of a rifle, but it mattered little. She wanted to see her quarry up close anyway. Was there a better place to witness his astonishment than right before his eyes?

"Did we win?" Thomas asked, looking over her shoulder.

She laid down the quill, then rumpled his hair. "Indeed, we did, Thomas. You are a splendid partner. Now, remember to keep our game a secret so we may play again. I would like to practice a few more times before we challenge anyone. If Stewart finds out, he will not allow us to train anymore, because he wants to be the best at this game."

He narrowed his eyes. "Aye, the dirty shite. The big cheater."

She was still chuckling hours later as she penned a letter to Stewart. Keeping a careful eye on Rose's door, she wrote:

Stewart,

Necessity requires me to leave Carlisle at once. Worry not, for my travels take me to the safety of Philadelphia, where I intend to toss all dignity at the feet of my father's widow. A letter received of late brings hope of a softening heart and word of ransom. I must go to her at once, as she is of changeable character.

She nearly signed the letter then and there, but a glass of Stewart's brandy and the danger of her upcoming mission poured honesty from her heart and into the quill.

Should I not return, rest assured that my silence bodes well. I will send word when I am settled, but pray, do not think the worst. I would be remiss if I did not put pen to paper to thank you for the kindness you have extended to me during these past few months. Oh, Stewart, how could we have known, on that day in June, when you sipped broth at our table, what lay ahead of us? I insist on seeing you repaid one way or another. If you have not heard from me by spring, please accept my mare as recompense for your troubles.

The mention of money turned her thoughts to his financial woes . . . and his plan for solving them. She pictured him walking with flawless Rachel Campbell and it made her face flush. *It's the brandy*, she assured herself. She turned her attention back to her letter, her throat constricting as honest words flowed out of the nib.

I expect a married man will read my next letter, a vexing thought, I confess. I have no right to my displeasure. You have justly pinned all hope on marrying a delicate and affluent quarry. Should it come to pass—and I pray God it does, for your sake—then I shall vow to be happy for you. Yet, I wonder, does she deserve you? Does she know the superior quality of the man courting her?

She pushed the brandy away, deeming it responsible for the undignified turn into candor, then retrieved it and finished it off.

Is she aware of your talent for melting the ice compressing a widow's heart? I have every confidence that I shall recover my loved ones. And yet, as I imagine them sleeping under my roof again, I see now how regret and longing shall remain my steadfast companions, and I think you know why. Only the memory of you, Stewart Buchanan, shall bring me comfort.

God preserve you, now and always.

Catrina

Tears pricked her eyes at the certainty of never seeing him again. In her mind, she watched him hand Hans a bilbo catcher. She saw him, too, surrounded by hay, when she asked him why he followed her to the farm.

Ye know why.

The unfairness of life galled her. She folded the letter angrily, then dropped it onto the table, where it lay crooked and easing open again, as if anxious to share the contents of her unsatisfied heart. She slammed her hand upon it to push herself up from her chair, then slipped into the warehouse, where her disguise awaited her next to Stewart's ledger book. Sighing, she shed her clothes . . . and all thoughts of Stewart Buchanan.

Chapter 22

Stewart tightened the sear screw inside a dismantled firelock, then stretched. His back ached from spending long hours hunched over his vise, but he could afford no rest. Not with Colonel Armstrong counting on him.

Two letters lay on his workbench. Both announced returns to Philadelphia. One, he recalled, invited him to a proper farewell over a cup of tea. Its polished words leaned forty-five degrees to the right in a graceful script penned with utmost care and precision. The other . . .

He picked it up and read the part ringing in his mind like an Angelus bell.

. . . regret and longing shall remain my steadfast companions.

Her admission coaxed out his own. God help him, he wanted the stubborn woman, not just for a night, but for the rest of his life. He could never marry Rachel Campbell now, not for every piece of gold in the king's coffers.

Rachel deserved the truth, which he'd delivered as she stood next to a carriage and surrounded by trunks. He expected and deserved her rebuke, not the slackening of features signifying her blatant relief.

"Oh, Mister Buchanan, you cannot know how happy I am to hear this."

His shock and humiliation must have been apparent, for she tried at once to salve his wounded ego.

"Forgive me. I fear you misunderstood me just now. Rest assured, I have always considered you a most admirable man, handsome and kind, and altogether worthy of any

woman's love. There are few men I would trust with my life. You, sir, are one of them."

She divulged a secret then, one she begged him not to share. She could not marry him or any other, as her heart already belonged to George Dawson, the lowly servant loading her trunks. In another six months, when Dawson's term of indenture ended, they planned to assume false names and flee to York City, where Dawson's uncle owned a prosperous grain mill.

It was a confidence Stewart considered breaking for the girl's own good. He wished her Godspeed, then raced home and pulled out a sheet of foolscap, knowing a courier could reach Lieutenant Campbell at Harris's Ferry by nightfall. Only the recollection of Mary Murray's unhappiness stayed his quill. He knew well the devastation caused by ill-fated lovers. In the silky sanctuary of a woman's heart, forbidden love smoldered forever. It gradually turned her to ash and then consumed every careless soul within reach. Would he sentence Rachel to the calamitous fate of lying under one man while dreaming of another? Nay, he would not, especially since the lieutenant would seek to suppress her rebellion by marrying her off at once. With Stewart out of the picture, it left only cocky, little Ensign Blythe. Stewart would not send Rachel into the arms of *that* swaggering fool. So, he bit his tongue and marveled at the slight girl seemingly made of iron. Good for her, choosing love over wealth.

Her mettle shamed him. The desire to present Catrina with his heart burned like whiskey in a wound. If he'd left when he first read Catrina's letter, he would be well on his way to Philadelphia, but circumstances did not allow it. As usual, Catrina's timing was utter shite. Had she stayed another day, she would know of Colonel Armstrong's command to assemble at Fort Shirley for a march on Kittanning. Stewart received his orders at Fort Lyttelton. He rushed home to muster with Armstrong's advance, which would move into Sherman's Valley within hours. He brought welcome news for Rose, too. Henry Mosebey had survived the attack on Ward's reapers, thanks to nature's call. He had been defecating in the woods when the attack occurred and fled on foot to Fort Lyttelton, where he begged Stewart to inform Rose of his wellbeing and ever-present affection.

Outside Stewart's shop, someone fired a musket, a frequent occurrence now with men funneling into Carlisle from every direction. Armstrong put out the call for fighting men. They answered in no small way. Overnight, bloodlust turned the town into a swarming city. The colonel's advance grew to nine companies made up of three hundred provincial soldiers, all of them volunteer frontiersman bent on revenge.

"Why'd she go and leave us again, Stewart?"

He flinched, rustling the letter he still held. He forgot about Thomas cleaning gun barrels in the corner.

"I told ye ten times, lad. She went to collect a ransom so she can try to get her loved ones back." He set Catrina's letter down gently, relieved she was heading toward the safety of Philadelphia. If General Braddock's rout at the Monongahela taught them anything, it was the terrible repercussions of defeat. Should Armstrong's expedition go awry, not even Carlisle could withstand Captain Jacobs's emboldened retribution.

The inner parts of Thomas's eyebrows formed points, turning his eyes to triangles. "She'll be back, though, right? Because, ye know, Stewart, Catrina and me, we need to practice our numbers and dress . . . Och, nae. Forget I said that." He returned to his work.

Numbers again. The word had been driving Stewart to the brink of madness since dawn, when Thomas started using it in every sentence.

He bit his tongue and counted to ten. Losing his temper would only send Thomas out of the shop crying, and he needed the boy's help if he wanted to see his bed before the cock crowed. "Concentrate on your work, son. She'll send word once she gets settled." He hoped so. Mercy, he hoped so.

"I've been thinking about numbers."

Stewart's cheeks burned. "Thomas, if I hear the word numbers again, I'm gonny go off my heed."

"It's just that . . ." Thomas rammed ticking down a barrel, then closed his eyes and shook his head. "Oh, my, I have the best idea for numbers. Och, sorry."

Jaysus Mighty. Stewart rubbed his eyebrows, then mouthed a prayer of forgiveness. If ever he wanted to be on God's good side, it was on the eve of battle. Taking the Lord's name in vain, even in thought, seemed particularly risky now.

Thomas pulled the cloth out of the barrel. "I know. I'll just practice wi'oot her. She left the money, after all."

Stewart laid his screwdriver beside Catrina's letter and tried to look nonchalant. "What money?"

"Well, I canny tell ye, can I? Because ye said I could nae say the word again."

Stewart faced the doorway to the main house. "Rose!"

She appeared with her sewing.

"What is this eejit on aboot?"

"Let me guess. Numbers and dress-up?"

"Aye, what is he on aboot? Now, he's talking aboot money."

Thomas's chin began to quiver. "Just forget I said anything. Besides, there's nae sense asking *her*. *She* threatened to cut my tongue oot if I mentioned it again."

Rose rolled her eyes. "Some silly game Catrina played with him."

Thomas shook the cleaning rod at her. "Ye know fine well it is nae silly. Ye're only saying so because ye know I'm better at it than Stewart. Ye *always* take his side, Rose.

I ought to go get the money and show the both of ye in one fell swoop."

Money again. Did Thomas rob someone? If so, he would tan the boy's hide.

Stewart crossed the room. "What money?"

Thomas pouted.

Stewart lifted the boy's chin with his finger. "I want to know right now what ye're on aboot."

Thomas wailed the open-mouthed yowl of a pinched toddler.

Stewart recalled Catrina's advice. *If you order Thomas to do something, he will do the opposite.*

He shook his head. "I thought ye said ye were better than me at this game."

"I am, Stewart." Thomas's cries surrendered to sobs. He wiped his nose on his sleeve. "I really am."

"If a man makes such a claim, he better be prepared to prove it."

"Do ye mean ye'll play?"

Stewart nodded, wondering what he was getting himself into.

Thomas jumped off his stool, his sorrow forgotten. "I'm gonny whoop ye so bad, Stewart." He raced into the warehouse.

Stewart followed him to the ledger.

Thomas scooped a pile of coins off the hardcover book. "We need to pick a character. I've been thinking aboot this all day. I say we dress a cabbage farmer. What say ye to that, Stewart? Ye ready?"

"Gi' me those coins."

Thomas's smile faded. He dropped the money into Stewart's palm.

"Where did these come from?" Stewart asked, examining coins blackened by soot.

"Catrina."

"For what?"

"The last game we played." Thomas sighed. "Honestly, Stewart, I expected ye to be better at this."

"Mayhap, we should go o'er the rules."

Thomas stabbed a finger at him and grinned. "Ahh, ye're trying to trick me. Ye know the rules fine well, ye big cheater."

"Indeed, I do, but your hesitation in confirming that *ye* know them makes me think ye're full of shite, Thomas Murray. I will nae waste my time playing wi' an amateur."

"Ha! We shall see who the amateur is, ye old-timer. Ye know as well as I do that we pick a character and then buy the goods needed to dress and supply him."

"That all?"

"Nay, it is nae all," Thomas huffed. "Ye have to write the cost of the items doon in this book." He thumped a finger against the hard cover of Stewart's ledger. "And, by jabbers, your sums better add up or ye're in a bucket of bubbly shite."

Stewart flipped the book open to reveal the items Catrina listed in the "goods sold" column.

"Thomas, who told ye aboot this game?"

"Catrina."

"Did she invite ye to play, or did ye find her playing it on her own?"

"She was practicing in here by herself, but I sneaked up on her." A wide grin turned his countenance impish. "Like a cat."

Stewart ran his finger over the list of items she purchased. *Tie wig, hat, shirt, breeches, leggings, hooks, line, fire starting kit, bedroll, tumpline, canteen, knife*. The total cost corresponded exactly with the amount of money he held in his hand. He closed his fist around the coins.

"What character did ye dress?"

"I canny say."

"Thomas Edward Murray, who did ye dress?"

"Ye're just trying to get the upper hand, 'cause if we use a trader again, then ye'll—" His face blanched. "Damn it. Well, there ye go. We dressed a trader."

A trader. Why would Catrina need a trader's supplies to go to Philadelphia? He scanned the list again. "No powderhorn or musket?"

Thomas nodded. "She had them already."

"How do ye know?"

"She said so. We were talking aboot how much money it saved her to already have them."

"Where did she get them?"

"Dunno."

"Did ye see them?"

He shook his head, then scowled. "Och, Stewart. She would nae cheat, would she?"

"Only one way to find oot."

~ ~ ~

Stewart found the carver covered in dust and shouting insults at his apprentice. "When I say don't move my horns, I mean don't move my horns!" He gave the boy a shove. "Now, find one marked Miller or you'll see no supper tonight."

"What can I do for you?" he asked when Thomas and Stewart approached his stall.

"Have ye made a horn for a woman recently?" Stewart asked.

"Aye. Elias Walker."

"Eh?"

"The woman's nephew. Said he was moving out with Captain Hamilton's company. Wanted a map to make sure he could find his way home."

"She ordered a powderhorn wi' a map on it?"

"And his name. Elias Walker, as I said." He rubbed the back of his neck. "Was I wrong to sell it to her? I don't want no trouble."

"Not at all. Indeed, your patron canny be the woman I know. Mine has no nephew."

"Her name escapes me. What was it, now?" The carver rubbed his chin and looked up to the sky, as if seeking divine assistance. "Hechwalder!" He snapped his fingers. "Anna Hechwalder."

Stewart touched his cap. "Nay, not her. Sorry for the bother. Come, Thomas."

They had just crossed the street when the carver called them back. He nodded at his apprentice. "My boy knows yours. Says it was *his* door he knocked on when I sent him to let the woman know her horn was nearly ready."

"Aye?"

"Aye. Says Anna Hechwalder answered the knock."

"He must be mistaken. I do nae know anyone named Anna Hechwalder."

"The boy has a foul mouth and a bad streak of laziness, but I've never known him to lie."

"What did Anna Hechwalder look like?" Stewart asked.

"Now, that I *do* remember. She had perfect teeth and the loveliest amber eyes. And her figure . . ." He whistled. "An autumn rose still in bloom . . ." He stared at nothing, apparently lost in Catrina's charm.

Stewart balled his hands into tight fists, momentarily rattled by the carver's admiration. "Did she pay for the horn?"

"Aye, with the blackest coins I ever did see."

Stewart ground his teeth together. The coins ripped out of Catrina's shift by the Robinson women had reflected the lamplight. Clearly, she obtained new ones since then. He guessed where.

"I had to chop through the beams to get the horse in here."

She cut into more than the barn, he knew now, and the logs scattered about Meyer's yard had not been dragged there by Indians. She hadn't sliced her arm in the barn, either, since pegs, not spikes, held that structure together. Only the cabin contained nails, not in the walls, but in the floor. If Catrina cut herself on a nail—and her wound certainly looked like it had been torn by a spike—then she did it while hacking through charred floorboards. She'd lied to him about her reasons for traveling to her ruined farm. She did not risk her life to see what she would be left with after the war. She went instead to retrieve a cache of coins, coins she used to further deceive him by outfitting herself for a long journey.

Fury turned his voice gritty. "You said she ordered a map."

"Aye."

"To where?"

"Kittanning."

His limbs turned to ice. She was not safe in Philadelphia, as formerly believed, but instead, hacking her way toward the devil's hot parlor, unaware of the provincial gun barrels about to point at her back.

"Come on," he said to Thomas. His face burned. His temples throbbed.

"We gonny go play numbers now?" Thomas asked.

"Aye, let's dress up another trader." He would head out immediately. She could not have gotten far.

As they passed the fort, muskets fired and officers shouted. A breathless man in Stewart's unit raced up to him. "They're calling us up. We drill in an hour and march at midnight."

Damn it. "How many of us?"

"Ten to advance tonight with the balance to follow at dawn."

He would not defy Armstrong, who was counting on all men to follow orders. Besides, the move into Sherman's Valley meant the potential for catching up to Catrina.

"But, Stewart." Thomas tugged on his shirtsleeve. "Ye canny go now. What aboot our game of numbers and dress-up?"

"We'll play one game, but we canny dress a trader." He tousled the boy's hair, wondering if Rose would care for him if he failed to survive the coming battle. "We must dress a soldier instead."

Chapter 23

Sound carried far in the wilderness. Thumps at daybreak warned Catrina of her nearness to Andrew Montour's village, sending her into the cover of a cornfield, where umber tassels adorned the stalks. A shrill dog pursued her there; she silenced it by crushing her only ball of pemmican and tossing it into the field. With the animal fixed on retrieving every nugget of the costly staple, she stole west to the sanctuary of the forest.

Her new course required crossing the creek four times, a troublesome consequence turned agreeable by late morning on the stagnant August day.

Hours later, on a deer trail slicing through a thicket, the sound of an axe splitting wood made her leap behind an oak tree. She padded from trunk to trunk in the direction of the sound, silent in her moccasins. At the curved end of a ridge, she smelled smoke.

Robinson's fort.

She was close. Too close.

She doubled back, careful not to rustle the laurel and planning each step before taking it. Sound was a fickle companion. It could turn from friend to foe in a switch of a mare's tail, bringing men—or bullets—upon her.

In spite of the delay caused by extreme caution, by the time the tree frogs began their opus, she stood atop the Conococheague, meeting her goal for the day. She cocked an ear toward the meadowlands below, labeled "H. Valley" on her horn. She would travel in an arc around that exposed parcel of land, then climb the sharp face of the Tuscarora, which loomed purple in the twilight. Bears, panthers, and serpents prowled the scree, but, God willing, no men would be upon it. Only a fool would climb it.

She wiped sweat from her brow. Though her hat did not breathe as well as a woman's cap, its shade prevented a worsening of the headaches she still suffered daily. Only willow bark tea seemed to dull them. To make some, she needed boiling water, and that required a fire.

The tie wig brought from Stewart's warehouse found its way into her packs early on. Wearing the sweltering accessory past Blue Mountain turned out to be sheer folly.

Though the sun was losing its grip on the day, a pastel moon promised a bright night. She debated the wisdom in pressing on.

Nein, she thought, recalling the vitriol in her enemy's eyes. When she met Captain Jacobs, she wanted to be as fresh as morning butter. The most dangerous part of her journey lay ahead, boding little chance for restoration. She should rest now or risk fatigue. Fatigue led to carelessness, and carelessness led to death.

The strap of her tumpline and blanket roll brushed against her tender crown as she lifted it over her head. Her gear fell to the moss, taking her mood with it. What if she rested now, only to arrive at Kittanning a day too late?

Casting aside her melancholy thoughts, she concentrated instead on the satisfaction of a job well done. Fewer miles separated her from her family now, thanks to fair weather and weightless clothes facilitating movement and wicking away sweat. Had she known the comfort to be found in breeches, she might have abandoned petticoats long ago. The only annoyance so far was the difficulty in answering nature's call. But the leggings. Oh, those wonderful, manly accoutrements, invented to bear the brunt of the forest's sharp edges. They delivered her to the top of the Conococheague with only a tiny scratch, and that on her cheek.

She took those buckskin saviors off now, delighting in the sudden coolness at her shins. She booted a mound of decayed heartwood out of a hollow tree, then spread out her oilcloth and blanket. It seemed a safe enough site for a cooking fire, which she made small and smokeless by digging a deep firepit and connecting it to a second hole by way of a tunnel to encourage draft. Within minutes, using only a few sticks, she had a white-hot fire seen only from above.

She had no time to cook the dried peas or parched corn she bought in Carlisle, so she settled for mushroom and nettle broth with a bit of willow bark dropped in. After it boiled, she kicked dirt into the holes, snuffing the fire without sending up a single wisp of smoke. She drank her supper from the pot and listened as the sounds of prowling night creatures broke the stillness of twilight. Some of those animals swishing through the leaves would deem her a flavorsome dinner. She kept the fowler close.

Using the last of the day's light, she rinsed her pot, repacked her belongings in case she needed to bolt, then carried everything inside the tree, where the ring of sapwood muffled all sounds but those she made. She stretched out on the unexpectedly comfortable bed, wondering why women relied so heavily on men. Weren't they capable of managing their own affairs? Did breasts make her less capable of crossing the frontier?

"Hmph," she muttered to the tree, pulling the fowler closer. The fault lay in archaic views alone. Weaker sex, indeed. Didn't a woman share a man's chores, even while suckling one child and dragging another behind? A man was stronger, sure, but wasn't she just as clever and brave? The precious time she wasted in waiting for men to help her sickened her now. First, Stewart. Then Colonel Armstrong. The men of the Assembly. The governor. The king!

Why, she had only to dust off the knowledge gained in her youth. Her play with Yellow Bear and his sisters did more than entertain her, she knew now; it taught her to survive. The memory of those lost souls gored her, and not just because she missed them. Like all Native women, Yellow Bear's mother endured crushing toil to keep a morsel of food in her children's bellies. How much worse was the situation for Marie, a throwaway slave? Was she still alive? Was Hans?

They had to be. Catrina would not consider the alternative.

Hold on, Marie. Mama's coming.

The strain of repressed tears drove her headache up the back of her skull. She succumbed to her pain, both physical and emotional, crying softly and wiping her tears on a sleeve that smelled, God help her, of a man she loved.

~ ~ ~

It took a day to find Aughwick Creek and another to skirt around Fort Shirley, where a wide swath of crushed meadow disclosed the path used by Captain Hamilton and his regiment.

What hope was there when provincial forces rolled across the frontier like heavy barrels? Perhaps, it was no accident. Perhaps, Colonel Armstrong intended to create the illusion of a great army. Trampling the goldenrod and foxtails would be a fine strategy if the enemy didn't possess the opposing talent of gliding about like mist. Not only would the war chiefs already know the precise number of soldiers within the fort's stockade, but also what each man ate for his morning meal.

She paused to catch her breath, then turned to judge her own stealth. In the forest of towering spruce trees, a single footprint dented the moss between two ferns. The mark was already springing back, erasing all evidence of use.

Near Standing Stone, yowls forced her to hide along the riverbank while ten painted men holding jugs danced around a fire. A day later, those drunken fools finally sobered up and departed, allowing her to move on, hungry and covered in mosquito bites.

She regained the lost time at Frankstown, where houses faced each other across a single street, a short leg of Kittanning Path. The village was utterly abandoned now, all doors hanging open and askew.

Did the residents lose hope . . . or their very lives? She imagined them as spirits peering through their black windows, their mouths locked in eternal screams for mercy. The thought quickened her step. She left the village with the hairs standing up on the back of her neck.

Two days later, while picking her way toward Burgoon's Gap, she remained jumpy from the experience and shattered by the fitful sleep it triggered.

Could spirits follow people?

A murder of crows flushed ahead, nearly stopping her heart. They cawed angrily at the thing disrupting their roost. Trusting their vigilance, she leapt off the path and into the forest, fuming at her carelessness. Spirits, indeed. It was the living she needed to fear!

Mindful not to disturb anything, she scuttled to an outcrop, where lichens and saplings clung to life in the sandstone's fissures. She crouched, her blood flogging her eardrums, her eyes locked on the path.

Voices.

She counted five men and two women passing by, all dressed in deerskin. They made no attempt at secrecy. Why should they, when the nearest gun—as far as they knew—lay miles away, at Fort Shirley?

A whiff of sweat drifted up from her armpits. Could they smell it, too? She pressed her arms against her sides and held her breath.

They continued east, halting every few steps to shout through cupped hands.

Panic nearly sliced her in two as she realized they were searching for someone. What if she wasn't alone in the woods?

The tallest among them mumbled and pointed at the ground where Catrina left the path.

She froze.

They clambered into the woods toward her, slipping like waxed thread among the trunks, ascending while shouting a word that could only mean "death."

Her hands squeezed the fowler like hickory hoops. She could never reload fast enough to shoot more than one of them, and with no wind to disguise her footfall, dashing away would bring them upon her. She needed a diversion. Wind, smoke, distant gunfire, flushing turkeys, anything!

Salvation rolled across the sky in a cloud so thick it obliterated the sun. Millions of wingbeats began as a hiss and amplified to a deafening roar. Bird droppings splattered on everything. Evergreen boughs undulated in the sudden change of draft.

Too frightened to care about the filth raining down on her, Catrina sprinted away, heading deep into the forest. She bounded over limbs and ducked under fallen trees, whacking her arms and gun against tree trunks and vines, knowing she was leaving one hell of a trail for her enemy to follow.

She ran until her lungs gave out and the forest turned deciduous, then slid inside a hollow chestnut tree. Breathless, she doffed her hat and inspected her arms, now coated with excrement.

Better than being dead.

It took hours for the flock to disappear.

When she finally stepped out of the tree, she entered a world gone white. Had it not been so wretchedly hot and malodorous, she might have thought the forest covered in snow. Careful not to slip in the mess, she descended into a hollow, where oaks protected the verdure like giant parasols. At their feet, a dozen or more frogs plopped into a clear pool. She knelt, her head thumping, to wash her face and arms.

Feeling quite unwell, she sat on her heels to mindlessly observe the water skippers flitting across the pool's surface. Her head pounded. Pain in her hip revealed a strain suffered during her getaway. To make matters worse, her northerly flight brought her close to the wetlands where, according to the carver, the Natives extracted lead for bullets. She could think of no more dangerous place to camp except, perhaps, Kittanning itself, yet four or five days away.

Though the pool would clean her skin and soothe her headache, it would exhale a cloud of mosquitoes after sunset. The footprints of many animals decorated the water's edge, including one with claws that left one-inch slices in the mud. Catrina flattened her hand inside one of those deep impressions and hoped *that* monster wasn't still thirsty.

She rose, then leaned the borrowed gun against a tree, bracing herself as vertigo removed all doubt about the wisdom in camping in the precarious spot. Her headache left her no choice; it must be relieved.

After stripping down to her shirt, she waded into the pool, glad to rid herself of filth. She floated on her back, sighing as the cool water eased her headache. So still was she that a brave sparrow came to splash in the shallows. Catrina lifted her head to inspect it, causing a ripple that propelled the bird to a low branch. There, it preened its feathers next to a tent of slender caterpillars.

With her headache reduced, she left the pool, clean at last, then slung her wet shirt over a limb. After spot-cleaning her stockings and breeches, she put them on again, along with loosely tied stays.

Better to sleep half-dressed than naked.

With her blanket wrapped around her shoulders, she grabbed the fowler and settled onto a bed of leaves to await nightfall. Her stomach rumbled miserably, and she pined for her lost pemmican. Instead, she ate wormy chestnuts gathered earlier, vowing tomorrow, she would find meat.

~ ~ ~

Birdsong woke her before dawn. In the treetops, she supposed, the winged creatures witnessed the sun's first peek at the new day. The grounded were less fortunate. For them, night persisted.

Wary of losing her supplies in the murkiness, Catrina felt her way to Stewart's shirt, only damp now, thanks to a breezy night she could not remember. She set her goods at her feet, then pulled on the garment, incredulous that she managed to sleep through the night.

A wail pierced the stillness and sent her reeling against a tree.

Mercy!

She held her breath and listened.

There. There it is again.

It sounded like a screaming woman. Or a child.

It cannot be. Can it?

It was one of the night creatures, she decided, those lethal marauders with a penchant for squealing. A raccoon, a fox, or sparring bobcats. Their fearsome cries sent many a man scrambling for his musket in the middle of the night. Why, even her uncommonly self-possessed father once shot through the door of their chicken coop to silence a pair of fisher cats.

She rolled up her bed and slung her tumpline across her shoulder. The screeches were worth investigating. She could steal a small predator's kill without firing a shot and cook it later at a safer place.

Though she could barely see her own fingers, Catrina started up the hollow. If she didn't beat the sun to the kill, she might lose it, since daylight drove nocturnal predators back to their dens.

The sound grew loud and familiar. She recognized it now as a porcupine, not the easiest animal to kill and dress, but certainly one of the tastiest. More importantly, she could eat it raw, since it ate only vegetation. Porkies were near-sighted and slow, which meant if she could avoid its quills, and if her hip didn't give her too much bother, she could chase and kill her quarry without the risk of shooting it.

The rodent fell silent for a time, long enough for daylight to strike the hollow. Supposing it smelled or heard her and waddled away, she was about to abandon the hunt when a faint whimper rose up from the far side of a moss-covered log.

She skulked closer, then peered carefully above the downed wood.

A pair of dark eyes stared back.

Her gasp made the boy scuttle back on his rump, but he did not scream. His cheeks glistened with tears. To his left lay a woman and a rattlesnake, both dead.

Though his skin lacked war paint, he was a miniature replica of her attackers. He wore no shirt and had no hair save the shock at his crown, which someone dyed red and speared with porcupine quills. His earlobes, which had been cut free, did not dangle in decorative hoops; they were missing altogether, suggesting he tore them during careless play. He rose, revealing a breechclout over buckskin leggings tied with beaded garters below his knees.

Catrina raced back to her former campsite, her mind struggling to process her discovery. She paced beside the pool, rubbing her forehead, desperate to collect her thoughts.

A child, next to a dead woman, and an even deader rattlesnake.

An idiot could piece it together.

"Alawa," she whispered to nobody. That was the word used by yesterday's travelers, and it must have been the woman's name. They were searching for her . . . and her child, roughly four years of age.

Fear shot to the ends of her fingers. She wrung her hands to ease the sting.

Would the searchers return?

Her concern for her own skin mortified her . . . until it didn't. She set out for the path, false apathy driving her across yesterday's bird droppings with reckless footsteps.

The boy is not my concern.

Emotion turned her lungs to bellows and her legs to thin ice.

Am I to save my enemy's child whilst they abuse my own?

She slumped onto a rock, her dizziness renewed, to cry into her hands. *Why? Why must I have a conscience?*

Taking no pains to stay quiet, she returned to the hollow, hoping the boy had already wandered off.

He hadn't. He sat cross-legged next to his mother's corpse, a tiny hand resting on her arm.

His sorrow melted icy bars off the doors of decency. He would slow her down and probably get her killed, but Catrina could not leave him behind.

She lay her musket on the moss, then approached him with her palms up, an unnecessary gesture, since he exhibited no alarm.

"You are one brave fellow," she cooed to him, knowing he didn't understand. "A child of *my* race would scream until he fainted." She knelt to touch his mother's stiff arm. "Alawa?"

He gave a quick nod, rose, then wilted against her bosom.

The familiar drape of a child in her arms undid her. Spreading her hands across his back, she pressed him close, feeling the jagged peaks of his spine and ribs.

Mercy.

"Here, now. When did you last eat?" she whispered, noticing a poultice of chewed leaves on Alawa's swollen ankle. The young woman looked to be in her early twenties, but a leathery patina made it hard to tell for sure.

Pushing the boy away, Catrina retrieved the snake, surprised to find it headless. "My goodness, even in her agony, your mama was thinking of you." She held up the snake. "This day will see you well fed, *mein guter Junge.*"

Catrina tucked the snake into her bag, gathered up her things, then carried the child to the path, now blissfully deserted. He was content to follow her thereafter, never falling behind, no matter how long her stride.

By late afternoon, they reached the area marked "Clear Fields" on her map. She allowed the child to inspect the carving on her powderhorn while she figured out what to do. They were both tired and hungry, and the snake was beginning to stink.

A mile off the path, she built a fire, for which the boy gathered twigs without being asked. After gutting and skinning the snake—an unexpectedly difficult task—she was pleased to find it possessed a pair of thick back straps. She was *not* pleased, however, when it writhed on the spit while cooking, a disturbing oddity that might have turned her stomach had she not been so hungry.

The boy stared at her while devouring his portion of the snake, ribs and all. He showed no outward signs of mourning. Did he miss his mother at all?

The fire was dwindling and their dinner nearly eaten when a flash of fur sent Catrina's hands to her gunstock. "Psst," she hissed, trying to divert the boy's attention from his fingers, which he licked, one at a time. "Boy."

Fright required no translation. As he met her eyes, he rightly judged her apprehension and slid next to her.

A low growl in the weeds below their campsite made the hairs stand up on Catrina's arms. Another emanated from a copse of pines to their right.

Wolves.

They were circling, preparing for the kill.

She jumped to her feet, then slid the tip of a dead branch into the fire. A flaming stick would hold the pack at bay until they were safely aloft. She looked up at two parallel branches of a sturdy beech tree, her main reason for choosing the campsite. Those in-the-event-we-need-them branches were vitally important now.

She lifted the boy into the tree.

He scrambled up to a thick limb and sat there, as still as a pine cone, while she snapped boughs from a neighboring hemlock tree and hauled them up with her supplies and the fowler.

Careful not to drop anything, she secured the fowler first, then wove hemp rope between the two branches, creating a springy platform. On this, she tossed the hemlock boughs for a mattress.

Catrina pulled the child to the platform, then tied him fast to it.

Minutes later, the wolves grew brave enough to creep out of the weeds, their teeth bared and heads lowered. Hackles raised, they pounced on the remains of the snake, fighting and snarling over the tiniest scrap of meat.

The yellow-eyed beasts circled the tree, yipping and growling with ferocity capable of curdling fresh cream. One grizzled veteran looked up at them. It leapt at them, snapping its jaws and sending up the stench of urine.

The boy flinched.

"Shush, now. They cannot get us." Catrina stroked his bristly head, knowing he didn't understand her. "They will go away soon."

For both their sakes, she hoped she was right.

Chapter 24

At Stewart's request, Captain Hugh Mercer sent a private from his company to question every man in the encampment, which now stretched from Fort Run to Aughwick Creek.

Private Arnold returned at midday with news of four women encountered during the fragmented march to Fort Shirley. The first was an Oneida woman who escaped her tormentors at Fort Duquesne, then avoided recapture by hiding in a beaver lodge. The rest traveled among friendly Senecas making their way to Shamokin.

Stewart poked the unnecessary fire in front of him, sending a shower of sparks toward the sun. *Someone* in the steady flow of men marching north and west to Fort Shirley should have seen Catrina. That they hadn't meant she was still ahead of him, or . . . He stared vacantly at the glowing chunks of wood, seeing Catrina instead, her wrists tied and shirt torn.

As the day wore on, he repeatedly steered his thoughts away from the visions of her capture assaulting him, but his mind refused to relent. He had too much damn time to think! Not one musket needed to be repaired. The battalion had enough firewood to smoke every ham in the province. Hell, he even volunteered for the watch, but Captain Mercer insisted on using his own men. Colonel Armstrong required patience alone, commanding all men to restore themselves in preparation for the coming march, which would be unbroken. Until the order to break camp came, Stewart could do nothing but fire-blister his knees and imagine Catrina's fate.

By dusk, his worries left him contemplating desertion and a moonlit trek alone. In a moment of weakness, he mentioned his temptation to another captain. His fellow officer rightly alerted Colonel Armstrong, who threatened Stewart with a public flogging.

"Can you imagine, sir, the danger in a careless man's captivity?" Armstrong roared at Stewart, who sweated at attention, his cheeks roasting and his heart pounding. The colonel's heels struck the hardened mud of the barracks floor as he paced in the lamplight with his hands locked behind his back. "God Almighty, Captain Buchanan, I don't need to tell you what our enemy is capable of. *Any* man would crack."

Stewart longed to defend himself, but the colonel was right.

"I am surprised at you. Imagine endangering our expedition over a woman. A woman!" He stopped to rub his eyes, which were hidden in shadow. "We waited so long for this moment."

"If I may, sir." Captain Mercer, a wiry, redheaded Scot, stepped forward.

Armstrong whirled on his heels. "You may not, Captain Mercer! Whilst I have the utmost respect for your work as a physician, I have not yet forgotten your support of the Jacobites. This is no mere rebellion, sir, and we are most assuredly *not* in Scotland anymore." He turned back to Stewart. "You, of all people, must know what is at stake here. A successful expedition will not only drive the enemy back but secure respect for our frontiersmen as first-rate fighting men. Campbell!"

He had no need to shout; Lieutenant Campbell stood only feet behind him.

"Aye, sir." Campbell's gorget flashed as he stood at attention.

Armstrong turned sardonic. "Assign a guard to this lovesick pup."

"Aye, sir."

God Almighty. Stewart shut his eyes to the humiliation.

"Open your eyes, you backwoods tomcat," Armstrong shouted.

Using the renowned doggedness of his race, Captain Mercer risked annoyance by speaking again. "Colonel Armstrong, sir, I beg your leave to hear me oot. Were we no' just discussing the benefits of sending a wee detachment to the fore?" He gestured to Buchanan, who prayed for lightning to strike him dead. "Since oor puir Romeo here wants to move on so badly, I say let him. Send him up to the beaver dams. Ye know fine weel there's no' a mair dependable man for the job."

Armstrong seemed to ponder this before leaning close enough for Stewart to smell ale on his breath. "What say you?"

Stewart would cartwheel to hell itself if it got him out of the colonel's headquarters. "I'll need men."

Armstrong straightened. "You shall have one only, so choose wisely. Advance to the beaver dams at Frankstown. Send your man back the moment the way is clear. We will break camp when he arrives. If you obey my orders, I hope to find you restored enough to move on to Cherry Tree. Disobey them, and I will have your balls. Do I make myself clear?"

"Aye, I'll hand 'em to ye masel', sir."

~ ~ ~

A hot breeze rolled up from the river and across former wetlands, drained now that all of Frankstown's beavers covered European heads. Their great dams once curved across a branch of the Juniata River here, turning low-lying willow and alder groves to artificial ponds serving as nurseries for salmon and trout. When the dams breached, the pools emptied, leaving a rich bottomland to grow up in cattails and saplings.

Stewart led his horse to a disused firepit in the middle of a sphere, where days of revelry had pounded the silt to a slab. He squatted to touch a rock.

"Warm?" Private Mosebey asked.

Stewart stood, then shook his head. "Cold." He surveyed the countryside. "She could be anywhere."

"You mean *they* could be anywhere."

"Aye, what did I say?"

"She."

"Did I?"

"Aye." Mosebey tried not to smile.

Stewart sighed and doffed his hat.

Surrendering to his amusement, Mosebey chuckled. "I won't tell anyone."

Stewart valued the private's discretion. He could bear no more ribbing. Thanks to Catrina, he now answered to everything from Pennsylvania Paramour to Sir Longs-A-Lot to Stewart the Swain. One bawdy Scot even declared, *Ye'd think a gunsmith could handle an o'erfilled shot bag. God's grace, man, go a ways intae the woods and fire a load oot the barrel.*

"Captain?"

Momentarily lost in disgrace, Stewart flinched. "Aye." He faced Mosebey, who looked especially leggy next to a horse meant for pulling a cart.

"The lads mean no harm. You know, about you being a Lovesick Laird and all."

Stewart winced inwardly. *Lovesick Laird.* There was a new one. He did his best to lie. "I do nae care what they call me as long as they follow my orders. Keep your voice doon." He scrubbed his sleeve across his forehead to mop up sweat. "I would like to keep my hair."

"Thing is," Mosebey lowered his voice, "they have a high opinion of you *and* Mistress Davis. It's just teasing. Nothing more. Why, just the other night, Charles Hambright was bragging about how Mistress Davis fixed his gun. Sam McClure stood up and declared he would take her to wife so she could fix *his* gun."

Stewart flapped the front of his shirt to cool the wildfire creeping across his skin. "That so?"

"Aye, and none of the lads liked it very much. Charles said Sam was blind if he couldn't see you and Mistress Davis as a fine couple.

"You know Sam. He could not let it go. Nearly came to fisticuffs until everybody said if he got in the way of you and the widow, they'd drown him in the river.

"So, you see, nobody despises you or your infatuation. They're just picking on you. I suppose it keeps their minds off their own longing, since every one of them lost or left someone behind."

Stewart cocked his head. "What aboot young Private Mosebey? Does *he* long for someone?"

Mosebey appeared to inspect the horizon. "You must know I do, sir, though I fear it shall never go beyond secret admiration. I have little to offer Rose. Alas, Captain, I'm not unlike this mare"—he patted the stubby horse—"willing and dependable, but not much to look at."

It saddened Stewart to find Mosebey thought himself unworthy of a woman's notice. He placed a hand on the young man's shoulder, feeling bone beneath the green wool of his uniform. Rose would have some job filling that out. "Would it be of comfort to know my hoosemaid never shuts up aboot ye?"

Mosebey turned his head fast enough to whip the tail of his brown hair. "You jest." His dark eyes were wide and glowing. "Pray, do not tease me. As you know, tender hearts can bear no cruelty."

It was Stewart's turn to smile. "Rose loves ye, lad."

The private exhaled as if punched in the gut. "I am relieved to hear it."

They stood in silence until Mosebey spoke again. "May I speak plainly?"

"Of course," Stewart whispered, "but remember where we are. Keep your eyes open."

"When the enemy razed the settlements, I enlisted for no other reason than to protect my dear Rose. I would die for her, sir."

Stewart believed him, and it filled his heart to bursting. A woman could do far worse than Henry Mosebey. He chuckled softly. "Do women know the power they hold o'er us?" He thought back to a day last spring, when he watched five male grackles tip back their heads and puff up their feathers in an impressive display for a lone female. He answered his own question without waiting. "If they do, we wallow in some heap of shite, aye?"

"Indeed, love does make a man go soft." Mosebey looked down at the firepit. "Why else would we risk our lives out here?"

Stewart suddenly regretted selecting the private for the dangerous mission. "We have only to chase the devil from our back door, and then we can go hame again."

"Aye."

Stewart handed him the reins. "Ride back to Fort Shirley. Tell Colonel Armstrong the way is clear. Go as fast as ye can wi'oot killing this animal. The sooner we get this disagreeable business o'er wi', the happier all of us will be. And, Mosebey," he said, as the private mounted the horse.

"Aye."

"I watched Rose grieve ye once. I do nae care to see it again."

Mosebey smiled and gave a quick nod. "Aye, sir. I'll do my best to stay alive."

With Mosebey gone, Stewart grew dejected. He had been certain they would find Catrina between Sherman's Valley and Fort Shirley. Now, even Frankstown offered no sign of her. He scanned the territory to the northwest, where clouds left shadows on the imposing wall of the Allegheny front. That looming impediment challenged the hardiest of men. Surely, a woman could not manage it alone. He watched the purple ridges until his eyes dried out, then found a safe place to wait with a knotted stomach for Armstrong to bring his men . . . and permission to move on to Cherry Tree.

Chapter 25

In the cornfield south of Kittanning, Catrina scratched at one of many insect bites rising out of a rash on her arm. She blamed the cornstalks for the inflammation, since two nights of reconnaissance brought her in contact with no other irritant.

She keenly felt the absence of her tiny companion, though sending him toward the plumes of smoke rising against the clouds had been the right thing to do. Her heart twisted at the memory of his lengthening shadow as he walked away from her on the wide path southeast of Kittanning. He had but a few miles to travel on his own—and each of them downhill—but the thought of deserting him vexed her.

He must have been found by now. God willing, he would soon end her misery by passing through the slice of Kittanning she could see at the end of the cornrow.

Though her hiding place provided a clear view of the southern edge of the village, it sustained clouds of biting insects, a bloodthirsty nuisance brought about by the remarkably wet summer. She waved at a gnat, aware the movement brought risk. The bugs were hellish, always flying into her eyes or up her nose. The furtive mosquitos were far worse. The only evidence of *their* presence came hours later in the form of itchy bumps.

Two days of surveillance revealed she did not suffer the scourge alone. The insect-repelling smoke of many bonfires blackened the wigwams. Yesterday, women and children heaped an unknown plant throughout the village. Catrina spent the day watching the largest pile, hoping to find Marie and Hans among those stopping to rub the leaves on their skin.

They did not appear.

Early this morning, she found the medicinal plant growing a few miles downstream. Its benefit lasted only a few hours, a detail she could have used earlier.

A gnat flew into the corner of her eye while another bit her temple. Desperate for relief, she smeared foul-smelling silt across her arms and face. She inspected her hands, now as cut and stained as any man's. *And to think I worried these might betray me.*

Hushed voices balled her up like a touched woodlouse.

A couple passed by, arm in arm. The warrior, clean and unpainted, leaned his head tenderly against a woman's. She had the thickest, darkest hair Catrina had ever seen.

Lovers.

When they were out of earshot, her thoughts drifted to Stewart, who was surely back in Carlisle by now. The letter she left for him would hopefully ease his torment and fortify his plot to wed Rachel Campbell. Though the idea of losing him pained her, Stewart's ledger made his financial peril quite clear and his plan apt. Marriage to the Campbell girl would set him to rights. He was an upstanding man in need of, and deserving, a woman's rescue.

I did that by leaving. I saved him from himself.

Though he never once spoke openly of his love for her, his actions left little doubt. She noticed the silky change in his voice when he addressed her. And then, there was the kiss by the corral, the feverish moment that turned her inside-out. If she required further evidence, she had only to recall the night she lay in his arms in the barn, and the words he spoke there. They traveled with her across the wilderness, returning to her memory again and again.

Why did ye come?

Ye know why.

They were trifling with danger, their journey across a bottomless pit of passion an uncharted voyage made on high seas and in gale force winds that would only lead to both of them going overboard. Lust had replaced Stewart's good judgment with recklessness, as it did with males of every species. Another fortnight and she would have succumbed to its promises, too.

He would have ruined himself for her.

She loved him too much to allow it.

The thought of her former bigotry pressed her deeper into the muck. How long ago those days seemed now. What would have happened if she had welcomed his advances in the valley that day, before learning of his plans to wed the Campbell girl?

She sniffed the collar of his shirt, where his scent mingled with hers among the threads. The odd intimacy brought tears to her eyes and a pain to her chest. She rubbed at her sternum, then huffed at a gnat and cautioned herself to pay attention to the task at hand.

Careful not to brush against any stalks, she sneaked through the cornfield. She found a row affording a better view of the longhouse, a building every woman seemed to pass at some point in her day. She would see Marie here. She was sure of it.

Finding Captain Jacobs might be a different matter altogether. The men of Kittanning did not move about the village. In fact, while the women scurried like ants from an overturned rock, the men did little else but play games and sit at fires. This morning, as she stood atop one of two hills overlooking the Allegheny and its twin villages, she watched them play a game with balls and sticks. Captain Jacobs did not appear among them. Perhaps, as chief, he considered spectatorship beneath him. Or, perhaps he held meetings with the Frenchmen in the village.

It was impossible to know which side of the river he inhabited, but the thirty cabins facing the Allegheny in the easternmost village provided a sensible clue. Their similarity to the cabins of Tuscarora Valley galled her. How dare he emulate the architecture he burned so callously? One of the structures even had a second story overshooting the first, just like Sam Bigham's fort. It was the only one of its kind, which meant it *must* belong to a man of rank. If the style of the fortress wasn't clue enough, the Frenchmen camped around it certainly were. They would not waste their time at the fires of lesser men.

She had no good plan of attack, but the portable soup in her sack would give her time to acquire one. The hills northeast of the cabins, prime territory for spying, must be explored. She would infiltrate the woodland tonight, before moonrise, and be ready to watch the cabins at dawn.

She resurrected the memory of her enemy's features and surrendered to fantasy. Captain Jacobs knelt in front of her, his scarlet face glistening with sweat and the copper bauble in his nose quivering. She shoved the gun barrel into his mouth—

A man's voice severed her odious thoughts. She dropped fistfuls of mud, which she had unwittingly squeezed into hard balls.

" . . . *froid au Canada,*" he said.

A Frenchman.

She caught only a glimpse of a buff sleeve with blue cuffs as he pushed a boy about Hans's size past the cornrow.

A Native woman came next . . . wearing a blue and white petticoat. Marie's petticoat.

Catrina's heart lurched. She covered her mouth to subdue the rapid breaths threatening to overcome her, smearing mud on her lips and cheeks. Sweat trickled down her temples and between her breasts. A headache detonated inside her skull.

Quiet. Stay quiet!

Her limbs quaked. She swallowed repetitively, though her throat felt as dry as overbaked cornbread.

What does it mean? What does it mean? Dear Gott, she is dead. My darling daughter is dead. Was that boy Hans? She replayed the scene in her mind. *Nein, those were not his clothes. That boy had no hair. But the petticoat . . .* She bowed her head to weep silently into her hands. *The petticoat was Marie's.*

Hours passed before she regained the strength to rise on legs without bones. She swayed, hollow-bellied and soulless, her very spirit trailing like a heavy cape as she made her way south. The temptation to run into the open nipped at her heels. Her pain could end. Today. She sank to her knees. *Hans*. She had to find him.

His plight gave her the power to rise again. She crossed the field seeing nothing but the fabric of Marie's petticoat. As she returned to the secrecy of a forest she once dreaded, the stolen garment gave her an idea. If she went to the northeastern woods, she could build a fire, then use its ashes to dye her hair. Moonset would see her back in the cornfield with a length of rope and a goal of snatching a woman her size.

The only thing left undetermined was whether she would let her unlucky victim live.

Chapter 26

It took Armstrong four days to reach the beaver dams. He did not send Stewart forward as promised. Instead, thanks to the tracks of two Indians near a freshly killed bear, the entire expedition broke camp a day later.

For the next two days, Armstrong, fearing they had been discovered, pushed his men and horses to the brink of exhaustion. Fifty miles from Kittanning, he ordered an officer to go ahead with a pilot and two soldiers to scout out the town.

Though Stewart volunteered for the job, Lieutenant Campbell sent Sam McClure instead, a matter that left Stewart chewing the inside of his cheek until it bled. Though the odds of finding Catrina evaporated a little more each day, a small part of him clung to the hope she was yet alive, maybe even walking along the path around the next corner.

If Sam McClure found her . . .

The thought consumed him as he marched, driving him too close to the man in front of him.

The frontiersman turned to glare and mutter, "Captain, ye're worse than a shepherd's dog, always nippin' at ma heels."

"Sorry."

"I can only go as fast as the man in front of me."

"Tell him to hurry up."

"Aye, an' the hunnert in front of *him*?"

They were weary and growing irritable, having covered over twenty miles already.

The scouts returned by mid-afternoon. The rapidity of their reappearance annoyed Captain Mercer, who argued passionately against their report. He claimed there was no way in hell they could have gone to Kittanning and back in such a short amount of time.

Standing on the road amid his officers, Colonel Armstrong questioned the scouts about the layout of the town. When their lack of particulars made it clear they never went the entire way to Kittanning, Mercer threw his hat. "Ye indolent bastards!"

Armstrong stormed off, tomato-faced. He returned a short while later, wiping sweat from beneath the white wig he should have left behind.

"We cannot afford the time it would take to send new scouts, and we certainly can't camp here. The enemy would most assuredly discover us, if they haven't already," he said.

Stewart wanted to murder Sam McClure.

Armstrong said to Campbell, "As I see it, we have no choice but to proceed posthaste." His voice bore the apprehension they all felt at their situation. "Tell the men to make ready."

Those at the rear of the long line had yet to make *unready*, for while Armstrong was off strategizing, they were still climbing the last hill. They no sooner came to a stop than the order to march reached them. They sipped water, then moved out, too tired to complain.

Near dusk, guides reported two or three Indians at a campfire just a few perches from the front. Armstrong sent two Iroquois scouts to investigate. He ordered the rear to retreat to make room for the front. This added miles to their journey and forced them back across territory they fought hard to claim earlier.

When the order to halt came, weary men collapsed where they stood. Some fell asleep at once, adding snores to the trill of unconcerned crickets and frogs.

Armstrong paced the road, his gorget flashing in the moonlight. He discussed strategy with his officers while awaiting the return of his scouts.

They arrived swiftly, reporting four shadows at a fire six miles ahead.

"I say we surround them," Lieutenant Campbell said.

Armstrong shook his head. "If even one escapes, the whole design will be discovered. Hogg!" He squinted at the darkness. "Where's Lieutenant Hogg?"

"Here, sir." The lieutenant stepped forward.

"You and your company will stay within sight of the fire until sunrise. We should be well situated in the cornfield south of town by then. Under no circumstances are you to fire before sunrise. Do you understand me?"

"Aye, sir." Hogg went to roust his men.

"How are the horses?" Armstrong asked Campbell.

"Drained, same as the men."

"Where's our infatuated Irishman?"

Judas's thirty pieces of silver . . . Stewart swallowed his chagrin. He stepped forward. "Here, sir."

"You have been to this town before, have you not?"

"A time or two."

"What can you tell me about the design of it?"

"Probably not much more than ye know already. The river cuts it in two. This path goes between two hills, right into the center of the town, all the way doon to the river. Captain Jacobs lives there in a log fortress. His relatives and fighting men live in cabins beside him. As I recall, there are fields of corn and squash to the south and steep hills to the east and northeast."

"Anything else?"

"Nothing useful."

Armstrong fell silent, evidently cultivating a plan. "The hills are to the north, you say?"

"Aye."

The colonel looked at Campbell. "What if we took a circuitous route, off the road here, and approached the village from the south?"

"Is it possible?" Campbell asked Stewart.

Stewart searched his memory for details of the landscape. "It's rough terrain. Lots of stone and downed timber. Horses will nae make it."

"But it is possible? It would bring us close?"

"Aye. Ye would eventually come to the river, south of the village."

Armstrong wasted no time in barking orders. "We will leave the horses here. Scaffold the baggage. Be ready in thirty minutes.

"We will split up here. Buchanan, you will take your company northeast. Travel around the end of the hill, then come back while it is yet dark. Form a line there close to the town. Be ready to cut off the enemy when I attack from the field. You will have to hurry, man."

"Aye, right awa', sir."

~ ~ ~

Well northeast of the village, Catrina cooked soup over an expertly sunk blaze. When her dinner bubbled softly, she sighed and lifted the tin cup off the tripod. It felt wrong to fill her belly while Marie rotted in some unhallowed pit, but her plan required strength, and strength came from sustenance.

Distant drumbeats rumbled across the frontier like stones in a barrel. They were lurid even at this great distance, broken only by occasional whoops and cheers. She knew not what prompted the revelry taking place under the glowing southern sky. Perhaps the villagers hailed the coming harvest, though the corn looked far from ripe. It was just as likely Captain Jacobs and his band of demons celebrated the harvest of a much different crop, a sobbing one struggling to stay upright on unsteady legs. Were they even now torturing those poor souls to amuse the French, those twenty vibrant peacocks who arrived at sunset in boats heaped with casks?

A clinking noise made her catch her breath and cock an ear toward the hollow below her campsite. Metal on metal meant white men, since Indians traveled silently. The French had no reason to range this far out of their way. Their alliance with Chief Shingas afforded them the luxury of using the main paths or, more importantly, the river, now that it had receded. Surely, her ears deceived her. A night bird must have made the sound, some western variety unknown to her.

There. Oh, sweet mercy, there it was again, like shillings in a cup.

Fear soured her stomach. She kicked dirt into her firepit, then sat quietly until her eyes adjusted to the darkness. Clenching her musket, she rose, then padded north, away from her supplies. She hid behind one tree, then another.

In the moonlit hollow, red flashed between tree trunks.

Her heart pounded so fiercely she feared the column of men might hear it. Red meant soldiers. Provincial soldiers! *Mercy*. She leaned back against the tree, closed her eyes, and exhaled softly.

Armstrong.

He would catch the village unaware. The raucous murderers would pay at last for their wickedness. Unless . . . Did the colonel know about the newly arrived Frenchmen? Not all of the casks they delivered held spirits. Many contained powder, something the colonel should know. He might also appreciate the accurate headcount she now possessed, thanks to days of monitoring the village. Her intelligence could only help him plan his attack. The trick was in reaching him without getting shot by his men.

She decided to dig up a coal from her fire and race to the end of the hollow with it. If she positioned herself well, she could blow on the coal as Armstrong's men caught up to her. They would send a scout to investigate the light. She could identify herself quietly, without betraying the line, and without risk of gunfire.

Moving swiftly and silently along the steep slope refreshed the pain in her hip and made her calves burn. She stopped to catch her breath against the silvery trunk of a beech tree, then closed her eyes and listened to salvation hustle northeast forty yards below her.

No time to savor it.

She whirled away from the tree—and crashed against a man.

He slapped his palm across her mouth, then threw her to the hard ground, landing on top of her and knocking her hat from her head.

"*Vous êtes qui?*" His hot words spattered vehemence against her ear. A blade stung her throat.

Catrina panted, firing snot and panic across his knuckles. With a Frenchman in the woods, it meant only one thing: the village's celebration was a ruse, a distraction meant to lure Armstrong into complacency. Despair replaced fear as she realized the Second Battalion was heading straight toward an ambush.

"*Vous êtes qui?*" the man repeated.

Though she understood enough French to know he demanded her name, she offered no reply. Her curves may be hidden by a man's clothes, but nothing could disguise her voice. Speech would disclose her sex . . . and lead to abuse.

He straddled her, making it hard to breathe. One of his hands remained clamped across her mouth. The other pressed a knife against her windpipe.

Her head ached unbearably. She saw double as she sought his eyes to gauge his integrity, but the moon hid his face in shadow.

Having received no response in French, he tried English. "I am nae gonny ask again. Who are ye?"

Recognizing him at once, Catrina shouted Stewart's name, but the palm smelling of smoke and linseed oil transformed his name into a nonsensical squeal. Tears streamed down her temples, both from relief and pain.

"What madness is this?" he asked, realizing at last he sat on a female. "I'm gonny take my hand awa' noo. Do nae scream, or I'll slit your throat where ye lie. Understand?"

She nodded.

He slipped his fingers off her lips.

"*Geh weg von mir, du irischer Teufel*," she whispered.

"Baby Moses in a wicker basket"—he lowered his voice—"Catrina?" His hat and knife thumped against the ground beside her head. The silhouette of his shoulders rose and fell as he struggled to trust his eyes and ears. He cupped her face in his hands. "Woman, I—"

His kiss finished the sentence for him, and although she allowed it, she did not return his passion, for sorrow occupied every corner of her heart now.

He crawled off of her, then knelt on the soft leaves beside her. "Forgive me. I should have asked for your consent. I've been so worried. How did ye manage to—"

"Stewart . . . Marie is dead." Saying it aloud made it more real. She felt faint. "I saw a woman wearing her . . . her . . ."

He pulled her into a tender embrace, dizzying her. "Och, pet. I'm sorry. I'm so sorry." He stroked her head as she wept, careful to avoid her crown. "And the lad? Hans? Have ye seen him?"

Hans. Ja, they must save Hans.

"Not yet." She withdrew from his embrace, then swiped her hands across her wet cheeks. "You must tell Colonel Armstrong there are Frenchmen in the village. I counted ten before, but twenty more joined them today. Their boats were full of powder casks."

Stewart helped her to her feet. "Nay time. The colonel and his men are already in position, in the cornfield south of the village. We have orders to march north around the end of this ridge so we can cut off any retreat. He will fire just after moonset." He eyed the sky. "We have only minutes left before the charge, I suspect. I wish I could take ye to the rear masel', pet, but I canny." He kissed her forehead. "I'll send ye back wi' Mosebey."

"You absolutely will not. I'm going with you."

He gripped her shoulders and hissed, "Listen here, you stubborn shite. This is nae place for a woman."

She forced herself to whisper. "Stewart Buchanan, it is high time you accept that I am in no need of protection. I am as capable as any man in your line. And, by the way, *Captain Capable*, you should tell your men they clank like a jailer's ring of keys."

He sniffled as he considered her words. "Aye, well, if ye're gonny hide in the woods, ye should pick a tree darker than a silver beech to lean against. Can ye shoot that thing?"

Though she could not see him well, she knew he meant the fowler. "Only better than most of your men."

"Then get your kit and come wi' me."

He led her to the front of the line, where men momentarily forgot the grim nature of their mission and smirked. Stewart muttered, "First man who utters a word will feel his teeth passing his windpipe." He allowed his threat to sink in. "Whisper doon the line. Every man is to secure his buckles and canteens. This lady heard us afore she saw us. Seems we're moving wi' a rattle." He stepped into line next to Catrina and whispered, "I received your letter. We have much to discuss."

"Ja, we do." She offered a knowing smile.

"First, we make war." Stewart grinned. "Com-pan-y, march."

They traveled the hollow with surprising secrecy thereafter, arcing around the end of the ridge, then doubling back on the other side, halfway up the slope, to form a line parallel to the village.

Once hunkered down, they lay their weapons across their laps and watched men below twirl and dip around their fires. Catrina sank behind a laurel bush, where the setting moon hid the full measure of her haggard condition. She grew drowsy while watching for Hans among the dancing shadows. Did he participate in the carousing, his mother already forgotten? She closed her eyes for what seemed a moment.

A thunderous volley thrust the line to its feet and opened the gates of Hell. She jumped up, her hands tight on her musket, surprised to find Kittanning bathed in diffuse light.

Gunfire flashed throughout the village, adding smoke to the tendrils of fog hanging at eye level.

"Make rea-dy," Stewart shouted. "Be careful," he said to Catrina. "I have something I wish to say to ye when this is o'er. Make damn sure ye stay alive long enough to hear it, aye?"

She nodded, then smirked as men with bayonets fixed them to their weapons. *This is it. Finally.* She summoned the memory of her enemy's face, its features having lost no detail in the passage of time. The black stripe still crossed his face below his nose. A copper triangle dangled there, just above his upper lip. Ebony dots, about the size of a man's thumbprint, speckled the red skin on his forehead and skull. Three lines began at the corners of his eyes and stretched toward his temples, where prominent veins zigzagged toward his grotesquely mutilated ears.

"Pre-sent!" Stewart's order echoed down the line.

The sound of so many hammers clicking to full cock sent a shiver of delight up her spine. Past the end of her barrel, women screamed and ran like mice before a wildfire. They dragged children along, stopping only to kick at drunken warriors languishing beside dead fires.

"Com-pan-y, march!" Stewart shouted.

As they moved away from the forest and onto packed earth, an explosion near the river sent a plume of smoke rolling up to spread out below the clouds.

"Steady," Stewart shouted.

Shots cracked and flashed like lightning in the cornfield and meadow. Others answered from the cabins.

Warriors streamed between the wigwams, their breechclouts flapping, discharging chilling whoops and transporting Catrina back to a fateful night in the Tuscarora valley. Rage turned her grip to granite and the heavy gun to a straw pillow.

Five yelping warriors charged with their axes cocked above their heads.

Catrina's pulse banged. Unmanageable trembling threatened to ruin her aim.

"Fire," Stewart shouted.

She pulled the trigger, hearing the whack of flint on steel. The lock flashed fire, and the gun kicked hard, spewing pieces of lead deep into her attacker's belly.

The ground bloomed red where he fell.

A tremendous volley eliminated the others.

She reloaded quickly, spilling some of the shot in her haste. In the sulfuric aftermath of gunfire hanging with the fog, she could barely find the end of her barrel.

"For-ward," Stewart shouted.

The line moved ahead, ready or not.

In the din, a woman screamed. "They'll kill us. God help us. They'll kill us!

Another shouted, "*Versteck dich hinter mir.*"

Captives. German and English captives.

Catrina shoved her ramrod into its groove, then followed the sound of their voices, waving away smoke and fog, until she saw them clasping hands and cowering behind a ramshackle hut. Had it not been for their familiar language, she would have mistaken them for Indians, for they were dyed brown and dressed in deerskin.

As she was about to shout to them, a man delivered a boy to a bald woman crouched among them.

Not wanting to shoot a captive by mistake, Catrina went down on one knee to carefully aim her gun at him.

He grabbed his prisoner's arm to wrench her away from the others. When she resisted, he pulled the child out of her arms. Off-balance, she stumbled, revealing her face to Catrina.

Marie.

Ignoring Stewart's orders to stay in the line, Catrina raced toward the hut. "Marie!" she shrieked as gunfire flashed and musket balls zinged past her head. "Marie!"

To her right, a warrior stabbed a bayonet at her.

She ducked and spun, then flipped her musket around to swing it by its barrel. The butt plate cracked against his skull.

He crumpled to the ground.

Marie's captor—she could see now he was an Indian—dragged her between the wigwams, toward the Allegheny, where frantic men were already paddling for Shingas's side of the river. He lifted Marie into a canoe, then handed her the boy.

Hans?

"Hans!" Catrina flipped her hat off her head as she ran, freeing her braid.

Marie wilted over her child while the warrior tossed paddles into the hull of the rocking canoe.

Not my babies, du Dämon. *You will not have my babies a moment longer!*

She stopped to aim her gun at him, oblivious to the combat around her and deaf to the whiz of lead balls.

Hans's arm poked through Marie's embrace to point at her. "Grandmama!"

Marie sat up. Her hand flew to her open mouth. Her eyebrows pulled together above the bridge of her nose. Then, as she recognized her mother, she screamed through her fingertips. "Mama, is it you? Is it really you?" She followed Catrina's aim. "Oh, Mama, no! Please, don't!" She leapt out of the canoe, dropped Hans, then spread her arms in front of the warrior.

He lifted Hans off the ground.

You will not have him, Du böser Höllenhund.

"Get out of the way, Marie," she shouted, tramping forward, her finger twitching on the trigger. "Marie, move!"

"Do not shoot him. Mama, please!" Marie clasped her hands as if in prayer. "I beg of you. Trust me."

What is happening? Had the warrior somehow entranced her? As she pointed the musket at him, she noticed he looked less . . . cruel than the others. He had helped Marie into the boat quite carefully, and he *handed* Hans to her instead of tossing him like a sack of seed corn.

She approached cautiously, still pointing the gun at him, to seek his eyes.

They bore no malice, only concern. He twisted his body to protect Hans, though the boy was squirming and screaming, "Grandmama! Grandmama!"

"Please," Marie cried. "I love him, Mama."

The words hit hard enough to spray blood.

Impossible!

She stepped back.

Was it?

Yellow Bear.

"Come with me." She shouldered her musket, then grabbed the warrior's hand, knowing Armstrong's men would correctly interpret the gesture and perhaps assume him of European lineage. "All of you."

They ran for the ridge, with Hans shouting something in Algonquian while bouncing in the man's arms.

Two warriors broke away from clubbing a soldier to pursue them. Behind them, Catrina caught the flash of copper baubles as Captain Jacobs ran for his fortress.

"Run!" She pushed Marie's man through a cloud of stinking gun smoke. He tumbled behind an outcrop of rock, landing on his back to keep Hans from striking the ground.

Marie dived beside him.

Catrina barely cleared the rocks before a lead ball shattered the sandstone just above her head. She wiped grit off her face, then rolled onto her belly. Wasting no time, she popped above the rock to fire at one of two warriors wielding knives. Though she hit only one, both men fell. She turned to see who fired the second shot and found Stewart reloading his musket uphill.

"Stay with him," she said, rising to her feet.

"Where are you going?" Marie squealed and grabbed a fistful of her breeches. "Mama, where are you going?"

Stewart started down the hill. "Catrina, stay put."

"I came here to do something, and I plan to do it!" She ripped free of Marie's grasp, then bounded away from their hiding place.

"Ye have your family back," Stewart shouted. "Let it go at that!"

"Protect them, I beg you," she yelled while running.

"This is madness," he bellowed. "Catrina!"

She dashed back to the village, overrun now with green uniforms and frontiersmen in tan overshirts. At Captain Jacobs's fortress, a bearded man laid fire to the logs. Another tossed pine knots onto the flames.

Inside the building, a man laughed in the face of death by singing. When a woman screamed, he interrupted his song long enough to rebuke her, an abusive sound Catrina would recognize in any language.

Shadows and coppery glints appeared at the garret window. Catrina ducked inside an abandoned wigwam to watch while reloading her weapon. Ready to fire again, she knelt on one knee, though she had no plans to shoot until she saw her enemy face to face.

Past the longhouse, she heard an English officer barking orders. "Prime and load. Come to rea-dy!"

Shots fired from the fortress's windows and loopholes as Captain Jacobs and his warriors did their best to repel Armstrong and his men. When they failed, the war chief tried to climb through the garret window.

Over my dead body. Catrina aimed from the doorway of the wigwam.

An explosion slammed her against the back wall. As the structure fell upon her, she fired her weapon at nothing. Dazed, with her ears ringing, she crawled out from under the pile of birch sheathing, into a sea of body parts.

Twenty yards away, Captain Jacobs rocked to his feet. He shoved an injured woman aside, then began to limp toward the river.

Catrina started toward him, her arms bleeding and her head pounding, but Armstrong's men lunged like dogs on a soup bone. They slit the war chief's throat—and the woman's—then pushed them over with the heels of their feet.

Catrina vomited, reeling on wobbly legs and not knowing what to do next.

A swarm of canoes provided the answer. Shingas was sending men—French men and painted warriors—leaving no time for confusion or disappointment. Already, they fired from the boats.

"Look!" She pointed at them and shouted to Armstrong's men, who were busy scalping the dead and setting fire to more cabins. "Look!"

The fight was about to worsen.

She ran northeast, choking on the pungent smoke obliterating the battlefield. A fresh volley forced her to take cover behind a pile of tree stumps. There, an armed warrior guarded five children. He had one eye.

She pointed her musket at him, forgetting she had not reloaded it. Fury erupted as she recalled his cruelty at her home. He had pushed her much harder than the others, laughing at her useless attempts to protect herself. Now, he smirked behind his trigger, which meant he either remembered her or knew her gun was empty.

A child pulled on his gun the moment he fired it.

Catrina jumped as a lead ball sprayed dirt across her feet. She gawped at the boy who caused the misfire. He had no earlobes.

The boy from Burgoon's Gap.

The child whirled to explain himself to the fuming warrior. When he'd finished, the warrior glared at her with his one eye, then thrust his chin toward the tree line.

Catrina raced away without argument, hurdling over bodies, crashing around wigwams, and not stopping until she reached the outcrop where she left Marie and Hans. They were gone, along with Stewart's line, now in full retreat.

Panting, she cupped her hands and shouted through the smoke. "Marie!"

They must be here somewhere.

Someone tugged on her shirt. "Come on, ye fool," Stewart shouted, his words tinny, the result of the earlier explosion. "They're safe, behind the line." He pulled her toward the trees.

A gunfight broke out at the river.

Shingas had arrived with reinforcements.

Catrina ran out of her moccasins, following Stewart into the trees toward home . . . with her family at her side, at last.

Chapter 27

In a wagon serving as a sick bed, Catrina dabbed the seeping wounds of an injured man. She wore no hat, for hers stayed behind in Kittanning, where propriety died in battle. Let them see her uncovered hair—what was left of it. What did she care?

Marie, on the other hand, lamented her baldness and state of undress. Stewart took pity on her and found a triangle of linen she could use for a scarf.

"Hush," Marie said to Ensign Baker, who moaned incoherently as she cleaned the gunshot wound on his arm. The former aide-de-camp wore no glasses now. He was one of thirteen men wounded in Armstrong's expedition. Seventeen others paid the ultimate price, earning shallow graves quickly dug into the lonely hills of the province.

Armstrong himself took a ball to the shoulder. Nobody had seen Captain Mercer since the start of the battle, which was a terrible loss, since he was not only an officer, but a skilled physician they needed badly at present.

Captain Hamilton found Lieutenant Hogg lying dead next to a gaunt horse on the path. According to two soldiers in Hogg's company, the "three or four" warriors Armstrong asked the lieutenant to monitor on the night of the attack turned out to be more than twenty. Hogg urged his men to stand and fight, but upon discovering they were outnumbered, their courage flagged. They ran, leaving Hogg to fight alone. Their undignified retreat did not serve them well, for all but one perished on the road less than a mile from the scaffolded baggage.

In spite of sustaining two shots to his belly, Hogg hid in the underbrush, then climbed onto a stolen Indian horse and rode away, leaving all of the battalion's horses and scaffolded supplies unguarded.

The Indians got to the supplies before Colonel Armstrong could, which meant another skirmish to recover the provincial horses. In the end, the Second Battalion grabbed the few animals they could, abandoned the rest, along with their supplies, and retreated to Fort Lyttelton as fast as the weary men could go. Even their retreat proved problematic, for they made the trek under constant harassment by their enemy, who fired from the shadows, then ran before men could pursue them.

They arrived at Fort Lyttelton on trembling legs and looking like men who didn't know if they were alive or dead.

Catrina wondered as she climbed out of the wagon: had the raid been worth the cost?

The seven captives shading themselves beneath a great oak tree said it was. Four more went with Mercer, wherever he was. According to Marie, Armstrong barely missed recovering over twenty others, whom Shingas sent to Fort Duquesne just two days before the raid. Hannah and Jane Gray were among them, a matter that destroyed John Gray, who took part in the expedition.

He sat among the captives now, as if being near them might somehow bring him closer to his loved ones. To his right, Taspecawen wrestled with Hans.

Marie's lover exhibited both courage and concern throughout the retreat to the fort, always taking pains to make sure Marie and her family were safe. Last night, he asked many questions about farming and the triune God. Catrina had to admit he possessed a bright smile, kind eyes, and with Marie and Hans, a gentle touch.

"I have not forgotten about Jacob, you know." Marie climbed down from the wagon.

"Nor have I."

Marie set a bloody bucket of water on the ground at Catrina's feet. "What happened to his . . ."

"They buried him at fort Robinson."

Marie blew out a breath. "I am relieved to hear it. Taspecawen was there that night." She handed a second bucket to Catrina, whose sore arms nearly dropped it.

"At the farm?"

Marie nodded, then stretched her back. "He took no part in Jacob's murder, or . . ." She looked up at her mother's hair.

"I am glad to hear that, at least."

Marie chuckled. "He did carry off your brass cauldron, though."

"The dirty *Arschloch*."

"I told him how much it meant to you. He swears he'll get it back somehow." Her expression turned serious. "Mama, I need to know. Do you judge me for . . ." She bit her lip and looked toward Taspecawen.

"For what, loving a man outside your race?"

Marie nodded, her eyes welling.

Catrina looked past her, where Stewart hammered a horseshoe at a makeshift forge. She laughed and shook her head. "Nein."

Marie sought the source of her amusement. Seeing Stewart, she raised a brow. "Indeed, Mama, it seems you lost more than part of your hair this summer."

Catrina blushed. "You are quite mistaken."

"Perhaps you only misplaced your bigotry, then. You've looked no less than ten times in Mister Buchanan's direction." She clucked her tongue and bent to empty her bucket. "Dear, oh, dear. Did your good deutsche self manage to cross the wide valley after all?"

Though the long walk from Kittanning provided ample time to share details of her injury and subsequent rescue with Marie, Catrina had kept her feelings for Stewart to herself.

There was little point in admitting her affection for a man intending to marry someone else. Besides, she had yet to speak to Stewart, whose rank and occupation kept him busy. "I owe him a great debt. There is nothing more to it."

"We owe all of these men a great debt," Marie replied.

Catrina followed Marie's gaze across the sun-speckled grounds, where Armstrong's battalion rested. Her eyes fell upon the scalps drying on hoops. "You *do* know that danger will trouble your newfound love. And judgment, too."

"I do, and I care not."

Catrina smiled at the girl who left Tuscarora Valley and returned a woman. "I always thought you took after my mother, docile to a fault." Emotion choked her words. "There may be a part of me in you after all."

She had been choking back tears since leaving Kittanning. She did not want to cry. Not yet, and certainly not in public. Her cries, when they came, would flume like the falls in New York Rose once described to her. There was much to celebrate. She and Stewart survived the battle, and her family was safe. The tears she shed for those blessings would be joyful. But the explosions at Kittanning worsened her headaches and returned her nausea and blurry vision. Her farm lay in ruin. The man she loved would marry someone else. And . . . She had killed people. Not as a soldier, but as a woman bent on revenge.

Remorse gnawed at her like a worm with teeth. It sent bile to the back of her throat and tears to prick her eyes.

Thou shalt not kill.

"We need fresh water." She picked up the empty buckets, then left for the stream before Marie could object or offer to accompany her.

In the flats below the fort, where sunbeams pierced the canopy of a verdant sanctuary, Catrina felt the blistering scrutiny of God upon her. She knelt before the stream, now a bed of glinting diamonds. As birds twittered praise around her, she confessed her sins and admitted she murdered men with hatred and revenge in her heart. Tears came singly, then in racking sobs. They kicked her soul into a heap. She cried until her sorrow was spent, then sat quietly, listening to the peaceful babble of the stream, wondering if God truly forgave sins.

A snapped twig behind her sent her pitching forward to wash her hands and face.

She rose in time to see Stewart parting the weeds. "I've been waiting all day to catch ye alone. What are ye doing doon here all by yoursel'?"

She stood, then dried her face on her sleeve, hoping he wouldn't notice she'd been crying.

He did. "What's wrong?"

There seemed little harm in telling him the truth. "I killed those men."

"Aye, and they killed Jacob. They tried to kill you, too. This is war, Catrina. People die in wars." He held out his hand. When she took it, he pulled her into his embrace. "It'll pass in time, pet."

She slipped her arms around his back, then laid her cheek against his homespun shirt, grateful for the comfort he offered. "Do you mind it?"

His heart pounded against her ear. "Killing folk? Of course I do. Nobody enjoys it."

"I did, a little."

"That's because ye're a mama bear, and they stole your cub. They'd be the first to admit they got what they deserved for it."

"Nobody deserves to die." The faces of her attackers would fade into history, but the men she murdered would haunt her forever.

Stewart pushed her an arm's length away. His voice turned soothing. "I can only tell ye this. It'll take time to heal. It always does." He pinched her chin. "We'll sort it oot. In Carlisle."

"I cannot go to Carlisle."

"Of course ye can." His eyes turned steely within their hollows, still ochre from the fists of men. "And ye will."

"I was thinking Marie and I would go back to the farm. A corner of the barn still stands."

"I remember." He kissed her temple, then her forehead. "We left some unfinished business in the hay there."

A pot of molten lead tipped over inside her belly. She ignored it . . . and his advances. "Marie's man seems keen to learn our methods."

He sighed. "I will nae let ye change the subject. Listen, ye're coming back to Carlisle wi' me. It'll be crowded, but—"

"Nein. Stewart . . ." She stopped short of mentioning the financial woes spelled out in his ledger.

"If ye think I make the offer oot of pity, ye're dead wrong. I want ye to come because . . . God help me, this is what I wanted to tell ye, the thing I said we needed to discuss. There's just no way around it. I love ye, Catrina. I have for a long time."

She wanted to press her forehead against his and tell him she loved him, too. Instead, she cleared her throat and said, "How unfortunate."

He threw his hat off his head. "Ye know something, Catrina Davis? Ye're more stubborn than any mule I e'er met. Are ye honestly gonny deny ye love me when your lips told me more than once how much ye do? I have your letter, remember? Ye left nae doubt."

She could not lie, not when the depressions of her knees remained in a muddy confessional only a few feet away. "I cannot deny it," she whispered.

He closed the gap between them. His lips tickled her ear. "Say it. Say the three words I long to hear."

"Two others keep me from it."

His head jerked back. "What two words?"

She held a finger in front of his nose. "Rachel." And then another. "Campbell."

Stewart burst into laughter. He whirled away, then clutched a small tree for support. "Aye." He wiped his eyes. "What a perfect wife she would make me."

Catrina felt her nostrils flare. She bent to retrieve her buckets. "You mock me."

"She's quiet and submissive—"

Catrina threw the buckets at him. "You delight in my anguish, sir!"

"And I'd never have to worry aboot her running off across the frontier." He sniffled and held his sides. "Oh, it's been years since I laughed so hard. I have to sit doon."

"I am glad you find humor in my misery. Go to your *gebrechliche Lilie*, then. Let me be." She stomped off toward the camp, swatting saplings and weeds out of her way.

The swish of vegetation behind her meant Stewart followed. "Wait. Catrina. Look at me."

She whirled to face him. "What?"

"Listen, ye bloody eejit, I broke off the courtship afore I left Carlisle."

"You did?" She attempted to veil her delight with concern. "Oh . . . She must be brokenhearted."

"Believe me when I tell ye she'll not pine for one tick of her fancy clock." He grabbed her wrist, then pulled her to him. "I told ye long ago. Some men appreciate a strong woman wi' her own opinions." He brushed a finger across one of her brows and licked his lips. "God help me, ye got plenty of those." He trailed kisses from her ear to her mouth, then rubbed his nose against hers. "Funny thing is, I want ye in spite of them."

She kissed him, hard enough to make him stumble.

He laughed, then whirled her against a tree.

She rested her forehead against his breastbone. "Oh, Stewart. What are we going to do?"

He hooked a finger under her chin to lift it. "We're gonny start o'er." He kissed her gently.

She tucked a strand of his graying hair behind his ear. "At our age?"

"They are nae measuring us for boxes just yet, Mistress. Besides, I have welcome news. I suppose ye heard what happened to Hogg."

Hogg's death was hardly welcome news. "Ja, Gott rest him."

"But did ye hear he stole a horse?"

"The Indian horse. Ja, I heard it mentioned."

"I've seen it. Hard used and mighty gaunt, the poor beast, but . . ." He stroked Catrina's arm. "Catrina, it's a stallion, one I think ye'll recognize."

Her hand flew to her mouth. "Not . . . Heinrich?"

"Aye. He's a bag of bones, but he'll live. Hell, in your hands, he'll thrive."

She threw herself into his embrace and wept. "Oh, I do not know what I did to receive such a blessing. Thank you, Gott," she whispered. "Thank you."

"So, ye see, ye have a brood mare and a stallion. And there's still Jacob's land. With Kittanning in ruin, we might stand a chance of reaping a harvest. Furs will start making their way east again. We'll build oursel' up. Thomas and Taspecawen will help, and Hans, when he's a few years older."

She looked up at him, her eyes strained from crying. "And if peace doesn't last?"

"Then we'll stay in Carlisle." He nudged her. "Say it."

She sighed.

"I mean it, now." He pressed himself against her, betraying his hardness. "Say it."

Heat spread from her belly and liquefied between her thighs. "I love you. There, is that what you want to hear?"

"Indeed, it is." His lips covered hers with hungry kisses.

"Ho-ly smoke," a man muttered.

They broke free of their embrace, then wiped their mouths on their sleeves.

"Oh." The man scanned Catrina's clothes. "Forgive me. I thought two lads were . . . Well, I don't rightly know *what* I thought. Anyway, Simpson sent me to find you. Said you might take a look at my fowler?"

"Aye," Stewart said, looking annoyed. "I'll be right up."

The man scratched beneath his cap. "I wasn't talking to you."

Catrina threw her head back in a hearty laugh. "I guess maybe we *will* make it, Stewart."

He led her away from the creek. "What man could fail wi' Catrina Davis by his side?"

With nothing but their broken hearts, a lame ox, and a torc they cannot sell without invoking a centuries-old curse, they head for the backcountry, where all hope rests upon getting their seed in the ground. Under constant threat of Indian attack, they endure crushing toil and hardship. By summer, they have wheat for their reward, and unexpected news of Henry's lost love. They emerge from the wilderness and follow her trail to Philadelphia, unaware her cruel new master awaits them there, his heart set on obtaining the priceless torc they protect.

Available on Amazon: **SCATTERED SEEDS**

THE SCENT OF FOREVER

Author Ann McConnell doesn't know she's reincarnated—or that she carries angelic DNA. She only knows she's alone and off the rails since Mike left her sitting in a fertility clinic. Now, her career is in a nosedive and Mike's all over Facebook with his girlfriend and new baby.

Battling despair, Ann focuses on renovating her ancestors' cabin. When she finds a gold torc hidden there, it amplifies her sense of smell and sends her into a tailspin. Curious about her ancestors and their powerful relic, she embarks on a journey to explore her heritage. Her quest steers her toward Somerled of Argyll, whose descendants she can now identify by scent. She travels to Scotland in search of his grave, unaware he's her 12th century soul mate. He's reborn, nearby, and trying to find her. So is her demonic stalker.

If Ann can't escape the foul clutch of a madman, it will spell disaster for reuniting souls, and—unthinkably—for humanity itself.

Available on Amazon: **THE SCENT OF FOREVER**

CPSIA information can be obtained
at www.ICGtesting.com
Printed in the USA
LVHW081232150320
650078LV00023B/2575